Creepy Hollow Adventures

Three Ghosts in a Black Pumpkin
The Power of the Sapphire Wand

Written by

Erika M Szabo and Joe Bonadonna

Illustrated by

Erika M Szabo

Golden Book Award Winner

Copyright © Erika M Szabo and Joe Bonadonna, 2017
Creepy Hollow Adventures 1 and 2

Second edition
ISBN-13: 978-1-943962-45-7
ISBN-10: 1-943962-45-6

This edition includes:
Three Ghosts in a Black Pumpkin
Creepy Hollow Adventures 1
Library of Congress Control Number: 2017904014

The Power of the Sapphire Wand
Creepy Hollow Adventures 2
Library of Congress Control Number: 2017914972

The first editions:
Published in the United States by Golden Box Books Publishing, New York.
Edited by Lee Porche
www.winddancerpublications.com
Illustrations and book cover by Erika M Szabo
www.authorerikamszabo.com
Book formatting, book interior, and illustration design by
www.goldenboxbooks.com

Once upon a time in the
Realm of Creepy Hollow,
Where bats and rats,
And cats and gnats,
No matter where you go,
Will follow.
Hobgoblin did bad things
In order to gain power,
From dungeons dark and deep
To his castle called Crag
Heap, his evil grew
Stronger by the hour…

Three Ghosts in a Black Pumpkin
Creepy Hollow Adventures 1
Erika M Szabo & Joe Bonadonna

Prologue

Hobart T. Goblin looked out the open window of his chamber high atop his castle of Crag Heap. Far below, he could see his courtyard, his servants and soldiers, and beyond that, the entire town of Goblin Acres. He watched his subjects performing their duties and going on with their little Goblin lives.

All this is mine, he thought. *But I want more and I will have more. I will have it all: Gnome Town, Gremlinville, Troll Haven, Impburg, Pixieland, Ogre Mountain...the whole world of Creepy Hollow will soon be mine!*

Standing only four feet tall, Hobart was nonetheless an imposing figure. His large, floppy ears fanned his face as he walked, and when his ears flopped forward his long beaklike nose stuck out between them like a pointing finger.

His thin lips broke into a grin, showing his sharp fangs as he jutted his pointy chin forward. "Once upon a time," he murmured under his breath, "I was just an ordinary Goblin, but look at me now! I am great, I am powerful, and I am Hobgoblin, the Master of Goblin Acres."

He turned from the window and lifted his skinny, green leg and huge foot to take a proud step forward. His boney knees bent and cracked as he took another step toward his favorite chair. He put his hands, with their claw-like fingers, on his hips when he saw his henchman standing on *his* chair.

"Ebenezer, get off my chair this minute!" Hobgoblin growled angrily. "Did you find the Wands?"

"Not yet, Master," said Ebenezer Rex. He didn't show fear and remained in the chair despite his master's angry words.

Hobgoblin let it slide because he needed him to do his dirty deeds.

Ebenezer was once a man, a very cruel and sick-minded man, who liked to hurt young children. When he was finally captured by the good witches known as The Trinity of Wishmothers, who rewarded good deeds and punished evil, Ebenezer was tried and convicted and turned into a Tasmanian Devil as punishment for his crimes. Although he served Hobgoblin faithfully, first and foremost in Ebenezer's cold heart was his desire to have his revenge on The Trinity of Wishmothers.

"Why didn't you find them yet?" Hobgoblin demanded. His big, floppy ears trembled with anger.

As wicked and mean as he was, old Ebenezer Rex was also cunning. He knew he had to pretend to be afraid in the presence of Hobgoblin if he, for his benefit, wanted to stay in his castle. "Forgive me great and powerful Hobgoblin," he said in a submissive tone of voice, although the mocking expression on his face betrayed him. "I went back to Celestria and searched all over, but all I could find, all I could locate, and all I could—"

"What *did* you find?" Hobgoblin interrupted, ignoring Ebenezer's mocking tone, for the time being.

"I found the thief who snuck into your castle and stole the three Wands, and then escaped right under our very noses," Ebenezer replied. He turned to a pair of Gnome soldiers standing guard at the entrance to Hobgoblin's chamber, and then snapped his fingers.

Nodding their little heads, the Gnomes vanished before Ebenezer could say *lickety-split*. "Ugh! They didn't wait for me to say my favorite word, again!" He fumed because he always wanted to say the word he made up, "lickety-split," before the Gnomes disappeared because he hated to say "as fast as possible."

The Gnomes reappeared in a jiffy and between them stood a tall, silver skeleton bound with iron chains.

"It took twenty Gnomes and ten Goblins to capture and render him powerless with those iron chains, Master," said Ebenezer.

"Ah, the famous Wishbone Jones," said Hobgoblin, gloating over the capture of his prisoner. "I had a pretty good idea it was you. The Trinity of Wishmothers always favored you, but they no longer watch over you and the other inhabitants of Celestria. The Realm of Spirits has no guardians now. The magic of the witch who turned your charred flesh to silver is of no use to you now. She cannot save your life this time."

Wishbone Jones stood over six feet tall. His right arm was slightly scratched, but the rest of his body was flawlessly covered with silver. One year ago, when he fought in the war against the Trolls, his body was badly burned. The Healing Witch found him barely alive when the fight was over, but all she could do to save his life was to turn his burned body into three inches of solid silver in order to protect his flesh and bones. Ever since that day, he became known as the Silver Skeleton.

Wishbone shook with anger as he took a step forward, pulling on the chains and dragging the Gnomes with him.

 Hobgoblin's eyes flashed with fear until his minions yanked hard on the chains and forced the skeleton to his knees. He smiled defiantly in the face of his captor. "Do what you will, Hobart. Do your very best. But you'll never find those Wands and will never be able to use their power. You and that stinking henchman of yours will be punished for the murders of the Wishmothers. And *that* you can count on."

Ebenezer laughed. "Hobgoblin is great and powerful, boneman. You don't even know how to free those ghosts from the pumpkin or where it's hidden!"

"Careful," Hobgoblin hushed his henchman quickly. "Don't give it away. Don't give him any ideas."

Ebenezer slapped his own mouth angrily and mumbled, "Oops, I almost did."

But Wishbone knew much more than his enemies thought he did, for the Healing Witch had told him everything she knew. "Trust me, I'll find a way, Hobart," said Wishbone, refusing to call him Hobgoblin. "I'll bring you both to justice and see to it that Creach Gillman is restored to his rightful place as the Mayor of Goblin Town."

"Good luck with that!" Hobgoblin said with a laugh. "He's in the Deep Dark Dungeon, where you'll soon join him." He turned to Ebenezer. "Have the Imps and Ogres torture this bonehead. Make him talk and then dispose of him. But don't stop searching for those Wands. Halloween is only thirteen days away and I must have those Wands before the chimes of midnight announce the first of November."

"Yes, Master. What about the black pumpkin?"

"Don't say another word, you fool! I'll take care of it."

Wishbone Jones gave a hearty, metallic laugh. "I know all about the black pumpkin, Hobart. I know what you've done. You won't get away with it, I promise you that."

"My name is *Hobgoblin*, you walking bag of bones!" roared Hobgoblin, his face turning red with anger. "Ebenezer, take him to the dungeon and begin his torture at once!"

Chapter 1

It was an unusually warm autumn day, and Grandma Sweet opened the front door. She loved it when the fresh, morning breeze flew through the rooms. The sun hung high in the eastern sky, big and bright yellow. The silver wind chime hanging from the roof next to the entrance made a strange but pleasant sound each time a gentle breeze touched it. Grandma found the wind chime hanging there almost two weeks earlier. Thinking it was a surprise gift from one of her friends, she named the wind chime Mister Bonejingles, because it looked like a jingly human skeleton.

Grandma Sweet felt the strange, quiet buzzing and humming in the air that hinted at the magic and mystery that comes only once a year on the morning of Halloween.

"You kids better not go too far from the house!" she called out on her way to the kitchen as she spotted Nikki and Jack rushing toward the back door. The smell of cookies baking in the oven was mouth-watering, and Grandma Sweet wondered why it didn't stop the children, as it usually did, from rushing out of the house.

The screen door flew open with a bang. Nikki Sweet and her cousin, Jack Brady, charged from the house, across the back porch, down the steps, and into the big backyard. Beyond the white picket fence lay Weeping Meadow, and beyond that, the small town of Diddlebury.

"It's Saturday," said Nikki, adjusting the backpack she carried with her everywhere she went. "No school!"

Jack had his favorite messenger bag on his shoulder, just in case he found some weird things to bring home. He thought wearing a backpack made him look childish, but the shoulder bag made him look cool.

"Better than that, it's Halloween!" Jack said. "Let's get out of here before Grandma changes her mind." He winked at Nikki playfully.

Nikki tugged on her left earlobe three times. "Okay, let's go. Ready?" she asked, leaning forward, getting ready for their usual race to the front gate.

"Why are you doing that?" Jack asked, staring at Nikki.

"Doing what?" Nikki asked, surprised.

"Pulling on your ear like that."

Nikki laughed. "Once I was nervous about a hard math test and Grandma told me to tug on my ear for good luck. I passed the test but I know it wasn't because I pulled my ear. It was because I studied hard. Now it's just something Grandma and I do for fun."

"That's cool," Jack said and nodded with a wide grin on his face. "My dad and I do something like that. When I was in first grade I told him I wasn't a baby anymore and didn't want him to kiss me goodbye when he dropped me off at school. So instead of a goodbye kiss, we started touching our pointing fingers together."

"That's nice. I wish I knew my dad…," Nikki whispered, and her expression turned sad for a second. But then she shook her head and grinned at Jack. "Think you can win this time?"

Jack was sure he could win their usual race to the back gate this time. He looked at Nikki and said, "Steady."

"Go!" Nikki said.

They raced each other across the backyard and toward the gate in the fence. Nikki, one year older than her mischievous cousin Jack, who was eleven, reached the gate first.

"I win!" she sang out victoriously.

"You always win," Jack complained with a sourpuss expression on his oval face.

Nikki tried to ease his sadness and made a mental note to let him win next time. "That's because I'm a year older than you," she said, trying to make him feel better.

Jack shoved his hands into the pockets of his jeans. He pushed his chest out like a fancy peacock, brushed a speck of lint from his T-shirt and boasted, "But I'm bigger than you!"

"Yup, it's true, but I'm faster than you!" Nikki said, not feeling sorry for Jack anymore. *You can forget it, buster! I'm never gonna let you win,* she thought.

Nikki opened the gate and they wandered over to the small, shallow creek running alongside the house. Not far from the creek, the leaves and branches of the weeping willows of Weeping Meadow danced in the breeze.

Jack had come to spend the weekend at Grandma Sweet's house. His parents were throwing a big Halloween party, for adults only, and didn't want their troublesome little boy running around and causing all kinds of mischief. Nikki was adopted by her grandmother after her parents died when she was a little girl. Although Jack's constant teasing about getting text messages every five minutes annoyed her, she enjoyed his visits and teased him back for taking pictures of every weird thing he found and posting them on Instagram.

"So, what do you want to do until we can go Trick or Treating?" Jack asked as he combed his fingers through his curly hair.

Before Nikki could reply her phone *pinged*, alerting her of the arrival of a new message. "I don't know," she mumbled while looking down and tapping her phone. "What do *you* want to do?" she asked.

"I asked you first," said Jack. "And for once, will you please put away your phone?"

Shaking her head, Nikki mumbled to herself, "Boys!" She put her cell phone in the pocket of her jeans, which she always wore with the cuffs rolled up above her ankles. "Fine, Jack. But if I see you take even one picture of a dead frog or a pile of dog poop, I'm going to slap you!"

"Fine! Whatever!" Jack said.

Nikki sighed. She knew he wouldn't be able to resist snapping even one photo of anything he thought was weird and cool. "So, what *do you* want to do today, Jack?" she asked.

"I don't know," Jack admitted. "I was hoping you'd have some ideas."

With a frustrated sigh and a shake of her head, Nikki's green eyes searched the clear water of the creek. "I want to look for river stones," she told him.

"Oh, you always look for stones," Jack whined. "Why do you collect those useless stones?"

"Because I like stones," Nikki said.

"You're such a...such a girl!" Jack huffed.

"And you're a dweeb," Nikki told him, shaking her auburn-haired head.

She ignored Jack and kneeled at the edge of the creek, reached into the water, and pulled out a shiny, bright blue stone. Scratching the side of her freckled nose, Nikki studied the stone for a moment. Then she wiped it dry on her T-shirt and put it in another pocket of her jeans.

Bored out of his mind, Jack pulled a book of matches from his bag and started lighting them one by one. Every time he lit a match, he'd watch it burn for a few seconds and then toss it in the river. When Nikki saw him doing this, she stood up and gently punched his shoulder to get his attention.

"Ouch!" he complained. "What was that for?"

"You know you're not supposed to play with matches, Jack," said Nikki. "Where did you get them this time?"

Jack shrugged and looked down at the grass. "I...um...I found them on the way to school today."

"Liar! Grandma buys this kind of matches. How many times did you get in trouble for stealing her matches, Jack?" Nikki's eyes flashed with anger. She snatched the book of matches from Jack's hand and punched his shoulder again, a little harder this time.

"Hey, that hurt!" He looked at her. "Now give those back!"

Nikki stuck the matches into her pocket. "You want them? Then take them from me." She knew Jack was a little afraid of her and he wouldn't push her to fight over the matches.

Glaring at her, Jack's blue eyes suddenly looked past her. "Nikki, turn around and look behind you."

"Jack, if you're trying to trick me so you can put your grabby hand into my pocket, it's not going to work."

Jack pointed. "No! Just turn around and look!"

With a sigh of frustration, Nikki turned and saw what Jack was pointing at. "That looks like a pumpkin," she said. "But it's *black*. I've never seen a black pumpkin before. Have you?"

"Nope," Jack told her, shaking his head.

The black pumpkin was sitting on the ground, near one of the willow trees at the edge of Weeping Meadow. They immediately forgot all about their argument and ran to look at the pumpkin.

"I think this pumpkin is rotten," said Nikki.

Jack grabbed the black pumpkin and held it up to his nose. "Doesn't smell rotten. Come on, let's take it back to the house and cut it open."

"It'll probably be filled with bugs and worms and other creepy-crawly creatures," Nikki said.

"That would be so cool," Jack said, wishfully.

Nikki shook her head and rolled her eyes, remembering the disgusting things Jack either brought home or took pictures of.

As they walked back to the house, taking turns carrying the heavy pumpkin, Jack glanced at Nikki. He grinned and thought: *I fooled you this time. You don't know that I have a box of stick matches in my pocket, and I'm going to play with them whenever I want to.*

When they got back to Grandma Sweet's house, they walked around to the front porch and sat down on the steps leading up to the front door. While Jack turned the black pumpkin over and over, studying it, Nikki felt the sharp edge of the matchbox poking her. She took it out of her pocket and put it on the step beside her.

"We need a knife to carve that pumpkin," said Nikki.

Jack pulled his phone from the pocket of his jeans. "Yeah, get one from the kitchen. But can I take just one picture so I can show it to my friends?" he asked.

"I guess so, Jack," said Nikki. "A black pumpkin *is* pretty weird."

"I wouldn't carve that pumpkin or take a picture of it if I were you," said a strange, chiming voice out of nowhere.

Nikki and Jack were stunned. They turned and looked around.

"Who said that?" Nikki demanded.

ENTER IF YOU DARE

"I did," the voice replied.

The two cousins could now pinpoint where the voice was coming from and looked up at Mister Bonejingles, the silver wind chime.

They jumped to their feet at the same time.

"How come you can talk?" asked Jack, feeling scared but curious. "You're not supposed to talk, Mister Bonejingles! You're just a wind chime."

"I am *not* just a wind chime."

Taking a step closer to get a better look, Nikki asked the silver skeleton, "Then what are you?"

"My name is Wishbone Jones."

"Where did you come from and how come you can talk?" asked Jack.

"I come from Creepy Hollow, a land that exists in another realm," said Wishbone Jones.

"Never heard of it," said Nikki.

"Of course you haven't," said Wishbone. "Few people in your world know of its existence, and those few are all children, just like yourselves."

"Well, my name is Jack, and this is my cousin Nikki," said Jack.

"I've been watching you two kids and it's very nice to meet you both."

Nikki took the wind chime off the hook and held it in her hand. "So how did you end up here, on Grandma's front porch?"

"That's a bit of a long story," said Wishbone.

"We have plenty of time before we go Trick or Treating," she said.

"Well," Wishbone began, "once upon a time I was a great warrior. I fought many battles until I was badly injured in the Troll War, protecting The Trinity of Wishmothers, who watch over Creepy Hollow."

"You mean…you don't mean you're dead, do you?" asked Nikki

"No, I'm alive but I'm not a flesh and bone man anymore," Wishbone told her.

"I'm sorry."

"Me, too," said Jack.

Nikki frowned and said, "Wait! Your body is silver. How can that be?"

"The Healing Witch turned my body into silver in order to save my life. That's how I became known as the Silver Skeleton of Celestria," Wishbone explained with a cynical tone in his voice.

"What's Celestria, Mister Wishbone?" Jack wanted to know.

"Celestria is the Realm of Spirits, where I live with my friends. It's a cemetery in Creepy Hollow." Wishbone cleared his throat with a metallic-sounding cough. "You see, in Creepy Hollow the spirits of the dead can live side-by-side with the living."

"Awesome!" Jack exclaimed.

"Wicked!" Nikki said, clapping her hands. "Okay, but now you're a wind chime. So how did that happen?"

"Well, let me tell you, and I'll try to make it as short as I can," said Wishbone. "It all began with a Goblin named Hobart. Hobart was just another ordinary goblin who had fallen on hard times. He lost his job and his home and had no luck at all. So one day he went to visit The Trinity of Wishmothers and begged them for help. Taking pity on him, the Wishmothers gave him a test in the form of three wishes. He was supposed to use the three wishes to help others, which in turn would help him and bring him good luck. But Hobart was greedy and he used the three wishes for selfish reasons. He wished for wealth and power and fame, so he failed the test. When he wished for power his body turned strong and his new strength made him overconfident and mean. The Wishmothers tried but they couldn't take away the three wishes they had granted him."

Nikki and Jack hung onto every word Wishbone said as he continued. "First, Hobgoblin used his wealth to build a great castle, which he calls Crag Heap, and he used his fame to attract a large band of followers. Then he used his power when he and his minions took over Goblin Acres and locked the mayor in the Deep Dark Dungeon."

"That Hobgoblin sure is one bad dude," said Jack.

"He certainly is," Wishbone agreed. "But wait, there's more. Hobgoblin wasn't satisfied with all that he had accomplished. He wanted more wealth and more fame, but most of all, he wanted more power…*magical* power. So he summoned one of his favorite minions, the Tasmanian Devil, who helped him murder the three Wishmothers and steal their magic Wands."

"Did Hobgoblin use the Wands?" asked Jack.

"Indeed, he did. He knew just enough magic to turn the power of the Wands against the ghosts of the three Wishmothers."

"What did he do to them?" Nikki asked.

Wishbone sighed; he sounded exactly like a wind chime swaying in the breeze. "He imprisoned them inside a black pumpkin."

Jack suddenly grew very nervous. He looked at the pumpkin and asked, "You don't mean *this* pumpkin, do you?"

"Of course he does!" said Nikki.

"Good thing we didn't carve it," Jack said. "But what happened to you, Mister Wishbone? How did you get here?"

Wishbone scratched his skull and said, "When the Healing Witch told me that the three Wishmothers had been murdered and their Wands stolen by Hobgoblin, I snuck into Crag Heap one night. I managed to steal the Wands from Hobgoblin and hide them somewhere safe. But as I was tiptoeing toward the door trying to find my way in the dark, a tiny flake of silver from my right arm got scraped off when I brushed up against a metal door frame. That piece of silver was enough for Hobgoblin to know that I was the one who took the Wands."

"How did you sneak into the castle?" Nikki asked Wishbone.

"The Healing Witch taught me a few spells, which in my present condition I can no longer use," he said. "I used the first spell to make myself invisible. Then, once I got away with the three Wands, I used some other spells to disguise them as a popcorn ball, a plastic mask, and a rubber bat."

"A baseball bat?" asked Jack.

"No, the kind of bat that flies. But this is a toy bat, made of rubber."

"Stop interrupting and let him talk, Jack," Nikki scolded him.

Jack's face turned red. "You do it to me all the time!"

"That's because you never know when to stay quiet!"

"Children, please. It's quite all right."

"So then what happened, Mister Wishbone?" Nikki asked.

"I hid the disguised Wands in three different places until I could find the black pumpkin, free the spirits of the three Wishmothers, and see to it that Hobgoblin and Tasmanian Devil are brought to justice," he said.

Nikki, always quick on her toes, said, "But you were captured. They found that piece of silver from your arm. I bet it was Hobgoblin who turned you into a wind chime."

"Yes, that's true. By turning myself invisible, I weakened the silver that protects my body. So a piece broke off. Using magic often has its drawbacks. They tortured me for days, but I didn't tell them where I hid the Wands. In his anger Hobgoblin turned my six-foot-tall, exoskeleton body into a six-inch wind chime," said Wishbone, sadly.

"I know what an exoskeleton is," Jack said proudly. "That's what protects the bodies of grasshoppers, spiders, and cockroaches, and all sorts of bugs and things." He stopped talking when Nikki gave him an angry look.

Nikki looked up at Wishbone and asked, "So how did you end up here, at Grandma's house?"

Wishbone explained, "Every year, for thirteen days up to and including Halloween, the inhabitants of Creepy Hollow can open portals that are special gateways between your world and Creepy Hollow. We call these the Ectomagic Gates. We use them to travel back and forth between our two worlds. But here on Earth, only children like you two can see the gates…and can see us."

Jack scowled and said, "So Hobgoblin brought you here."

"Yes," said Wishbone. "He used my own magic key to open a gate and bring me and the black pumpkin here. Then he hung me here, on your Grandmother's front porch."

"This Ectomagic Gate," said Nikki, "does it open here, at Grandma's house?"

"The gates open wherever we want them to open," said Wishbone. "However, come midnight tonight, we won't be able to open any more gates until next year. Those are the rules."

"You said Hobgoblin used your key to open the gate," said Jack. "Does he still have it?"

"No, after using it he tossed it in the creek before he went back to Creepy Hollow. Naturally, he has his own key, but using mine and then leaving it here got rid of any evidence that might point to his involvement in my disappearance."

"What does this key look like? Maybe we can find it," said Nikki.

"You already found it. I can feel it," Wishbone told her.

Jack and Nikki looked at each other with eyes wide open in amazement.

"The blue stone!" she said, removing the stone from her pocket.

"Wow! Your stones are not useless after all," Jack said, smiling at Nikki. Then he turned to Wishbone. "You can use the stone and go back home again, Mister Wishbone."

"Look at me," said Wishbone. "Do I look like I'm in any kind of shape to do *anything?*"

Nikki looked thoughtfully at the blue stone in her hand and placed it on top of the black pumpkin. "Can we use it to take you back to this Celestria where you live?"

"If I told you the magic words, you could," said Wishbone. "But you...you mean you would really do that for me?" His voice was filled with emotion and hope.

"Sure, why not? We have nothing better to do," said Jack.

"We'll help you. Tell us what to do," Nikki told Wishbone.

"Oh, thank you!" he said. "Okay. You just have to hold the stone out in front of you and say these magic words: *Snappy fingers, cracking bones.*"

Jack gave Nikki a skeptical look, but then shrugged his shoulders. "If a wind chime can talk, then I guess some dumb magic words can work, too," he said.

Nikki picked up the shiny blue stone, held out her hand and recited, "Snappy fingers, cracking bones!"

Suddenly she and Jack heard the snap and crackle of static electricity, and a strange humming noise. Then, a few feet from them, a vortex opened up—a gateway shaped like a wheel of swirling light set inside a shimmering blue doorway.

"Now what?" Nikki asked.

"Just walk through it as if you're walking into another room," Wishbone replied.

Jack and Nikki exchanged glances of uncertainty, then he shrugged, she nodded, and together they walked toward the Ectomagic Gate, taking Wishbone and the black pumpkin with them. As soon as they stepped through the gate they vanished from Grandma Sweet's front porch faster than Jack could unwrap a Snickers bar, which is the only thing he could do faster than Nikki could.

Chapter 2

When Nikki, Jack, and Wishbone emerged from the other side of the Ectomagic Gate, it closed behind them without a sound and vanished. Nikki was a bit disappointed; she had expected something more spectacular, such as entering a magical world with fairies and unicorns. But Jack couldn't have been happier, for they had entered a gloomy cemetery. Delicate, silvery spider webs graced the leaves and branches, from which hung Jack O'Lanterns and strings of twinkling green, purple, and orange lights. The cemetery was filled with tombstones that cast eerie shadows on the ground from the sun hiding behind huge, dark clouds.

Nikki watched curiously as dark clouds floated above the graves, but when one cloud melted into a grave and disappeared, she realized that those weren't clouds at all. They were bluish-gray and silvery-white ghosts.

"Welcome to Wormbelow," Wishbone said to Nikki and Jack.

"I thought this was Celestria," said Nikki.

"Oh, it is," Wishbone told her. "Celestria is the real name of our realm. Wormbelow is just our nickname for it. Almost everyone who dwells here calls it that."

Jack looked a little confused. "Why did you name it Wormbelow?" he asked.

"Because the soil is very rich and more worms live here than in any other parts of Creepy Hollow," Wishbone replied.

"But…why *below?*" Jack looked at him questioningly.

Nikki rolled her eyes at him. "Duh, Jack! Where do worms live?"

Jack frowned thoughtfully and scratched his head. Then his eyes went wide. "In the ground," he said, smiling. "Worms live below the ground."

"Took you long enough," said Nikki.

"Wormbelow is a more fitting name for other residents of Celestria, as well," Wishbone cackled. "The bodies of everyone who died lay below ground, but their ghosts float above. They're celestial beings and I think that's where the name, Celestria, came from."

"This place is totally awesome," said Jack. He pulled out his phone. "I've got to take some pictures." He took a picture but when he tried to post it on Instagram, he couldn't. He mumbled, "What's going on? I don't have a single bar. Check yours, Nikki."

Nikki took her phone out of her pocket, stared at the screen and said with a disappointed look on her face, "Me neither. Not a single one. There's no reception here."

"Hey, look!" Jack showed Nikki his phone. "I took the picture but now it's just a blur. What's going on?"

Wishbone chuckled, "This is Creepy Hollow. We don't have such things as Wi-Fi, cellular towers, or the internet here. And you can't take pictures, either. This is a secret place. Nobody in your world, other than you and a few other kids, are allowed to know about it."

"That's bad!" said Nikki, wondering and worrying what they would do if they had to call home for help. She frowned and put away her phone.

Jack was disappointed, but he shrugged. "So, Mister Wishbone," he said, putting his now useless phone back in his pocket. "What do we do now? What do you want me to do with this pumpkin?"

"We need to take it to the Wishmother's mausoleum, just a little further," Wishbone said.

Jack looked confused. "What's a mausoleum?" he asked.

"It's like a grave," Nikki explained, "except that it's above the ground, not below it. It's like a small house."

Jack nodded. "Oh, I see. The Wishmothers' bodies are buried in the house, but their ghosts are now stuck inside the black pumpkin."

They heard shuffling sounds and saw two tall figures emerge from the darkness of the line of trees by the graves and slowly walk toward them. Jack and Nikki looked at each other, uncertain whether they should be afraid or not. One of the figures was a black cat that walked like a man, and the other was a young woman who looked like a Goth vampire.

Wishbone, still being held by Nikki, shook his whole bony, silver body. "My friends are here," he said happily.

Nikki and Jack sighed in relief.

"Wishbone, you've come back!" cried the man-like black cat.

"I see you're still a snappy dresser," Wishbone laughed, eyeing his friend's colorful outfit. "That brown vest over a blue shirt, blue-striped pants and leather boots with the pouch dangling from your leather belt really suits you. I wish I could wear decent clothes, but look at me…" Wishbone's voice turned sad. "Curse that evil Hobgoblin!"

The tall cat hissed.

The woman's silver eyes flashed with anger. She lowered her head for a moment and wiped the tears from her eyes.

She likes him, she likes him a lot, Jack thought. *And I bet Mister Wishbone likes her, too.* In many ways, the woman reminded Jack of his classmate, Peggy, who always dressed in black clothes. He had a huge crush on her but was still too shy to talk to her.

"I missed you so much," the pretty Goth woman told Wishbone. "After we heard what that awful Hobgoblin did to you, I went to the Seer Witch. She said you'd be found on the Other Side by children who would bring you back to us." She took a step forward as her black gown trailed behind her, and flipped her long black hair over her shoulder.

"Yes, I'm back, but look at me now." Wishbone sighed, gave an admiring glance to the young woman and thought: *She still wears the turquoise headband I gave her. She didn't forget me. And she still paints her nails black.* He fought back the feelings of sadness and hopelessness that were creeping up on him.

"It doesn't matter," she said with warmth in her eyes. "You're still you."

Yeah, I'm still me, Wishbone thought bitterly.

Nikki admired the young woman's lace gloves and sparkling rings and thought: *She really likes turquoise. Goth. She's definitely Goth. She's so pretty with her pale face, and her clothes suit her very well. She's a lot taller than me, too. I wonder how old she is. She looks about eighteen-ish*, Nikki guessed, impressed by the older girl's clothing and behavior.

Wishbone desperately wanted to avoid the tall woman's eyes, which were filled with pity and sorrow. He nodded to Nikki and Jack. "Let me introduce these *very* special children, my dear," Wishbone told the tall woman. "Nikki found my Key Stone to the Ectomagic Gate. Jack found the black pumpkin and brought it back with us."

The black, humanlike cat took a step forward and said excitedly, "Wonderful! My name is Otto, but I prefer to be called Catman. I'm the caretaker of Wormbelow."

"How come you look like a cat and can talk like a person?" Jack asked.

"That's because I *am* a person. Or was, I should say," said Catman. "You see, long ago I had a black cat named Poe, who was my best friend. He lived all of his nine lives and then got sick and was close to death." Tears formed in his eyes and he turned away.

Noticing Otto's distress, Wishbone said, "The only way to save Poe was for Otto and Poe to become one person."

"That is so cool," Jack said.

Catman wiped his eyes with his paw and turned around to continue his story. "So the Wishmothers granted my wish, and now Poe and I are one. We are Catman."

Nikki and Jack clapped their hands. "Awesome!" she said.

The Goth girl flashed a smile at the children with her plump blue lips and introduced herself. "My real name is Hannah, but I prefer to be called Ghoulina. It suits me much better, don't you think?"

"Oh, yes, I think so," said Nikki.

"Me, too," said Jack.

"And my first name is Bob," said Wishbone. "But since I became the Silver Skeleton, everyone started calling me 'Wishbone.' I don't mind. I kind of like it."

Jack couldn't stop himself from laughing out loud.

Nikki gave him a puzzling look. "What's so funny, Jack?"

"It's their names…Otto, Hannah, and Bob."

"What is so funny about our names?" Ghoulina asked indignantly.

"Your names are palindromes!" Jack boasted when he saw the puzzled looks on their faces. *Ha, Nikki doesn't know, but I know*, he thought, feeling smug.

"What's a palindrome?" asked Catman.

"A palindrome is a word or name that's the same whether you spell it forward or backward," Jack explained. His happy grin turned sour when he saw the disapproval on Nikki's face, but he continued anyway. "You know, like racecar, level, radar, and a lot of other words."

"Well, now we all know. We're palindromes." Ghoulina shook her head, looking irritated.

Nikki gave Jack an angry glare. His ears and cheeks turned red. "I'm sorry," he said. "I didn't mean to be a know-it-all or to make fun of anyone."

"No worries, Jack," Catman said, trying to ease the tension. "Ghoulina is just a little irritated because she's hungry. She hasn't eaten a thing all morning."

Jack, suddenly frightened, took a sharp breath.

Nikki lifted her hand as if to protect her neck, and asked in a hoarse voice, "You mean you haven't drunk any blood today?" She cleared her throat and then it dawned on her. "Wait, the sun's out. Vampires don't come out during the daytime."

Ghoulina walked up to her, put her pale hands on her hips and stared down at Nikki. "I am not a vampire, little girl. I am a Ghoul," she said.

The initial shock wore off quickly and Nikki got angry that the older girl seemed to be trying to intimidate her. "Well, how was I supposed to know that?" She stomped the ground with her foot. "*You* live here. I'm just visiting!"

For a moment, Ghoulina's silver eyes flashed angrily, turning from silver to red, and then from red to yellow, and finally back to silver again. Nikki took a step back. She shifted her weight, as her martial arts *sensei* taught her, and got ready to fight in case Ghoulina attacked her and Jack.

If she's not going to drink our blood, then she's going to eat us! Jack thought, growing frightened. But he stood his ground next to Nikki and stared Ghoulina in the eye.

Then Ghoulina started laughing and her unexpected reaction startled Nikki and Jack.

"You know what, kids? You're both smart and brave. I like that," Ghoulina said.

"You scared the daylights out of me!" Nikki huffed, feeling puzzled but relieved.

"Oh, sorry," Ghoulina said. "I didn't mean to scare you. It's my eyes. I can't control my eyes when I feel annoyed and hungry."

"Um…forgive me if this offends you, but you don't look like a Ghoul," Nikki said. "Ghouls look like ugly monsters because they eat meat, dead meat. Don't they?"

Ghoulina curtsied and laughed. "Yes, Ghouls who eat meat look like ugly monsters," she said. "But I don't eat meat."

"If not eating meat makes a Ghoul look as pretty as you are, then I'm changing my diet," Jack said and, in his mind's eye, he pictured Peggy giving him admiring glances when he walked into his classroom looking tall, dark, and handsome. Ghoulina's pleasant voice snapped him out of his daydreaming state.

"Why, Jack! How nice of you to say that," Ghoulina replied. "I'll tell you about that, later. Right now, we have to talk about what we're going to do. Thanks to you, we have the black pumpkin, and Wishbone is back. But now it's time for you to go home and we have to make plans how to free the Wishmothers."

"We can help," Nikki said, looking at Jack for approval.

"Sure, I'm in," Jack replied. "Just let us know what to do."

"Thank you for your offer, we really appreciate it," Ghoulina said. "But you have helped us a lot already. We can't put you in danger. You must open the gate and go home."

"No, we want to help!" Nikki said.

"Hannah is right, we can't let you help us," Wishbone agreed. "We have to get the wands back and the places I hid them are dangerous."

"Please let us help," Jack begged.

"We want to help and we will be careful," Nikki added.

Ghoulina, Catman, and Wishbone talked in hushed voices for a few minutes, and then Ghoulina said, "Alright, but you must do as we tell you and at the first sign of danger we will send you home. Do you have ideas of what we should do?"

Nikki looked at Ghoulina and then counted down the tasks on her fingers. "First, I think what we need to do is to figure out how to get Wishbone back to his right size and free the ghosts from the black pumpkin. Right?" she asked.

Ghoulina nodded. "Exactly! We need a plan."

Jack raised his hand. "I have an idea," he said.

"Let's hear it," said Wishbone. "What's your idea?"

"If any of you have a knife, we can cut open the pumpkin and free the Wishmothers," said Jack.

Startled by Jack's suggestion, Catman hissed angrily, Ghoulina took a horrified breath, and Wishbone shook himself in Nikki's hand, making his silver bones ring and chime in alarm.

"No!" Wishbone protested. "We can't do that. That's the worst thing we could do, and the worst thing that could happen to the Wishmothers."

"You mean, worse than being trapped inside a black pumpkin forever?" asked Nikki.

"Oh, yes, yes indeed," said Catman, licking one of his paws.

"What do you mean?" asked Jack. "Seems like the right way to free them. Just cut them out of there with a good sharp knife."

"Boys and their simple ideas. Cut it, hit it, and kick it. But this is not that simple!" Ghoulina moaned.

Nikki laughed out loud, but when she saw the hurt expression on Jack's face, she whispered, "Sorry, Jack."

Ghoulina walked over to Jack, placed her pale hands on his shoulders and quietly said, "I'm sorry too, Jack. I didn't mean to hurt your feelings, but most boys your age don't think about the consequences before they do something stupid or even dangerous."

"Nu-uh, not me…well, not usually. I didn't mean to be hasty, it's just…it seemed like a good idea," Jack said, quietly accepting Ghoulina's apology.

"It's alright," Ghoulina said. "You didn't know, so let me explain. To carve into that black pumpkin would not only cause harm to it, but doing so would also destroy the ghosts of the three Wishmothers forever."

Jack took a sharp breath and said, "Oh, we don't want that!"

"No, we don't," Ghoulina said and looked at the others. "Let's go over to the Wishmothers' mausoleum. We will explain everything, and then figure out what we're going to do."

Everyone nodded in agreement and followed Ghoulina.

Nikki glanced at the sky just as a witch riding a broom flew by, accompanied by whispering ghosts and squawking ravens. A number of ghosts poked their heads out of their graves to look around and see what was happening. A pair of big, fat spiders dropped from nearby treetops, dangling by silvery strands of webbing, and reminding Nikki of nosey neighbors. A gentle breeze whispered through the cemetery, bringing with it the smells of chocolate, pumpkin pie, and fresh popcorn. Both Nikki and Jack felt safe and comfortable among the granite tombstones and in the company of their new friends.

Having grown tired of carrying Wishbone in her hand, Nikki gave him a nice, comfortable home in her backpack. She propped him up inside of it in such a way that allowed him to lean over her shoulder to see and hear everything going on.

Nikki smiled at Ghoulina. "Just to be sure. . .you and Catman are *not* ghosts, like the Wishmothers?" she asked her.

"No," Ghoulina replied with a shake of her head. "Catman is alive and he is the sexton here…the caretaker. I'm an orphan, and I wasn't always as you see me now because I was born a Ghoul. But the Wishmothers granted me the wish to change my appearance, and this is the look I chose. Ghouls have their own magical powers, too, for healing and such things. But we are not powerful like the Wishmothers. We do not possess the magic to grant wishes."

"I'm an orphan, too," Nikki said. Then suddenly she realized something. "You're the Healing Witch who saved Wishbone's life!"

Ghoulina and Wishbone exchanged sad and affectionate glances. "Yes, I am," she said. "I came here to study with the Wishmothers because I always wanted to become a Guardian of Celestria one day. But sadly, they were murdered before I could complete my training."

"And once the Wands are returned to the Wishmothers, I hope they'll be able to restore my body and make me a man again," said Wishbone.

"But here we are now, with no Wishmothers to guard our realm," said Catman, meowing like a very sad cat.

"Their spirits will be trapped forever inside the black pumpkin unless we can restore their power and set them free," Wishbone explained.

"But they'll still be ghosts, right?" Jack asked.

"Yes, I'm afraid so," said Catman. "After all, they *are* dead, and nobody has the power to raise the dead."

"But remember what I told you," Wishbone reminded Jack and Nikki. "In our world, the ghosts of the dead are always around and can interact with us, if they desire to do so. The Wishmothers may not have all the powers they once had, because they're dead. But at least they'll be free, instead of being trapped inside that cursed pumpkin."

"And I believe that you are the special children who can help us free the Wishmothers," said Ghoulina. "Humans can do things here that the rest of us can't do."

Nikki gazed into the air, imagined herself as her favorite TV show character, *Zinja: Warrior Girl* and thought, *I'll be the heroine who saves the Wishmothers.* As she was picturing herself in a long dress just like the one Ghoulina wore, her gaze fell on Jack. Seeing the dreamy expression on his face made her smile. *Jack is daydreaming of being a superhero, too.*

Coming back to reality, Nikki shook the sweet daydream out of her head and said, "So as I see it, job one is to get the Wands and bring them back here, right?"

"Spot on," said Catman. "Wishbone, where did you hide the Wands after you disguised them?"

"One Wand is disguised as a popcorn ball, and it's hidden in Red Crow Forest," Wishbone told them. "Another is a plastic Halloween mask hidden in the Cave of Spooks. The third Wand is a rubber bat that I hid in the belfry of the old, abandoned Tower of Shadows."

Ghoulina stopped and pointed at a large, stone building standing under a tall weeping willow tree. "Here we are. That's the mausoleum of the Wishmothers over there," she said. The mausoleum was a small, rectangular building made of gray stone, with two pillars, brass doors, and stained-glass windows.

"Oh, good," Jack mumbled. "This pumpkin is getting too heavy."

The late morning was peaceful and quiet as everyone sat in a circle in front of the mausoleum. Ghoulina took the black pumpkin from Jack and set it on the grass in front of her. Jack sat down between Nikki and Catman, then took his messenger bag off his shoulder and put it behind him.

"So you hid the Wands in plain sight, as everyday items, Wishbone. Excellent idea," said Ghoulina, her flowing black dress immaculately clean and perfectly fluffed out on the grass around her in a most lady-like manner.

"Yes," said Wishbone. "Now the first thing we have to do is summon the Wishmothers."

"But you told us they're trapped inside the pumpkin," said Nikki.

"And so they are," Catman told her. "But even without their Wands, they still have certain magic powers. Wishmothers are very much like the genies of your world." He turned and nodded to Ghoulina. "You studied under them, Ghoulina. You're the only one who can do this."

"Do what?" Jack asked.

Ghoulina winked at Jack, blew on her black fingernails, rubbed her hands together, and said, "I will summon the Wishmothers."

Placing her hands on the black pumpkin, Ghoulina closed her silver eyes and started rubbing the pumpkin while she chanted:

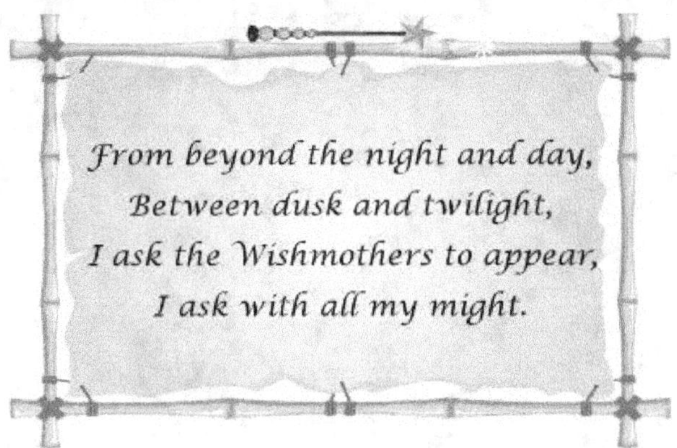

A moment later, the black pumpkin uttered a soft whooshing sound and three clouds of light blue mist emerged from inside of it. Each cloud began to take on a shape of its own, and then the shapes turned into the ghosts of very imposing-looking women.

But these were no ordinary, transparent ghosts made of light and mist and shadow, or ghosts that looked like bedsheets with holes for eyes. No, these three ghosts were finely dressed in elegant gowns and wore strange-looking hats and long, flowing capes.

Catman clasped his hands together and purred with delight.

As the three spirits floated above the pumpkin, Nikki and Jack saw that each had a black, iron chain wrapped around her wrist, and these chains were attached to the pumpkin.

Ghoulina bowed her head. "Welcome, Wishmothers," she said. "Your passing has all Celestria grieving. But now we have come with the hope of setting you free.

"I see," said the tallest Wishmother. "You have found the children who can help us. Please introduce us."

"Certainly," Ghoulina said. She nodded to the two cousins and then pointed to the first Wishmother. "Nikki and Jack, this is Prunella Pickles," she said.

First Nikki stood up and bowed, and then Jack followed her example.

"I see that you are well-mannered," Prunella Pickles said, her voice reminding Nikki of her school principle. Tall and willowy, Prunella had a thin, stern-looking face. "Welcome to our realm, children," she added.

"Thank you, Wishmother Pickles," said Nikki.

Jack was too afraid to say anything, so he just bowed again.

"I do declare, you two are the cutest children I have seen in ages," the second Wishmother said in a soft voice with a Southern accent. She curtsied and added, "My name is Gladiola Scales."

Nikki replied, "It's very nice to meet you, Wishmother Scales."

Jack stuttered but finally managed to say, "Hi!"

"My name is Minerva Terrapin," said the third Wishmother. Her chubby figure and warm smile reminded Jack of Grandma Sweet.

Nikki was startled but not surprised to see that all three Wishmothers had silver eyes, the same as Ghoulina. That made sense because Ghoulina was studying to be a Wishmother.

Prunella Pickles gave Ghoulina a stern look. "Have you been studying and practicing, child?" she asked.

"Yes, Wishmother Pickles," Ghoulina replied. "It's very difficult without your guidance, though. But we've come here to tell you that we promise to retrieve your Wands and free you from the prison of that black pumpkin."

"And how, may I ask, do you all plan to accomplish that?" asked Minerva Terrapin.

"Wishbone will guide us to where your Wands are hidden, and we shall return them to you, Wishmother," said Ghoulina.

"You know that even with our Wands there is little we can do to help you and to free ourselves from the curse of Hobgoblin's evil magic," said Prunella Pickles.

"We'll find a way, Wishmothers," Catman promised the ghosts.

"Surely you all must realize that the longer we remain chained to the black pumpkin, the number of times you may call upon us becomes fewer and fewer," said Gladiola Scales. "If you do not hurry, we will be trapped inside the pumpkin forever."

"And then you, Ghoulina, will never be able to finish your training and become a Wishmother in your own right," said Minerva Terrapin.

"I know, Wishmother," Ghoulina told her. "I know."

"The Seer Witch told Ghoulina she had a premonition that two children would come here to help us," said Wishbone. "Jack found the black pumpkin and Nikki found my Key Stone. We believe they are destined to find the answer to how we can set you free."

The Trinity of Wishmothers remained silent as they looked at Nikki and Jack, observing and studying them for a few minutes.

Everyone was tense as they watched the Wishmothers, nervously waiting for their decision.

"Yes, the children are the key to our future," Minerva Terrapin finally said.

"I do believe you are correct," Gladiola Scales agreed.

"But how will they know what to do?" Ghoulina asked.

"They will know," Prunella Pickles replied. "Together they will find the answer."

The tall, willowy Wishmother stared directly at Nikki, who felt embarrassed and uncomfortable under the penetrating gaze of her eyes.

"We must return soon to the prison of the black pumpkin," said Minerva Terrapin. "I can feel it pulling us back in."

Nikki could see the chains around the wrists of the three Wishmothers growing taut. The chains pulled them closer and closer to the pumpkin.

"We have little time left," said Prunella. "And while there is truly nothing we can do without our Wands, we are still Wishmothers. We can still offer some help."

"What do you all have in mind, dear?" Gladiola asked her.

"Each of us can give the children a wish to be granted for future use when they're in need," said Prunella. "Three wishes they will be given, which they must share but must not waste on foolish and frivolous things. Do you children understand?"

Nikki bowed. "Yes, I do, Wishmother."

Jack nodded. "Me, too!"

"Know this, children," said Wishmother Minerva. "Because you are humans from the Other Side, Hobgoblin's wicked magic cannot harm you."

"But there will be other dangers on the road ahead that you may face," Gladiola told Jack and Nikki. "Do you all understand this, my darlings?"

"I do," said Nikki.

"Ditto," said Jack.

"Very well, then," said the Wishmother. "My sisters and I wish you luck and ask you to do this as fast as you can before it is too late to free us. Farewell."

Quicker than a blink of an eye, the trio of Wishmothers were pulled back inside the black pumpkin.

The graveyard of Wormbelow grew still and silent.

"Now what?" Jack asked, daring to break the silence.

"We should leave at once," said Catman. "The sooner we start, the sooner we finish."

"Catman, as caretaker, you have the keys to the Wishmothers' mausoleum," Wishbone told him. "Hide the black pumpkin inside and lock the door."

Without a word, Catman hurried to do just that.

Ghoulina said, "We must go find the Wands and bring them back here. Are you two ready?" she asked, looking at the children.

"I'm ready," said Nikki.

Jack replied with a determined look on his face. "Me, too. Let's go."

The small group started walking across the cemetery.

Chapter 3

After they had walked across the cemetery and a large wooded area, they reached a winding road paved with black stones.

Jack complained, "I'm tired of all this walking. How far do we have to go?"

Ghoulina frowned and thought, *It was a mistake to let them come with us. He's just a whiny little boy, he will slow us down.*

Nikki watched Ghoulina's expression and could guess what she was thinking. Feeling embarrassed, she growled at Jack, "You're always bored and tired of something! You wanted to help, so stop complaining."

"Well, I can't help it. Walking is boring and my feet hurt, too," Jack said.

"And you're making my head hurt," said Nikki. "Now be quiet like everyone else!"

"Maybe you should open the portal and go home," Catman said. "This is too much for children."

"No! We're not going home until the Wishmothers are free. Ignore Jack. He's always complaining for no reason," Nikki said, giving Jack an angry look.

Catman didn't say anything but exchanged worried glances with Ghoulina and Wishbone.

Jack sulked in silence as they walked down the black stone road toward Red Crow Forest. From inside Nikki's backpack, Wishbone leaned over her right shoulder and pointed them in the right direction.

The road curved to the left and to the right as it took them through fields and meadows, past rivers and waterfalls, up hills and down hills, and along the borders of towns and villages.

The sun was nearly overhead, almost noon, and its warmth made it feel more like early summer, instead of late autumn. Jack and Nikki kept reminding themselves that they weren't in Diddlebury anymore, and the world of Creepy Hollow was quite different from the world they called home. But Nikki thought it was a pleasant day, and it felt as if they were out for a noon-time stroll.

Although Jack didn't have much to say, every now and then he would remind everyone that his legs hurt and his feet were sore. Nikki ignored him, but Ghoulina looked concerned.

Nikki, aware of Ghoulina's concern and afraid they would be sent home if Jack continued complaining, asked him, "Remember Grandma's favorite saying?"

"Yeah," Jack mumbled. "She always says, 'No use complaining when you can't change a thing.'"

"So, stop complaining already!" Nikki huffed.

"Okay, okay. I will just stop nagging," Jack replied, wanting to have the last word.

Nikki opened her mouth to tell him off, but when Ghoulina touched her shoulder and winked at her, Nikki changed her mind and didn't say a word. *We girls, we know,* she thought, feeling a bond forming between Ghoulina and her.

As they walked on, heading west toward their first destination, they saw Ogre Mountain rising in the distance, far to the north. The top of the mountain was covered with snow, and its peak hidden by mist and clouds.

"That's where the Giant Oafs live," Ghoulina told Jack and Nikki.

"They rarely come down from the mountain," said Catman. "It's cold up there and that's just the way they like it."

"I hate cold weather," said Jack. "But I love playing in the snow."

"Yeah, that's all you do in winter…play in the snow," said Nikki. "You should come over to Grandma's and help me shovel her sidewalk once in a while."

"I would, Nikki," he said. "But she only has one shovel."

"We can always share it, Jack," she said. "Haven't you ever heard of sharing?"

"Sure I have," he said. "Don't I always share my movies and games with you?"

Nikki sighed and said, "Yeah, I guess you do."

Wishbone chuckled. Catman and Ghoulina looked at each other and shook their heads.

"Kids!" she moaned, but not unkindly.

"They should be seen but not heard, right?" Catman asked her.

"As right as rain," Ghoulina told Catman and winked at him playfully.

Nikki and Jack frowned, but then started laughing when they realized they were just being teased.

"No, it's not right, Catman. Children should be allowed to speak freely when they have something to say." Ghoulina changed her mind as she remembered how the children were hushed by the caretakers and teachers all the time in the orphanage where she grew up.

"Yes, you're right." Catman admitted. "I was just kidding around. I always hated it when adults bullied and threatened kids into silence when I was a young lad."

"Children should speak their minds," came Wishbone's chiming voice. "But they shouldn't blab and they must learn when to keep quiet."

Nikki frowned, looked at the group, and said indignantly, "I think Jack and I have heard enough of teacher-ish stuff for today."

"Yeah!" Jack agreed happily because he hated to be lectured.

"Look!" Ghoulina pointed ahead, glad for the chance to change the touchy subject.

They saw a long line of hills filled with caves of all sizes.

"That's Gremlinville, where the Gremlins live and work," said Wishbone. "A number of them now serve Hobgoblin, as do a lot of Gnomes, Imps, and even an Ogre or two."

They walked in relative silence, admiring the unusual sights. Fields of bright blue grass lay on both sides of the road. Farther away they saw a narrow, purple river that emptied into a small, purple lake. They saw green roses, red sunflowers, black tulips, and palm trees no taller than themselves, with big leaves shaped like hands. It was a whole new world to them, strange and exciting. But for as much as they enjoyed the sights, they always kept in mind the possible dangers that lurked everywhere and worst of all…the possibility that Hobgoblin might somehow find out what they were up to.

After a while, Nikki's stomach began to growl. "I'm getting hungry," she said, having not had anything to eat since breakfast. "Is anyone else hungry?"

"Now that you mention it, I still am," said Ghoulina.

"Me, too," said Jack.

"You're *always* hungry," Nikki said to him.

"I suppose we can stop to eat and rest," said Catman.

"Trouble is, we didn't think to bring any food with us," said Ghoulina.

"That's definitely going to be a problem," said Jack. "Nikki, what do you have in your backpack?"

"I can tell you that," said Wishbone.

"What's she got in there, Mister Wishbone?" asked Jack.

"Well, there are a couple of comic books, a notebook, a few pens, two flashlights, and rocks…lots of rocks," said Wishbone.

"Nikki collects rocks," said Jack. "She's got rocks in her head, too."

"And you got peanut butter in yours, Jack!" said Nikki angrily. Her stomach growled again. "I'm starving! I wish we had something to eat."

"Oh my," said Wishbone. "Bad call, kid. Bad call."

Ding!

From somewhere in the distance, a bell rang. A moment later, a blanket and a picnic basket appeared on the blue grass right in front of them.

"Well, there goes your first wish," said Ghoulina.

"I wasted one wish," Nikki said, feeling guilty. "I'm so sorry, but I was starving."

"Well, we can't take it back, so let's eat!" Catman said, eyeing the food basket.

"Not me," said Wishbone. "I haven't eaten since the day I turned to silver."

"That's sad, Mister Wishbone," said Jack. "I'm sorry."

The companions sat down on the blanket and Nikki opened the picnic basket. "Wow! Cakes and cookies, candy and water bottles…and hot dogs and hamburgers. We got all kinds of food here."

Jack and Catman wasted no time finding something to eat. Jack, as usual, made a pig of himself by taking a huge bite from the juicy burger and stuffing a handful of chips into his mouth.

Nikki was about to take a bite of her hot dog when she noticed that Ghoulina was still standing but not eating anything. "Would you like a hot dog?" Nikki offered her.

"I'm a Ghoul," said Ghoulina. "Ghouls don't eat hot dogs."

"She eats corpses, Nikki. You know…dead bodies," said Jack.

Nikki frowned with disgust. "Gross! Do you eat zombies, too?" she asked.

"Get real!" said Ghoulina. "Zombies don't count as corpses. They're the living dead."

"And zombies eat only people who are alive," said Nikki.

Jack nodded. "Yep!" he said.

Catman laughed and winked at Ghoulina. "Do you eat cats?" he asked her.

"You know very well I don't," Ghoulina replied.

"Well, you can't eat me," Wishbone said, joining in on the conversation. "I don't have any meat on my silver bones."

"As if," said Ghoulina. "Not even a dog would gnaw on your skinny bones."

"So, you just eat dead people, right?" Jack asked Ghoulina.

"No, I do not eat meat, dead or otherwise," she said.

"Jack and Nikki eat dead meat," Catman teased Ghoulina.

Nikki grabbed another hot dog, smeared it with mustard and relish and said, "But Grandma cooks it first."

"Now *that* is totally disgusting," said Ghoulina.

Jack stuffed his mouth with the other half of his burger. "Hey, have you forgotten, Nikki?" he said with a mouth full of food. "Ghoulina doesn't eat meat."

"I'm a vegetarian," Ghoulina told Jack. "And it's not polite to talk with your mouth full, young man."

"So what does a vegetarian ghoul like to eat?" Nikki asked, opening a bottle of water.

"You know," Catman said, laughing. "Dead leaves, flowers, plants, and vegetables."

Ghoulina gave Catman a look that froze the laughter in his throat. "I'm glad to see you're enjoying yourself and having fun at my expense," she said.

Catman gave her an apologetic look but when Ghoulina winked at him with a smile on her pretty face, he realized that she wasn't angry, she was just teasing him.

Jack asked, "So you never eat cooked food?"

Ghoulina shook her head. "I like my food raw. I eat vegetables, leafy greens, and fruit," she replied.

Reaching into the picnic basket, Nikki pulled out a plastic bowl filled with carrots, peas, radishes, and celery sticks, and handed it to Ghoulina. "These are not cooked," she said.

"Thank you, Nikki," Ghoulina said as she reached for the bowl, sat down, and started eating.

After their accidental but very much appreciated break, Nikki, Jack, and their three companions set out again on the road. Their stomachs were full, which put them in a much better mood. While teasing each other and laughing during lunch, old friendships had been renewed and new friendships had been forged.

They reached the banks overlooking the violet waters of the Purple River, which curved to the left just ahead of them. To their right stood the edge of Red Crow Forest, which was encircled by a wall of gigantic cactus trees. Two huge, red brick crow statues stood guard on each side of the path leading into the woods. Dark, menacing trees loomed high above the entrance. Strange and eerie sounds echoed from deep within the forest. The squawking of birds, chattering of squirrels, and the chirping of insects was deafening.

"Well, here we are," Wishbone announced, leaning against one side of Nikki's backpack and looking over her shoulder. "Red Crow Forest. We enter here."

"How far do we have to walk, Mister Wishbone?" asked Jack.

"Oh, not very far at all," Wishbone told him. "Perhaps a half hour's walk, at most."

"And you remember where you hid the popcorn ball Wand?" Nikki asked.

"Of course I do, young lady," Wishbone replied, almost sounding as if he'd been insulted.

Catman hissed softly. "You'd better be sure of that, Bones," he said.

"I surely hope so," Ghoulina added. "All this walking has gotten my lovely gown all stained and dirty."

Nikki looked at the Goth Wishmother-in-training. Sure enough, mud, road dust, grass stains, and twigs stuck in the lace had made a mess of her lovely dress. But then Ghoulina gave her gown a shake, whispered a spell under her breath, and suddenly it was all clean again.

"There! That takes care of that," she said.

"Neat!" Jack told her. "You have to teach me that trick. My Mom is always complaining about the mess I make of my clothes."

Ghoulina laughed and mussed up Jack's hair. "Shall we continue?" she suggested.

"Yes, I guess," said Nikki.

"You should pull your ear for good luck," Jack murmured under his breath.

"That's just a game, Jack," Nikki said with a nervous laugh. She saw Ghoulina watching her and felt embarrassed.

Ghoulina smiled and said to her, "We can use all the luck we can get."

Nikki shrugged and thought, *It wouldn't hurt, and just in case…*and then she quickly tugged her earlobe three times.

Catman led the way into the forest, and although they didn't see any of the forest's denizens, they could hear them moving and fluttering about the tree tops and through the underbrush. There were palm trees growing in Red Crow Forest, too, but these were unlike any palm trees Nikki and Jack had ever seen. In fact, they weren't even sure if they *were* palm trees. These had big fat trunks gnarled and twisted like the roots of an ancient oak tree. The branches and huge green leaves drooped like weeping willows. There was one other odd thing about these trees, too:

"Pumpkins!" Nikki cried out in amazement. "Pumpkins grow on trees here?"

"Indeed they do," Wishbone told her.

"They grow in patches on the ground, where we come from," said Jack.

"Well," said Wishbone. "You'll soon see why I hid the magic popcorn ball here."

Catman wiped the dust from his long whiskers. "How much farther do we have to go?" he asked.

"Just up ahead, where the path forks left and right," Wishbone replied.

"Which fork do we take?" Ghoulina asked, sounding impatient.

"Why, the right one, of course," Wishbone told her.

Upon reaching the fork, they continued walking on the right path for another quarter hour or so. Jack grumbled and complained all the way about his tired and achy feet. Nikki told him to stop whining a number of times, but he ignored her.

"Jack, I'm warning you!" Nikki said, losing her patience. "If I hear one more peep out of you, I'm going to say the magic words, open the gate, and send you home. You're not a baby anymore. Stop complaining!"

"Okay, okay!" replied Jack, feeling embarrassed. "Not a peep, promise."

Jack walked quietly after that and finally, Wishbone called the group to a halt when they reached a small clearing. It was surrounded by pumpkin trees, darkness, and the echoes of squawking crows.

"Third tree on the left, next to the gray rock," said Wishbone. "Catman, go stand next to the rock and look up at the tree. You can't miss it."

Catman trotted over to the palm tree and looked up. "I see it!" he said. "It's high up between the branches, but thanks to having Poe's abilities, I can climb up to get it."

Removing his boots, Catman sunk his needle-sharp claws into the trunk of the tree and started to climb. He almost reached the orange popcorn ball that hung concealed between the pumpkins when a thin branch snapped under his weight.

Ghoulina shouted and everyone ran to the tree to try to catch the falling Catman. He meowed in fright but flipped his body in the air and dug his claws into a thicker branch, breaking his fall.

Everyone gave out a relieved sigh when he started climbing again, this time being more careful. He reached the branch where the popcorn ball was hidden and pulled it free. He hurried back down to rejoin the others.

"You got it!" Nikki said with delight.

"I've never seen an *orange*-colored popcorn ball," said Jack. "Why did you make it orange, Mister Wishbone?"

"There is no better way to hide it from prying eyes, among all the orange pumpkins, Jack," Wishbone explained.

"Very clever," said Ghoulina. "Now I suggest you put the popcorn ball inside Nikki's backpack, Catman. Then let's get out of here. This place is giving me the creeps. Listen."

Faintly at first, but slowly growing louder, the flapping of wings and the squawking of a great flock of birds echoed in the distance. Then, far ahead of them, the sky darkened with large, red shapes heading in their direction.

"Shrieks!" Catman yelled. He grabbed his boots and quickly put them on.

"What are Shrieks?" Nikki asked him.

"The Red Crows that inhabit this forest and gave it its name," Catman told her.

"But crows are black!" Jack hollered over the growing clamor of the birds.

"Not in Creepy Hollow," said Ghoulina.

The sky grew even redder and darker with the oncoming flock of crows.

"What are we going to do?" Nikki asked, staring at the sky. She grew more afraid as the Shrieks drew nearer and nearer.

"We run!" proposed Catman with fear in his eyes as he picked up a thick, broken tree branch that was lying on the ground.

They turned and ran for their lives but could not outrun the flock of Red Crows.

"Why are they coming after us?" Nikki asked.

"Because they saw Catman take something from one of their trees," Ghoulina told her.

"But they didn't even know it was there until we came to get it, because they didn't guard it. And the Wand is not theirs, it belongs to the Wishmothers," Jack said defiantly.

Ghoulina shook her head. "That doesn't matter to them. Their rules say that anyone is allowed to bring something to their forest but nobody is allowed to take anything away," she said. "Stop talking and keep running!"

"Nobody told me that rule," Jack mumbled, speeding up.

They ran as fast as their legs could carry them. But the Red Crows closed the gap and swooped down to attack, cawing and squawking with anger.

"Guard the children, Ghoulina!" Catman called out. "I'll try to hold them off." He stopped and turned, and then started swinging the branch as if it was a baseball bat.

Bam! Wham! Slam!

Catman snarled and whacked three of the Shrieks, sending them tumbling through the air. But the flock of Red Crows swarmed in and surrounded him.

"We're doomed!" screamed Wishbone.

The branch was a blur in the air as Catman kept swinging it, fighting off crows that tried to peck and scratch him. He knocked down two more Shrieks, but more swarmed all over him.

"Cover your eyes and your faces, kids," Ghoulina told Jack and Nikki. She herded them under a pumpkin tree and stood guard in front of them with her arms outstretched.

Jack buried his face in his hands. "Why don't we use Nikki's rocks and throw them at the crows?" he suggested.

"What kind of rocks do you have, Nikki?" Ghoulina asked.

"Just…just some rocks I found in the creek back home," Nikki told her. She was trembling with fear but tried hard not to let her voice give her away. "You know. River stones."

"Ah, yes. Wisdom Stones," said Ghoulina. She turned, reached into Nikki's backpack, and pulled out a fistful of stones. "These will do nicely. Catman, come back here!"

Swinging his branch and battering crow after crow, Catman slowly backed away and rejoined the others. Though he had killed or knocked unconscious a number of Shrieks, they continued the attack as more crows stormed in.

Ghoulina's silver eyes flashed and, turning to face the army of Red Crows, she tossed her handful of rocks high into the air, raised her arms, and chanted a magic spell:

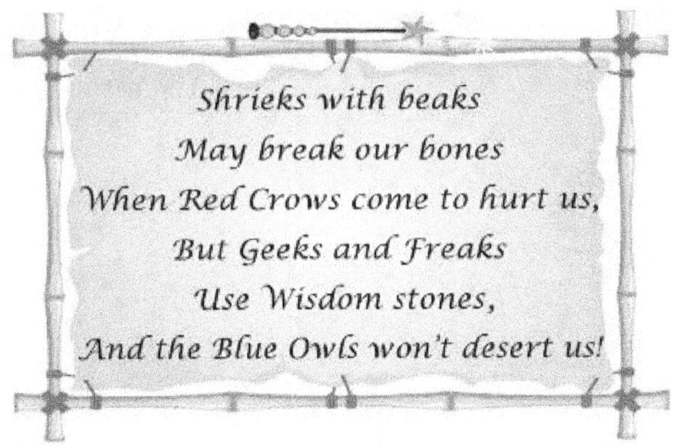

Suddenly a huge dome of blue light encircled the companions, protecting them, and the stones Ghoulina tossed into the air turned into an army of bright Blue Owls.

The Crows shrieked and tried to flee as the Owls hooted, flapped their wings, and attacked them.

Red Crows squawked and Blue Owls screeched as they clashed in battle, their beaks nipping and snapping at one another. For a moment, the sky looked as if a purple tornado was swirling in the air. Feathers, both blue and red, floated to the ground. Bodies of fat, Red Crows tumbled from the sky and crashed into the ground and among the treetops. Soon the rest of the Red Crows gave up. They turned, flapped their wings furiously, and flew back the way they had come. But the Blue Owls weren't finished with them yet. With a great hooting cry, the Owls set off after the Shrieks and within moments both flocks of avian warriors disappeared from view.

Catman wiped sweat from his brow. "That was close," he muttered. "Thanks for saving us, Ghoulina."

"You fought well and bravely, Catman," Ghoulina said. "But we owe our thanks to Jack." She turned and ruffled Jack's hair. "That was brilliant, Jack. Stone the crows. Just brilliant!"

Blushing, Jack said modestly, "Oh, it was just a thought."

Nikki gave Jack an affectionate punch in the shoulder. "I'm proud of you. You were scared but you still used your head," she told him.

Jack puffed up his chest, smiled, and took a bow.

Chapter 4

The five companions emerged from Red Crow Forest, huffing and puffing from running so fast and hard. Nikki passed around the last of the water bottles and everyone took a moment to quench their thirst and catch their breath.

"Is everyone okay?" asked Ghoulina.

Catman purred and nodded.

"We're fine," said Nikki.

"Except for a few scratches and a ripped shirt," said Jack.

"What happened back there, Wishbone?" Ghoulina asked. "Did you encounter the Shrieks when you first hid the popcorn ball?"

"No, I didn't," said Wishbone. "In fact, I had no trouble with anyone or anything when I hid the other two Wands, either. But as you said, bringing something in is no problem, but getting it out again is not that easy."

Catman scratched behind one ear. "And don't forget, you were the mighty Silver Skeleton when you hid the Wands," he said, "not a talking wind chime."

"You had your own magic then, too," Ghoulina told Wishbone.

"A whole lot of good it did when that menacing Tasmanian Devil caught me," said Wishbone, sounding disappointed and a little embarrassed.

"He ambushed you, with help from Gnomes and Goblins," Catman told him. "They had Hobgoblin's evil magic to protect them. They outnumbered you, trapped you, and overpowered you. You can't blame yourself for that."

Nikki felt great sorrow for Wishbone when she saw the sad expression on his face, and to change the sensitive subject she asked, "Where do we go next?"

Thankful for the interruption, Wishbone quickly replied, "To the Tower of Shadows, where I hid the second Wand, disguised as a rubber bat. There was an ancient city there a long time ago, but it was destroyed during a war. Only the old tower remains standing."

Afraid she might lose the Key Stone, Nikki took it out of her pocket and put it in her backpack.

"Good thinking, Nikki," Wishbone said. "We don't want to lose it."

"How far is this Tower of Shadows?" Nikki asked.

"Not far," Ghoulina answered. "Both Catman and I know the place."

Jack yawned and whined, "I don't care how far it is. I'm tired. All this walking and running hurts my feet."

"Quit complaining, Jack," Nikki snapped.

"I'm not complaining," he said. "I'm just stating a fact. Walking hurts my feet and it's boring, too."

"Were you bored in Red Crow Forest?" Wishbone asked.

"No, but as I said, walking all the time is boring."

"You're always bored with things, sooner or later," Nikki told Jack.

"I wouldn't keep talking about this if I were you," Ghoulina advised Jack.

"Why? Is there some kind of rule against it or something?" asked Jack.

"Not exactly," said Ghoulina. "But if the Witch of Boredom hears you, she'll come and kidnap you. She hates Halloween and Creepy Hollow, and she'll take you to her land where fluffy bunnies hop, lions eat apples and play with lambs, and snakes bring candy to all the kids. It's all happy, smiling faces…and *so* boring."

"Sounds good to me," Jack said. He laughed teasingly, but the world of the Witch of Boredom didn't really sound appealing to him.

Ghoulina's eyes flashed from silver to red and back again. In her anger, she missed the mocking tone of Jack's voice. "Then you're a real doofus, Jack," she told him.

"Who's a doofus?" Jack demanded, quickly forgetting that this was supposed to be another teasing match to pass the time.

"You're a doofus," Ghoulina said angrily.

"Oh, yeah?" Jack sniffed and tried to find some insult to throw back at Ghoulina.

"Yeah," she said. "You're a doofus, and that's that."

Jack gritted his teeth, momentarily at a loss for words. Then he said, "Well, I know what I am. So what are you?"

Ghoulina threw her hands up in the air in disgust. "Kids!" she moaned.

"Stop it, you two!" Wishbone demanded from Nikki's backpack. "Ghoulina, you're almost a grown woman. You should know how to control your anger and words."

"All right, I'm sorry," Ghoulina mumbled as she bowed her head. "But Jack, you can be really annoying sometimes. Admit it."

Jack put his hands in his pockets, stared at the ground, and kicked some dirt with his foot, feeling embarrassed. "Well, I'm just so tired, and my feet still hurt," he said with a sigh. "I wish we had a couple of trail bikes and could ride everywhere we have to go."

"No!" hollered Nikki.

Ding! Ding! Rang the invisible bell again, and moments before its echoes faded away, two bicycles materialized out of thin air.

"Now you've done it, Jack," said Nikki. "Another wish wasted."

"Yeah, like you wasted one on food and candy," he told her.

"Well, there's nothing we can do about it now," said Ghoulina. "Jack, you really *are* a doofus. Trust me on that."

Jack's face turned red, and he was livid. "Listen, ghoulie girl," he said. "I wish you'd…"

Nikki clapped her hand over Jack's mouth before he could finish his sentence. "Enough, Jack," she said. "You were brave and smart back there in the forest, but now you're acting like a kid half your age. It's time to shut up now before you waste our last wish!"

Not daring to speak, Jack glared at his cousin, walked away, and sat on the grass, pouting.

"Well," said Catman, "as long as we have the bicycles, we might as well use them."

"But how will *we* ride?" asked Ghoulina. "I never rode on a bicycle, and I'm wearing a silk dress which I don't think is made for a bike ride."

Nikki said to Catman, "You ride with Jack, on the crossbar. He'll show you how to sit sideways and hang on. Ghoulina, you can ride with me. We just have to make sure your hair doesn't blow in my face and your gown doesn't get caught in the tires."

"What about me?" Wishbone asked.

"You stay in my backpack," Nikki told him.

Ghoulina and Catman exchanged wordless glances, and then both shrugged in resignation.

"May the Spirits of the Wishmothers help us all!" said Ghoulina.

With her long hair tied back in a ponytail and her gown pulled up to her knees, Ghoulina sat sideways on the crossbar of Nikki's bicycle.

"This is fun!" Wishbone said from his spot inside Nikki's backpack.

"Fun for you, maybe," Ghoulina told him, but this was her only complaint.

Sitting in the same position on the crossbar of Jack's bicycle, Catman's black fur was ruffled by the wind rushing past them as they rode to their next destination.

"Think you can teach me how to ride a bicycle, Jack?" Catman asked.

"I don't know, Catman," Jack replied. "You might be too old."

Catman's laugh sounded like a cat's happy meow. He let go of the handlebar with one paw, but lost his balance and almost fell off the bicycle.

"You may be right, Jack," he said.

They rode on for about half an hour or so, detouring around the borders of Troll Haven.

Trolls are very protective of their farmlands, bridges, and huge stone houses. But because sunlight turns Trolls into stone, they only come out at night. So they hire Gremlins and Gnomes to guard their realm during the daytime. Although Gremlins and Gnomes are not as frightening as Trolls, the five companions still kept to the back roads to avoid being seen. They rode their two bicycles over dusty trails and narrow paths through the woods. Wishbone instructed them when to turn left and when to turn right.

Finally, they emerged from the woods and saw a grim landscape spread out before them. Nothing grew there and nothing lived there. What few trees and ruins were left had been burned black by whatever evil power had destroyed that ancient land. The smell of smoke still lingered in the air. Everything was covered in soot, and the whole area was like a desert covered with black dust and gray ash. Only one tall building had been left standing; the dark bricks from which it was built were stained and damaged, but not destroyed.

Wishbone pointed to the structure. "There it is," he said. "The Tower of Shadows."

Nikki and Jack peddled their bikes slowly and carefully through the ash, cinders, and debris of that long-forgotten city. When they reached the tall stone tower, their passengers, Catman and Ghoulina, hopped off the bikes.

"Why in the name of the Wishmothers would you hide a Wand in this miserable-looking building?" Catman asked Wishbone.

"Because it's supposed to be haunted," said the silver wind chime leaning against the side of Nikki's backpack. "And no one in their right minds would ever come here."

"Except us," Ghoulina said, winking at Wishbone.

"Haunted by what?" Nikki asked, sharing a frightened look with Jack.

"Shadows, of course," Wishbone replied.

Jack laid his bike on the ground and stared up at the tall tower built of black bricks. "Sure looks like it's haunted, Mister Wishbone," he said. "What kind of shadows?"

"Nobody really knows," Wishbone said with a shrug. "Perhaps they're shadows of grief and sadness. Maybe the shadows are the memories of the people who once lived in this land. Dark and bitter shadows left behind, shadows of evil thoughts and emotions, things like anger and hatred, jealousy and intolerance."

"But you saw nothing when you hid the disguised Wand in this place?" Catman asked. "You weren't attacked by anything?"

Wishbone shook his little silver head. "No, I already told you."

Nikki looked first at the dark and gaping entrance to the Tower of Shadows, the door to it now long gone. The bell that had once topped the tower and rang out across the unknown realm lay broken, burned, and rusted on the ground, not far from the entrance. There were plenty of windows, so there would be enough light inside the tower, making it easy for them to see when they climbed up to the belfry to retrieve the Wand disguised as a rubber bat.

This place gives me the creeps, thought Nikki. Feeling scared, she said, "Wishbone, it's too bad you're not the mighty warrior you were the first time you came here. Nobody would dare try to hurt the Silver Skeleton, right?"

"Except for Hobgoblin and his Tasmanian henchman," said Ghoulina, sighing.

"Yes, and now I'm just a helpless wind chime," Wishbone replied woefully.

"If the Wishmothers had changed you back to your normal size, we wouldn't have to worry about anyone or anything," Catman said to Wishbone. "If you had returned the Wands to them right away, instead of hiding them, we wouldn't be here right now."

"And if the dog hadn't pooped, no one would have stepped in it!" Wishbone said angrily. "Look, Catman. I told you before…I *had* to disguise and hide the Wands. Hobgoblin's henchman was after me with his entire army, and I knew they would spy on the Wishmothers, hoping I would try to take the Wands back to them. If Hobgoblin had gotten his dirty hands on the Wands again, it would have been game over for all of us. Just look at me and you can see what sacrifices I had to make!"

"Sorry, my mouth is running faster than my brain," Catman purred softly.

"Listen, everyone," said Ghoulina. "Arguing about what should have been done doesn't solve anything. We have to focus on what we have to do *now*."

"You're right, Ghoulina." Catman bowed his head, feeling ashamed, and then turned to Wishbone to apologize. "Sorry, man."

"It's okay," Wishbone replied."

Jack glanced at Nikki and, trying hard not to show fear, he asked, "So what do we do?"

Nikki laid her bike on the ground and smiled back at Jack, putting on a brave face, but the butterflies in her stomach told her that she was just as nervous as he was about entering the tower. "Let's not waste any more time. Let's get the Wand and then get out of here," she said, looking at the others.

Ghoulina smiled at Nikki and Jack, trying to ease their visible tension. "So what are we waiting for?" she asked.

Catman carefully led the way into the Tower of Shadows, with Jack, Nikki, and Ghoulina following closely behind them. Wishbone leaned over Nikki's shoulder from inside her backpack to see where they were going.

Pale sunshine poured through the broken windows, providing them with just enough light to see. The inside of the Tower was a mess, with cobwebs in every nook and cranny, and broken bricks and wooden beams scattered all about the floor. There was dust and dirt and ash everywhere, and puddles of mucky water. The entire place smelled musty. Insects of all kinds scurried about, and even a few skinny rats darted back and forth through the debris of the ruined interior.

This must have been a cool-looking place a long time ago, thought Jack.

"What a dump!" said Ghoulina, pulling her gown above her ankles so it wouldn't get wet and dirty.

Nikki looked at the long flight of wooden stairs leading up to the belfry. It looked too old, weak, and rickety to support their weight all at once. "You sure those stairs can hold our weight, Wishbone?" she asked.

"Sure thing, kid," he replied. "Just hold onto the railing and don't look down."

With Catman still leading the way, the five friends climbed the stairs, slowly and carefully. Even Jack, who liked to race up and down stairways, taking two steps at a time, was being extra careful where he put his feet.

It hardly took them any time to reach the belfry.

"So where's the rubber bat?" Ghoulina wanted to know.

"Hanging from that beam directly above your head," Wishbone told her.

Ghoulina looked up, and so did the others. There, hanging by a piece of string, was the black rubber bat.

It's too high! Nikki thought.

And indeed it was.

"No one can reach it, Mister Wishbone," said Jack. "You were six feet tall when you put it up there. With your reach, it's probably eight feet up there."

"I can't reach it, that's for sure," said Catman.

Ghoulina shook her head. "Neither can I, and certainly Nikki and Jack can't reach it, either. We need something to stand on, and there's nothing, not even a box or chair."

"I can stand on Catman's shoulders," Nikki told them. "I just need a boost."

"Great idea!" said Jack. He quickly kneeled next to Catman, interlaced his fingers together and made a stirrup with his hands. "Climb aboard, Nikki!"

"The string is tied to the beam in a bow, the way you'd tie your shoes," said Wishbone.

Catman squatted to make it easier for Jack and Nikki. "Ready, steady, go!" he said.

Adjusting her backpack and making sure Wishbone was safe and sound, Nikki put one foot in Jack's hands. He grunted and groaned when he lifted her up so she could climb on Catman's shoulders.

"You eat too much, Nikki," Jack said.

"And you talk too much," she told him.

As soon as Nikki sat on Catman's shoulders, he carefully rose to his feet so she could reach up, untie the string, and retrieve the rubber bat.

"Got it!" Nikki said. "Okay, Catman. Squat down again and I'll hop off."

A gentle breeze blew into the tower, bringing with it the smell of old and rotting newspapers. No one paid any attention to it.

Once she was standing on her own feet again, Nikki studied the black rubber bat. *Just a simple little Halloween toy, but it's really a powerful magic Wand,* she thought. *Wow!* She handed it to Jack and said, "Please put this inside my backpack."

"Excuse me, Mister Wishbone," said Jack, making room for the rubber bat inside Nikki's backpack, placing it right next to the orange popcorn ball, the two flashlights, and the blue Key Stone.

"No problem," Wishbone told him.

Suddenly they heard ghostly sounds. One voice laughed and another one sighed. The echoes of both voices drifted up toward the ceiling.

"I think this is a good time to get out of here," said Nikki.

"I think that's a very good idea, Nikki," said Ghoulina. She turned and led the way back down the stairs as more strange sounds echoed all around them: dripping water, something being dragged across the floor, a squeaky door, and footsteps on the belfry above their heads…

They hurried toward the entrance when something dark and shapeless brushed past them.

Catman hissed painfully and grabbed his arm. "Something just burned me," he said. "I can smell the singed fur."

Holding his arm gently, Ghoulina looked at it and said, "Yes. A patch of fur has been singed. And part of your vest, too."

"Just like in the forest," said Nikki. "Bringing something in is a lot easier than taking something out."

Suddenly all the pale sunlight pouring in through the broken windows and damaged roof was replaced by an eerie, violet light.

"Nothing like this happened the last time I was here," said Wishbone.

Jack was the first to see them. "Look!" he shouted with fear and excitement. "The Shadows are all around us."

Sure enough, emerging through the floor, sliding down the walls, and crawling on hands and knees across the ceiling was a great horde of man-shaped Shadows. Their violet-colored eyes shone brightly. They hovered in the air, swirled over the floor, and floated toward the companions.

"Run," Wishbone told everyone. "Run!"

"Follow me," Ghoulina shouted, heading for the way out with everyone else running in a single file behind her. Catman brought up the rear.

When they had almost reached the entrance, a dozen more Shadows drifted into the Tower, blocking the way out.

"Ouch!" Catman yelped. "One of them just burned me again."

"Don't let them touch you!" Ghoulina warned everybody.

The Shadows closed in all around them.

"What are we going to do?" Nikki asked.

"We have to fight our way out," Catman replied.

As more of the Shadows drew close enough to touch, Catman jumped in the air and kicked one of them across the chamber. The thick leather soles of his boots protected his feet from being burned, but every time he kicked one Shadow into some dark corner, two more took its place.

"Stay behind me, children," Ghoulina told Jack and Nikki. "I got this." Raising her arms and pointing her fingers at the oncoming Shadows, she chanted as her thumbs turned black and streaks of crimson light shot like laser beams from the tips of her fingers. But the beams passed right through the Shadows, causing no damage or harm to the dark phantoms.

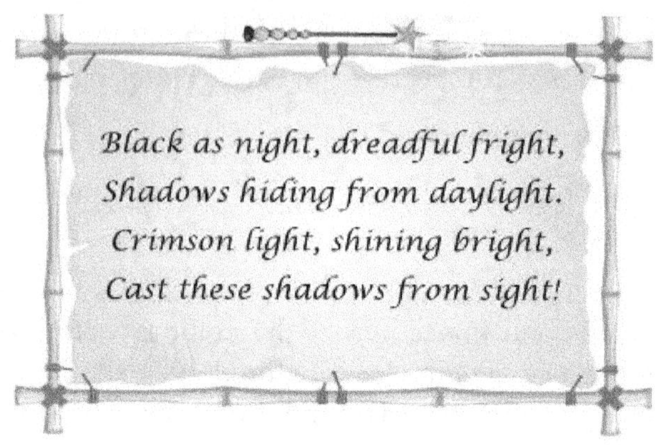

"My spell isn't working!" Ghoulina said, panicking. "Or my power is growing weak." She hitched up her gown and kicked at one of the black silhouettes. "Protect the children, Catman!"

"What do you think I'm doing?" Catman wailed. "But this is like trying to fight rain or clouds. *Ouch!* Rain and clouds that burn you when they touch you."

"Oh, if only I was bigger," said Wishbone.

Ghoulina cried out in pain as a Shadow made physical contact with her and burned her arm. "Stay close, kids," she told Jack and Nikki. "We'll get out of this somehow." She tried her magic finger-beams again, but it was no use. "It's like the magic of this world doesn't affect these Shadows."

Catman kicked and hollered every time a Shadow laid a hand on him. He picked up a burnt piece of wood and swung it at the Shadows, hitting them again and again while his booted feet kept up their part of his defense.

"Ruin my gown, will you?" Ghoulina let out a high-pitched scream whenever the Shadows touched and burned her. She kicked at them and picked up whatever objects she could find on the floor to throw at the Shadows. "Catman, we have to do something!"

"I know! But what?" Catman replied, feeling frustrated.

"Oh, my," Wishbone moaned, ducking inside Nikki's backpack when a shadow tried to melt his head.

Nikki and Jack exchanged frightened but confident looks.

"You thinking what I'm thinking?" Nikki asked Jack.

"If you're thinking about the flashlights, I am," Jack said.

"Yep! If Ghoulina's magic doesn't work, maybe the magic of *our* world will," said Nikki.

Jack grinned at his cousin. "Excuse me, Mister Wishbone," he said, once again rummaging through Nikki's backpack. He pulled out the two flashlights, happy that Nikki carried them. He made a mental note not to tease her ever again about her full-of-stuff backpack. He tossed a flashlight to Nikki. "Ready? On three."

"Two," she said.

"One!" Jack yelled and flicked on his flashlight almost exactly at the same time Nikki turned on hers.

Bright, almost blinding beams of white light shot from the lenses of the flashlights. Nikki and Jack waved their flashlights back and forth as if they were lightsabers. Shadows screamed and shrieked each time a light beam touched them. They tried to retreat, but the cold, blazing white light of the flashlights, the science and *magic* of Jack's and Nikki's world, burned and dissolved them, turning them into *nothingness*. Within moments the Shadows were vanquished.

"Quick thinking, kids. Great job!" said Catman.

"Guess they'll have to give this place a new name," said Jack, flicking off his flashlight.

Nikki nodded. "I hereby proclaim it to be Flashlight Tower!" she announced with glee.

"I am proud of you children," Ghoulina said as they hurried out of the building.

"Me, too," said Wishbone, poking his head out of the backpack again.

"Jack and I aren't hurt," said Nikki. "But Ghoulina, you and Catman have been burned. How bad is it?"

"Not too bad, Nikki," Ghoulina replied, sweeping her slender fingers over her injuries and ruined dress, and murmuring a spell under her breath. "See? All better. I'm glad my magic is back again. I was worried when it didn't work inside the tower." She laughed as she healed Catman's burned skin and restored his clothes.

"My whiskers," Catman whispered, touching his face. "My whiskers are gone. Can you grow them back, Ghoulina?"

"Of course," Ghoulina smiled as she caressed his face and murmured a spell under her breath.

"Phew, they're back! Thank you, my kind lady. You know, cats feel dizzy without whiskers." Catman bowed.

"I know, and you're welcome," Ghoulina replied.

Feeling relieved, Catman said, "I suggest we get out of here as fast as we can. This place makes my fur bristle, and we have to move on to our third and final mission."

"Where are we going to next?" Jack asked.

"To the Cave of Spooks," Wishbone answered.

Nikki and Jack didn't like the sound of that, especially after what had just happened in the Tower of Shadows.

Chapter 5

Nikki, Jack and their companions rode their bicycles past Pixieland but didn't have time to stop to enjoy the amazing sights and attractions. They were on a mission. Come midnight, they would not be able to open another Ectomagic Gate, which meant that Nikki and Jack couldn't return home until next October. They were concerned about that and knew that Grandma Sweet would be worried out of her mind. But they tried not thinking about it and remained hopeful that everything would be all right.

It was already late in the afternoon as they rode their bicycles over hills, through marshlands and still more back roads and forest paths. But this final part of their journey was becoming more and more difficult because the underbrush was growing thicker and all tangled with roots and vines.

"Are we almost there?" Jack asked. "It's getting harder and harder to ride through this forest. Pretty soon we won't be able to use the bikes at all."

"We're here," Wishbone said just as they emerged from the woods.

They came to a stop in a clearing not far from the edge of a deep hole in the ground. Rising straight from the bottom of the chasm was a gigantic stone pillar, and on top of that sat a great dome, with a dark cave facing them. Spanning the chasm stretched a sturdy but narrow footbridge leading directly to the cave. The bridge was tied securely with rope to four wooden posts that were driven into the ground. Beyond the far side of the chasm stood more dense forest, with trees so tall they almost touched the sky.

"There it is," said Wishbone, "the Cave of Spooks."

"I don't like the looks of it," said Jack.

"Me, neither," said Catman.

"I have a very bad feeling about this place," Ghoulina whispered.

"Looks like we'll have to leave the bikes here and cross the bridge on foot," Nikki said. "The wheels will get stuck between the floorboards or whatever you call those things if we try to ride across."

"Yes," said Wishbone, "and we'll have to be very quiet when we cross the bridge."

"Well, Mister Wishbone, before we go across I want to know more about these Spooks that live there," said Jack.

"There's not much to tell you," said Wishbone. "Long ago a band of rebellious ghosts refused to live in Wormbelow. They wanted a place of their own. Then, one October night, they snuck into your world and stole hundreds of boxes of Halloween costumes from various department stores, so they could dress up as different characters. But then their leader, Lord Rattlegrim, discovered that whenever they wore the Halloween costumes, the magic of your world turned them into solid creatures. They weren't ghosts anymore: they had real flesh, blood, and bones."

"Just like us, Mister Wishbone?" asked Jack.

"Just like you," Wishbone replied. "That's why they're called Spooks, because when they wear their costumes they have bodies and they're no longer ghosts."

Nikki found this interesting and a little disturbing, too. But as always, her curious mind had questions. "What happens if they take off their costumes?" she asked.

"They turn back into ghosts," Wishbone told her.

"So how did they end of up here?" Nikki asked.

"When the Wishmothers found out what Rattlegrim and his rebels had done, they banished the Spooks to this cave, to remain here forever," said Wishbone. "But remember, the Wishmothers are kind and merciful, so they gave them one night a year when they can leave and enjoy themselves in Creepy Hollow, as long as they harm no one."

"That's why there's a bridge here," said Catman. "The Spooks can't float across the chasm when they're wearing their costumes because they have physical bodies. So they need the bridge, just as we do. But if they take off their costumes, they can't leave the cave. And they never take off their costumes because they don't like being ghosts."

"Sounds awfully complicated to me," said Jack. "But I get it. I wouldn't want to be a ghost, either."

"Did you see the Spooks when you hid the last Wand here?" Ghoulina asked Wishbone.

"Yes, I did," he replied. "But they kept to the shadows and didn't bother me."

"Because you were the powerful Silver Skeleton then, Mister Wishbone, and they were afraid of you," said Jack.

"Right you are, Jack," Wishbone replied sadly and with a heavy sigh.

"So what do we do now?" Nikki asked.

"We proceed cautiously and try very hard not to anger the Spooks," Wishbone replied.

Nikki swallowed the lump in her throat. "Will our flashlights help us if they come after us?" she asked.

"No," said Wishbone. "The Spooks fear only two things: losing their costumes, and fire. They are *very* afraid of fire."

"What happens if they lose their costumes or they catch on fire?" Nikki asked.

"Without their costumes, the Spooks turn back into normal ghosts that can float through the air," said Wishbone.

"But then they can't leave their cave," said Jack. He put a hand inside one of his pockets and stared at the Cave of Spooks. *I'll have to remember both of those things,* he thought.

"Well, I've had enough of the history lesson," Ghoulina said impatiently. "Let's hurry up and get this over with so we can get back to Wormbelow before it gets dark."

In single file, they walked across the bridge. Nikki didn't like heights and would not look down; she kept her gaze focused on the cave at the other side of the bridge. Jack, however, stared down into the deep chasm and enjoyed every minute of it. *Too bad I can't take pictures,* he thought. *My friends would be so jealous!*

They reached the end of the bridge without any difficulties and stood together at the entrance to the dark Cave of Spooks. No sounds or smells came from inside the cave, although a soft, green light illuminated the interior, just beyond the entrance from where they stood.

"How are we going to do this?" Nikki asked.

"You, Catman, and I will lead the way in," Wishbone replied. "Jack, you stay behind us, and Ghoulina will bring up the rear."

"Why am I always the last in line?" Ghoulina asked with a wink and a laugh.

"How come I'm always stuck in the middle?" Jack whined.

Quietly, slowly, and carefully, they entered the cave and proceeded down a tunnel illuminated by soft, emerald-green light. Soon they discovered that the light came from the stones built into the walls and ceiling.

"Look at all the boxes. The labels say they're all Halloween costumes," Jack said in a hushed but excited tone.

Piled along the tunnel walls on both sides were hundreds and hundreds of boxes.

Many were empty, but many more were still unopened, with pictures on their lids of superheroes, pirates, and villains, characters from famous horror movies, and aliens from outer space.

"These Spooks must be master thieves," Catman purred.

"The best," said Wishbone.

"Any sign of them? The Spooks, I mean," said Nikki. She felt the hairs on the back of her neck standing straight up, and her arms were covered with goosebumps. The things they had encountered in Red Crow Forest and in the Tower of Shadows had taught her to be more cautious and wary…and more afraid, too.

"Nope," said Catman, his bright golden eyes reflecting the cave's green light.

Ghoulina looked around. "So where did you hide the mask, Wishbone?" she asked.

"I hid it in an empty costume box, just up ahead," he replied.

They walked deeper into the tunnel until it opened into a huge chamber softly lit by the emerald glow radiating from the stone interior of the cave.

"Tell me which box to look for," Nikki told Wishbone. She was eager to find the disguised Wand and get out of that cave as fast as possible.

"There, to your left," said Wishbone. "Third stack of boxes, fourth box in the pile."

While Catman and Ghoulina kept watch, Nikki and Jack dug through the pile of boxes until they found the one Wishbone had pointed out. Nikki grabbed the box and held it while Jack opened it.

"Look, it's a pumpkin head," Jack said, removing the plastic mask from the box.

"It's called a Jack O'Lantern, Jack," Nikki told him.

"I knew that," he said.

"Fine, now put it in my backpack so we can all get out of this spooky cave," Nikki said in a voice louder than she had intended.

This was easy, Jack thought. *But wait, it's never been this easy. What's going on? I wi... No! I can't wis...* Jack stopped himself just in time before he wasted the last wish.

When he stuffed the mask inside Nikki's backpack he noticed that the green light in the cave grew brighter. *Here we go*, he thought. *I knew it wasn't going to be easy.* He watched in horror as menacing figures emerged from the shadows at the far end of the cave. They wore Halloween costumes of robots and zombies, cartoon characters, and famous monsters such as vampires, mummies, and werewolves.

Nikki turned her head and saw more of them emerging from what she realized were dark holes carved into the walls of the tunnel behind them.

"We're trapped. What do we do now?" Nikki asked, growing more frightened.

"I'll handle this," said Ghoulina. She raised her arms high into the air and started chanting:

Ghoulina never had a chance to finish her spell because a Spook dressed as Frankenstein's monster grabbed her and threw her against the wall. She landed on a pile of costume boxes, moaning and rubbing her head.

"Hannah!" Wishbone cried out, unable to help her.

Jack raced over to Ghoulina. "She's hurt!" he called out.

"I'm okay," she said, smiling reassuringly at Jack. Then she frowned and massaged her forehead. "But I… I can't remember the rest of the spell."

Not knowing what to do, Jack kneeled beside her and put his arm around her. "Don't worry, Ghoulina," he said. "I'll think of something."

"You'd better think fast, Jack," she said. "Turn around."

Jack turned just as a group of Spooks walked toward them. Three of them wore mummy costumes and two were dressed as werewolves. Each of them held a box containing a Halloween costume. The sixth, in a Count Dracula costume, held a wooden scepter, the symbol of his authority.

"Just great! It's Lord Rattlegrim," Wishbone whispered.

"Wishbone Jones, how nice of you to honor us with another visit, and this time you brought along some friends," Rattlegrim said in a hissing, creepy-sounding voice. "The last time you were here to do whatever it was you came here to do, we could do nothing to stop you, because you were the great Silver Skeleton. But now I see that the rumors are true. You are nothing but a silly little wind chime."

"You'd better let us go, Rattlegrim," said Wishbone. "The Wishmothers won't be too happy with you if you don't.

Lord Rattlegrim cackled like an old witch. "I hear they're dead and their ghosts are imprisoned in some kind of magic pumpkin," he said. "I have a feeling that this visit may have something to do with the Wishmothers' missing Wands, curse those old hags!"

Catman snarled like an angry tiger. "You shut up about the Wishmothers!" he said.

"Go lick your behind, kitty," spat Rattlegrim.

"What do you want with us?" Nikki demanded.

"What do I want, little girl?" Rattlegrim asked. "Why, I want each of you to choose one of these costumes my five companions have in their hands."

"Then what?" Nikki asked the Lord of the Spooks.

"You will become one of us," Rattlegrim replied.

Nikki's body shivered with fear. She turned and glanced at Jack, who was comforting the injured Ghoulina. *I hope he's got something up his sleeve because I sure don't,* she thought.

"I suggest you choose your costumes wisely because it's the only choice you'll get," said Rattlegrim.

The five Spooks carrying the costume boxes stepped forward.

Then, with a loud and menacing roar, Catman charged one of the werewolves, his claws ripping the mask from the Spook's face. The Spook's costume vanished in a flash, revealing him for what he was: a ghost. But he wasn't a ghost like the Wishmothers or any of the other ghosts Nikki had seen in Wormbelow. No, he resembled a white sheet, with two black holes for eyes. The Spook uttered a shriek and floated up to the ceiling.

Swallowing her fear and summoning her courage, Nikki dashed forward and ripped the Dracula mask from Rattlegrim's face. He screeched and dropped his scepter when his costume dissolved and he turned into a white-sheeted ghost.

Floating toward the ceiling, Rattlegrim shouted to his minions, "Don't let them get away!"

The Spooks closed in on Nikki, Catman, and Wishbone.

Catman grabbed the fallen scepter. "See to Jack and Ghoulina," he told Nikki as he raced forward, swinging the scepter like a club and attacking the Spooks.

While Catman battered one Spook after another, Nikki ran back to join Jack and Ghoulina. The Spooks blocked the entrance and slowly crept forward, leery of Ghoulina and what magic she might still possess.

"Jack, what are we going to do?" Nikki asked.

Jack turned to Ghoulina as she started throwing costume boxes at the Spooks. "Didn't Wishbone say the Spooks are afraid of fire?" he asked.

"Yes!" said Ghoulina, rising to her feet. "But I don't have the magic to conjure fire."

"I do," said Jack. Reaching into his pocket, he pulled out the box of stick matches he had hidden from Nikki.

Pulling a match from the box, Jack scratched it against the striker on the side of it. The match ignited at once and Jack held it out in front of him. The small flame burned brightly.

The Spooks stopped and started to back away, afraid their costumes would catch on fire. Jack threw the match on the cave floor, right at their feet, and then quickly lit another match. The Spooks retreated farther and then vanished back inside their dark holes.

"That was brilliant, Jack!" said Nikki.

"Indeed!" said Ghoulina. "But we have to save Catman and keep the Spooks from chasing after us."

"You just leave that to me," Jack told her. He tossed the match onto a pile of costume boxes. "Hurry, Catman, get out of there."

Jack lit a third match and tossed it onto another pile of boxes. The cardboard boxes and the costumes inside them began to burn, bright flames climbing higher and higher.

Kicking and clubbing Spooks left and right, Catman heard Jack call to him. He retreated quickly but didn't turn his back to the Spooks. He fought them one at a time, sending Spooks crashing into walls and tumbling to the floor. He managed to knock the masks off a few of the Spooks, and they floated toward the ceiling.

The costume boxes piled against the walls of the tunnel were now burning like a huge bonfire. None of the Spooks dared pursue Catman when he got close to the flames and finally reached his friends. Lord Rattlegrim floated down from the ceiling and drifted toward the cave entrance, where he hovered just above the floor.

"You may have escaped me," he screeched. "But you'll never escape Hobgoblin, you hear? When he finally rules Celestria…"

The roar of the fires drowned out whatever he might have said next.

"Let's get out of here!" said Wishbone.

"You don't have to tell me twice," Jack replied.

With the three disguised Wands now tucked away inside Nikki's backpack, they made it back to safety. Black smoke billowed from the mouth of the cave, accompanied by the howls of angry Spooks.

"You okay, Hannah?" Wishbone asked Ghoulina.

Ghoulina smiled at him. "I'm fine, Bob. Don't worry," she said.

"Hold up for a moment," Catman told the others, stopping to throw Rattlegim's wooden scepter into the chasm. Then he used his sharp claws to slash at the ropes that secured the bridge to the posts on their side of the chasm.

Nikki and Jack watched in silence and then, seconds later, the bridge collapsed into the chasm and slammed against the side of the pillar atop which perched the Cave of Spooks. The bridge hung there, still tied to the other two posts, but now useless.

"That should hold them until they can figure out how to repair their bridge," said Catman.

"The Wishmothers were too lenient when they punished the Spooks, and will have to get tougher with them now," said Wishbone. "Those cursed Spooks can no longer be allowed to roam free in their costumes on Halloween night. They've grown much too dangerous."

"But first we have to actually *get* the Wands back to the Wishmothers," said Ghoulina, cocking her head to the side and narrowing her eyes. "Do you hear that?"

Nikki and Jack nodded at the same time. From off in the distance came the sounds of howling, growling, and yowling. Then Nikki spotted movement at the far side of the clearing.

"What now?" Jack asked nervously.

"That looks like a dog. It's coming this way," said Nikki.

"That's no dog," said Wishbone. "That's a Tasmanian Devil, and his name is Ebenezer Rex. He's tracked us down!"

The Tasmanian Devil raced toward them, leading six Goblins riding huge, black beetles as if they were horses.

"We can outrun them on the bikes," said Jack, leading everyone back to where they had left the bicycles.

Once they were mounted on the bicycles again, Wishbone said, "I know a shortcut through the woods that will take us back to Wormbelow."

"Then show us the way," Nikki demanded. She was glad that the Spooks couldn't leave the cave without their costumes. But she had a hunch that what was coming after them was even worse than the Spooks.

They got on the bikes and rode faster than ever before. Nikki and Jack took off with Catman and Ghoulina sitting on the crossbars and hanging on for dear life. Wishbone shouted the directions into Nikki's ear, and Jack followed her lead. Soon they were riding through the forest, trying to outrun their pursuers. But in this part of the woods, the underbrush grew thick, with tangled roots and vines and all sorts of shrubs and plants which slowed them down.

Behind them came the sounds of pursuit, closer and closer.

"I wi…" Jack caught himself before he finished the word. "I mean, Ghoulina, can't you make us fly with a spell?

"I wish I could," Ghoulina said, her voice glum. "But I don't have that much power, Jack."

"We're too slow," Jack grumbled.

Then suddenly his wheels got caught in the soft moss and tangled roots that covered the ground, and his bicycle tumbled over. Catman leaped off the crossbar, but Jack fell with the bike on top of him. A moment later, the wheels of Nikki's bike got snarled in twisted roots and her bicycle fell over. But she and Ghoulina managed to jump free before the bike hit the ground.

"Nikki! My foot is caught in some sort of root thing!" Jack called out for help.

Ebenezer Rex and his Goblin cavalry were drawing closer and closer.

Nikki and Ghoulina hurried over to where Jack had fallen. Catman tried to pull the bicycle free, but it was too tangled in the undergrowth and wouldn't budge. They tried to free Jack, but the thick vine was wrapped tightly around his ankle. The vine was too tough and thick for even Catman's claws to slash apart. It would have to be untied, and that would take too much time.

"We have to leave the bikes here and go on foot," said Catman.

"They're coming closer." Wishbone warned.

Nikki knew they wouldn't be able to free Jack and get away in time before their pursuers caught up with them, so she had a decision to make, and she had to act fast. Taking off her backpack, she removed the two flashlights and then handed the backpack to Ghoulina.

"Take the Wands back to the Wishmothers," Nikki told her friends. "I'll free Jack and we'll slip around the other way and meet you in Wormbelow."

"What?" Wishbone said. "You'll never find your way back there alone."

"And you won't get away from Ebenezer Rex, either," said Catman. "Someone has to stay to defend you kids. So I'm staying."

"No, you have to go with Ghoulina," Wishbone told him. "Your sense of hearing and smell are far better than hers. You can warn her to hide from the pursuers. I'm going to stay with the children."

"Bob, you can't defend the kids in the state you're in," said Ghoulina. "You must go to the Wishmothers and ask them for help so you can fight Hobgoblin."

Wishbone sighed. "You're right," he agreed, reluctantly. "I'm useless like this."

"Everyone, please, stop arguing," Nikki told them. "Even if we can't get away, you know where they'll take us, so with the Wishmothers' help you can rescue us. Catman, you must protect Ghoulina."

"But we can't leave you here alone," said Ghoulina.

"Listen to me," Nikki said. "If we all get captured, Hobgoblin will take the Wands away from us, and then Creepy Hollow will be in big trouble. You *have* to take the Wands back to the Wishmothers. Now get going!"

"No, Nikki," said Jack. "Don't be hard-headed. I think I twisted my ankle, so even if you can cut the vines off my leg, I couldn't run fast. Leave me here and go with them."

Nikki shook her head. "No! I'm not leaving you, Jack." She turned to the others and said, "Jack can't run and I'm not leaving him behind. Now go before we're all captured. Don't worry. Even if they capture us, the Wishmothers said that Hobgoblin can't hurt us with his magic. We'll be all right."

The growling of the Tasmanian Devil grew louder and closer.

Ghoulina looked at Catman, sighed and said, "Nikki's right. We have to split up. The most important thing is for us to keep the Wands from falling back into the hands of Hobgoblin." She and Nikki nodded to each other.

"Don't worry," said Catman. "We'll find you."

"I know you will," said Nikki, still trying to untie the vine from around Jack's ankle. "Go already, hurry!"

Her heart heavy with fear but her soul filled with courage, Nikki watched Ghoulina put on the backpack and start running with Catman at her side. Soon they were swallowed up by the forest and no longer in sight.

Nikki finally managed to untie the vine, pull Jack free and help him to his feet.

"Are you okay, can you stand?" she asked.

"It hurts but I'll try."

They heard a voice from not too far behind them.

"There they are!"

Nikki and Jack turned their heads. The Tasmanian Devil and his Goblins were only about fifty yards away.

"Come on, Jack," she said. "Let's go to our left, circle around, double back, and try to outrun them."

Jack nodded and they started running.

Nikki knew she could outrun their pursuers, but when she looked over her shoulder she saw that Jack was limping and had fallen behind.

Their pursuers were only about twenty yards away, and the Tasmanian Devil was even closer. Nikki could smell his foul breath.

"Are you okay?" she asked Jack without stopping.

"I can't run any farther. My ankle hurts too much," he said, wincing.

Nikki stopped and ran back to help her cousin, but before she could reach him the Tasmanian Devil charged forward, caught up with Jack, and bit his leg.

"No!" Nikki shouted.

Jack moaned in pain and fell to the ground with the Tasmanian Devil hovering over him.

"You get away from him!" Nikki screamed, then she picked up a broken branch and threw it at the nasty beast.

Ebenezer Rex ducked and the branch flew over his head. He snarled and showed his sharp teeth. "Try that again, little girl, and I'll bite you, too."

In spite of the Tasmanian Devil, Nikki rushed over to Jack and kneeled beside him.

"Jack, you're bleeding," she said.

"Of course. Like twisting my ankle and can't get away wasn't enough, this *dog* had to bite me and now I'm bleeding!" he grumbled.

"One more peep out of you and I'll eat your leg!" snarled Ebenezer.

The six Goblins mounted on the giant black beetles now gathered around them.

"Don't try anything funny," Ebenezer warned Nikki.

"*You* can just shut up, you mangy mutt!" Nikki said, too angry to be afraid of the talking beast. She flicked on one of the flashlights and shined it in Ebenezer's eyes.

The Tasmanian Devil blinked, turned his head, and growled. "That doesn't scare me, little girl," he said. "Now get that light out of my eyes or I'll bite you, too."

Realizing there was nothing she could do, Nikki shut off the flashlight. She was glad that her friends had gotten away, although she was worried about what was going to happen to Jack and her. *But the Wishmothers will know what to do,* she thought. First, though, she had to see what she could do to help her cousin.

"Does it hurt?" she asked Jack.

"What do *you* think?" he replied. "There's a handkerchief in my back pocket. Take it and wrap it around my leg. Wrap it tight to stop the bleeding."

Just as she reached for Jack's pocket, she heard a high-pitched voice behind her, "Did you have to bite him, Ebenezer?"

Nikki turned around. Behind her, sitting atop a big, horned beetle was an ugly goblin with green skin, floppy ears, and a pointy nose.

"I didn't bite him all that hard, Master," the Tasmanian Devil replied.

"Yes, you did!" Jack yelled angrily.

"I just wanted to make sure they wouldn't get away, like the others," said Ebenezer.

"We'll catch up with them one way or another," said the Master. He grinned wickedly at Nikki and Jack. "Welcome to Creepy Hollow, children."

"Some welcome this is," said Jack, wincing in pain.

Nikki glared at the Tasmanian Devil's master. "Hobart T. Goblin, I presume," she said.

The eyes of the ugly little green creature flashed with anger. "My name is Hobgoblin!" He turned to the Goblins and said, "Put them on the beetles and let's go. We'll capture the others when they come to free these humans."

Chapter 6

It was late-afternoon by the time Wishbone, Ghoulina, and Catman returned to Celestria and the graveyard they called Wormbelow. Catman wasted no time unlocking the doors to the mausoleum. He got the black pumpkin and placed it on the steps. Ghoulina rubbed the pumpkin, spoke the incantation, and summoned the ghosts of the Wishmothers.

Still chained to the black pumpkin, The Trinity of Wishmothers floated in the air above the pumpkin.

Wishbone quickly told the ghostly trio everything that happened since they set out from Wormbelow earlier that day to find and bring back the three Wands.

"So that's what happened and now we must rescue the children," he said when he finished. He was still inside Nikki's backpack, which Ghoulina had placed on the steps next to the pumpkin.

"We're truly sorry that the children were captured, but we had to split up to avoid all of us being caught," said Ghoulina.

"Nikki knew that getting the Wands back here to you was very important, Wishmothers," said Catman, purring sadly.

Ghoulina nodded and told the Wishmothers, "It was Nikki's decision, and we had to respect her and the decision she made." She sighed heavily. "Jack and Nikki are brave kids, and Nikki showed real, adult courage when she made that decision. They sacrificed their own safety and put their lives in danger to make sure we got the Wands back to you."

Catman cried out mournfully. "What are we going to do?"

"The Wishmothers will think of something," Ghoulina whispered.

"We can't let the children suffer at the hands of Hobgoblin," said Wishbone.

"No, we cannot and we shall not," said Wishmother Minerva Terrapin.

Prunella Pickles, held up her index finger. "But first things first," she said.

"Oh, child, you saw that mangy, good-for-nothing Ebenezer Rex *bite* that poor little boy?" Gladiola Scales asked.

"Yes, I looked back and saw that evil creature bite his leg, but there was nothing I could do. We *had* to bring the Wands to you," Ghoulina replied.

"Then we have very little time, I'm afraid," said Minerva.

"We know!" Catman hissed impatiently

"What do you mean?" asked Wishbone.

Prunella shook her head. "We don't have any idea how that bite might affect Jack," she said. "He is not from our world. The bite of the Tasmanian Devil may be poisonous to him."

"You mean…he could die?" Ghoulina asked, suddenly realizing that the children could be in more danger than she thought.

"I'm sorry, honey," said Gladiola. "But that may, indeed, happen."

Wishbone wailed loudly from inside Nikki's backpack. "No! We must do something to save them."

Catman turned to Ghoulina. "You're a Healing Witch," he said. "Can't you do something, like brew a potion or come up with a spell?"

"Yes, I have herbs from which I can make a healing potion," Ghoulina told him. "But first I have to make the potion and then we have to *get* it to him in time."

"He and Nikki are no doubt locked away in the Deep Dark Dungeon," said Wishbone, his silver bones rattling and chiming as he trembled at the memory of that place.

"Ghoulina, show us the Wands, dear," said Minerva.

Ghoulina kneeled on the steps and reached inside Nikki's backpack. She swatted angrily at the two nosy spiders that dropped from the tree and dangled in front of her face on their silvery strands. When the spiders scurried back up to the treetop, she took out the orange popcorn ball, the plastic Halloween mask, and the rubber bat. She also took out the blue Key Stone.

"Nikki put this in her backpack to keep it safe," she said and showed the blue stone to the Wishmothers. "She could open the portal and go home if the Key Stone was still in her pocket."

"But what about the bite wound on Jack's leg? They might not have medicine for that in the human world," said Wishbone. "You must make the potion that could heal him."

"Yes, you're right! I must hurry home and gather the herbs. I can brew the potion fast. It would only take a few minutes."

Prunella was in deep thoughts for a few seconds and then she said, "Everything is happening just as the Seer Witch told you, Ghoulina."

"What do you mean?" asked Catman.

"Their destiny led Jack and Nikki to the Key Stone and the pumpkin, and it is their destiny to help us," Gladiola explained. "Only they can set us free from the pumpkin."

"But what about your Wands?" Wishbone asked. "Can't you use them to free yourselves? Can't you use them to restore my body or at least make me the Silver Skeleton once more, so I can go and rescue the kids?"

"The Wands are useless to us for now, Wishbone," Minerva said in a sympathetic voice.

"What?" he said.

"How can that be?" Ghoulina asked. "We've risked the lives of the children to bring the Wands here!"

"Because now we can see that you changed the Wands when you disguised them, Wishbone," said Prunella. "You changed their nature and their power."

"But I didn't know," Wishbone moaned. "I didn't know!"

"Oh, my word," said Gladiola. "We are not blaming you, dear Wishbone."

"Then how can we rescue the children?" Catman asked, casting a frightened and worried look at the Wishmothers.

"Two of the Wands must first be used by Nikki and Jack in order to remove the spell that Wishbone used to disguise the Wands," said Prunella.

"What about the third Wand?" Ghoulina asked.

"You hope to become a Wishmother one day, do you not, child?" Minerva asked Ghoulina.

"Yes, I do," Ghoulina told her.

"Then you must use the third Wand, dear," Gladiola said.

"But how?" Ghoulina asked.

"Give us a minute. We need to discuss the possibilities."

The companions waited nervously while the Wishmothers put their heads together and whispered to each other. After a few minutes Minerva announced, "We have a plan."

The Wishmothers told them what must be done. Ghoulina hurried home to brew the potion, and took Wishbone with her. Catman wished them good luck and went to fulfill his part of the plan.

Beneath the castle of Crag Heap, the dungeon was dirty, cold and damp.

When Nikki and Jack were thrown into the cell, they saw only one barred window. It was at ground level, about fifteen feet above the dungeon floor. But that was too high above and there was no way for them to climb up and escape. The door of the cell had iron bars, but the spaces between them were too narrow to squeeze through. Outside the door, two Goblins stood guard. Water dripped down the stone walls of the cell, cobwebs hung in every corner, and bugs of all kinds skittered across the hard, cold floor.

Nikki was grateful that there weren't mice or rats scurrying about. But her main concern was for Jack, who under normal circumstances would have been excited to see all the bugs, and trying to catch them. But he just sat there in the middle of the cell because he didn't want to touch the damp wall. His face was pale and his forehead beaded with sweat.

"You don't look so well, Jack," Nikki said, squatting in front of him.

"I don't feel so well," he told her. "Oh, Nikki, what are we going to do? How are we going to get out of here?"

Although their flashlights had been taken from them, Hobgoblin's men had no idea what the cell phones were. After they examined the phones and decided that the small objects were harmless, they let Jack and Nikki keep them.

"These phones are useless," said Nikki. "I should have taken Wishbone's Key Stone out of my backpack so we could open the Ectomagic Gate and escape. We'll just have to hope he and the others come rescue us."

Jack swayed and moaned, "I feel so weak and dizzy."

Nikki sat down on the ground behind him so he could lean to her back for support. She knew there was nothing else she could do for Jack.

Jack coughed and moaned painfully. He was sick, and Nikki knew it. She suspected that the bite of that nasty Tasmanian Devil was poisonous, and she was very worried about her cousin. But she would not let Jack see her being worried and would not tell him she was sure he had been poisoned. They were both frightened and concerned about being stuck in the dungeon, and there was nothing they could do about it.

"How's your ankle?" Nikki asked.

"Still swollen, but it doesn't hurt a lot," Jack told her.

"What about your leg, where that nasty beast bit you?"

"It hurts a lot! But at least it stopped bleeding. You did a good job making that tourniquet with my handkerchief and bandaging my leg."

"I learned a thing or two in the Girl Scouts," Nikki said.

Jack moaned again. "This is my fault," he said. "If I hadn't wished for those bicycles, we wouldn't be here."

"None of this is your fault, Jack," said Nikki. "Things just went wrong and things just happened. We'll get out of here, I promise you."

"But how?" he asked. "How?"

Nikki had no answer to that.

The cell door creaked as the Goblin Guards unlocked and opened it. The guards stood at attention as Hobgoblin marched into the cell, followed by the mangy and foul-smelling Tasmanian Devil, Ebenezer Rex.

"I hope you two are comfortable," Hobgoblin said with a grin and a sarcastic tone in his voice. "I'm sorry the accommodations aren't up to the standards of a five-star hotel, but it's the best we can do."

"Trying to be funny doesn't suit you. What do you want, you filthy Goblin?" Nikki demanded.

"Don't make me tell you again, you brat. My name is Hobgoblin!" he growled angrily.

Ebenezer snarled. "Let me take a bite of that nasty girl, Master," he begged.

"Not yet, my pet," said Hobgoblin. "I have plans for them."

"You know what you can do with your plans," Nikki told him.

The Tasmanian Devil growled. "I can chew and swallow you in less than five minutes, little girl," he said.

Afraid but unwilling to show it, Nikki stood her ground. "Go ahead, and you'll have the worst case of indigestion you've ever had," she said.

With a growl, Ebenezer crept toward Nikki and Jack. Nikki jumped to her feet, her hands clenched into fists, ready to defend them both.

"Heel, boy. Heel!" Hobgoblin shouted at his henchman. "All that can wait."

The Tasmanian Devil howled with frustration but did as his master ordered him to, and he sat down on his haunches.

"How did you track us down?" Nikki asked Hobgoblin.

"One of the Shrieks in Red Crow Forest told me what happened there," he said. "Then, once you entered the Cave of Spooks, Lord Rattlegrim sent one of his messenger bats to tell me where to find you."

"So what do you want with us, Hobgoblin?" Nikki asked.

The ugly, big-nosed and floppy-eared goblin rubbed his hands together. "I want to know what your friends are up to," he said. "I want to know what they did with the Wands and what they plan to do with them."

"We won't tell you anything," Jack said defiantly, before a coughing fit stopped him from talking.

"Your cousin is very sick," Hobgoblin told Nikki. "If you talk, I'll give him some medicine to make him well again. If not, well...you'll talk. I have ways of making you talk."

Nikki swallowed the lump of fear in her throat. "Are you going to torture us?" she asked.

"I'm going to torture *you*, while he sits there and gets sicker and sicker," Hobgoblin replied. "Your choice, little girl. Talk or face the consequences. I'm a patient fellow, so I will give you one hour to decide. After that...well, you'll see."

"Yeah, you'll see, and I'll have a nice dinner," said Ebenezer.

"Oh, go chase your tail, you mangy mutt!" Nikki said angrily.

The Tasmanian Devil growled menacingly, but Hobgoblin grabbed him by the back of his neck, picked him up, and tossed him out of the cell.

"One hour, missy," Hobgoblin said to Nikki. "For your cousin's sake, I hope you make the right decision."

 Hobgoblin turned and left the cell, and the guards locked the iron-barred door.

Jack's stomach growled and then he threw up. "I don't feel so good," he said. "Hobgoblin said something about medicine for me. I'm scared, Nikki. Am I going to die?"

When he started crying, Nikki's heart ached and despair started to creep into her thoughts. *This ugly creature is not kidding. They will torture me and it will hurt a lot. I'm so scared, but Jack is even in bigger trouble! What will happen to us if the others can't get here on time to rescue us? Grandma will never find out what happened to us... No! I'm not going to cry! Jack can't see me cry...* She changed positions in order to sit next to him and hold his hand. "I'm scared, too, Jack. We'll get out of this. Trust me. And you're not going to die!"

Despite putting up a brave face, she had to turn away to hide the tears that flooded her eyes.

Back in Wormbelow, the plan to rescue Nikki and Jack was ready and everyone knew their part.

Ghoulina brewed the potion as fast as she could, and double-checked the ingredients with Wishbone. When it was done, she murmured a healing spell while she strained the liquid into a vial and put it into Nikki's backpack. Then she removed the rubber bat and put it in the pocket of her gown, leaving the popcorn ball, the plastic mask, and the blue Key Stone safely tucked away in the backpack.

"Don't forget the tea for Catman," Wishbone reminded her. "His voice must be crystal clear."

"Oh, I forgot. Thanks." Ghoulina quickly prepared the tea and, picking up Wishbone, she made him sit on her shoulder while they hurried back to the Wishmothers.

When they got back to the mausoleum, the Wishmothers gave instructions to everyone, and then Minerva asked, "Ghoulina and Catman, you two know what you must do, right? You know the spell and know how to use it?"

"Yes," said Ghoulina. "Once we hear Wishbone give the signal, I will go into action."

"And you, Catman?" asked Prunella.

He finished drinking the honey and ginger tea Ghoulina had made for him. He sang a few notes like a singer practicing his scales and said, "I'll be ready to do my part. Thanks for the tea, Ghoulina. My voice box is in good shape now."

"Absolutely marvelous," said Gladiola. "Wishbone knows his part, too, so everything is set."

"Remember, Ghoulina," said Minerva, "you and Catman must cause a disturbance at the main gate to Crag Heap Castle."

"Yes," said Ghoulina. "A distraction, to help Wishbone do his part."

"Exactly," said Prunella.

"You must force the residents of Goblin Acres to flee to the safety of their homes, and hopefully empty out the castle," said Gladiola.

"What sort of distraction are you planning?" Wishbone asked because, while Gladiola had told him what to do, he didn't hear what the others talked about.

Ghoulina smiled at him. "Thanks to Prunella and Minerva, we have a good plan. No time to explain, you'll see," she said. "You just send us the signal when you're ready, and then the bats and cats will hit the fan."

"Remember, Wishbone," Minerva reminded him, "Jack must put on the mask."

Prunella nodded and said, "And Nikki must take a bite of the popcorn ball."

"And you, my dear Wishbone, don't forget…you must also take a bite of the popcorn ball," said Gladiola. "Is everything clear?"

"Got it," said Wishbone.

"Good," said the Wishmother.

"Should your mission succeed, and it will, return here on the double," said Minerva. "Bring us Hobgoblin and Ebenezer Rex. They must pay for their crimes."

No one asked what if they did *not* succeed. They all knew what would happen if they failed.

"What about Nikki and Jack? What about you, Wishmothers?" Catman asked. "How will we free you from the black pumpkin?"

"There is a way, Catman," said Prunella.

Gladiola fussed with her gown. "There is always a way," she said.

"The children will know by instinct what to do," said Minerva. "Trust them. But remember, you have to be back here before midnight or else the Ectomagic Gate can't be opened for another year and the children will be trapped here."

Nikki and Jack sat huddled together in the middle of the cell. Time was running out. It had been over a half hour since Hobgoblin had come to give them his ultimatum. They had no plan, no ideas, and Jack was growing sicker by the minute. He had thrown up again and still felt nauseous. Nikki was becoming more scared and worried with each passing minute.

"What are we going to do?" Jack moaned.

"I don't know," said Nikki. "I have no idea. We'll have to trust in our friends and hope the Wishmothers can save us."

Suddenly, Jack snapped his fingers. "I've got it! We have one wish left!" he said enthusiastically, before another coughing spell hit him with full force. Once he was able to catch his breath he croaked, "We can *wish* ourselves free."

"We can't do that, Jack," said Nikki.

"Why not?" he asked. "We *have* to. It's our only chance of getting out of here."

"Look, Jack," said Nikki. "I've been thinking about those wishes and about what happened to Hobgoblin when he used his own wishes for selfish reasons. I don't want to be turned into some Goblin or Gnome, and I don't think you want to be, either."

"What do you mean?" he asked.

Nikki held up her finger. "First, I used one wish by accident, just because we were hungry. That was a selfish wish." She held up another finger. "Second, you wished for bicycles because your feet hurt from walking. That was a selfish wish, too."

"But we were hungry and we could travel a lot faster on the bicycles, and nothing bad happened to us because we made those wishes." Jack coughed again and his stomach growled. "Well, I *did* sprain my ankle and get bitten by that Tasmanian Devil," he said after he was done coughing.

"I'm sure it's a test," Nikki told him. "The Wishmothers want to know if they can trust us. We failed twice already and we can't fail with the third. We must use the last wish for an *unselfish* reason."

"Nikki, I'm feeling very sick," Jack whispered weakly. "I'm dying."

Although she feared the worst, she said fiercely, "No, you're not dying! We will be rescued, you'll see! Ghoulina, Catman, and Wishbone will be here soon."

"Are you kids okay?" They heard a familiar voice from above their heads call to them.

"It's Wishbone!" Jack said with hope in his voice.

Nikki rose to her feet, looked up at the window, and saw Wishbone's tiny head poking through the bars. He had the straps of her backpack wrapped around one arm. *He must have dragged my backpack all the way here,* she thought. "You found us. I'm okay, but Jack's real sick."

"Here, catch," Wishbone told her. He pushed her backpack through the bars of the window, and Nikki caught it. "There's a vial of medicine in there that Ghoulina prepared for Jack. Have him drink it all and he'll be fine in a few minutes."

Nikki rushed over to Jack, opened her backpack, and handed him the vial filled with green liquid.

"Drink it all," she ordered him.

Jack pulled the cork from the vial and started drinking the medicine. Although he made faces because it tasted so bad, he didn't stop until the vial was empty.

"Where are the others, Wishbone?" Nikki asked, walking back to the cell window.

"Outside," he told her. "Be careful, now. Two of the Wands are in the backpack, too."

Nikki frowned. "Just *two* Wands? Where's the other one?" she asked.

"I'll explain in a moment," said Wishbone.

Then the six-inch Silver Skeleton jumped down to the floor and walked over to Jack.

"How did you get here?" Nikki asked Wishbone. "What are you planning to do?"

"There is no time to explain," he said. "Trust me and do as I say. We've got a good plan." He turned to Jack. "How do you feel?"

"I'm feeling a whole lot better already," he said with relief. He looked at the bite wound on his leg. "Look, the wound is totally healed and my ankle doesn't hurt anymore."

"Good," said Wishbone. "Nikki, give the plastic mask to your cousin. Jack, put on the mask. Nikki, you have to take a bite of the popcorn ball and then give me a tiny piece of it."

Nikki removed the plastic mask from her backpack and handed it to Jack. "What's going to happen, Wishbone?" she asked, taking the popcorn ball out of her backpack and eyeing it suspiciously.

"Magic," he said. "Hurry now. The sun is going down."

Jack put on the plastic Jack O'Lantern mask.

Nikki took a bite of the orange popcorn ball and gave a small piece to Wishbone. They chewed and swallowed, and then she returned the rest of the popcorn ball to her backpack.

For a moment, nothing happened.

Then...*wham!*

There was a bright flash of purple light, and Jack was instantly dressed in a tight-fitting warrior costume. He looked just like a superhero.

"Hey, I even have my slingshot!" he said with a laugh.

Then there was a flash of golden light, and Nikki was suddenly wearing the costume of a warrior as well.

"I'm Zinja, the Warrior Girl," she said. "And I have nunchucks, too!"

Nikki and Jack felt strong, brave, and capable of doing great, heroic deeds.

There was a third flash of light, this one all silver and white, and suddenly the once six-inch Wishbone Jones stood there in all his six-foot glory.

"Finally! Being only six inches tall is no fun at all," Wishbone said.

"What do we do now?" Nikki asked.

"We break out of here, free Mayor Gillman, and find Hobgoblin and that scraggly little Tasmanian Devil."

Wishbone put his fingers in his mouth and whistled louder than Nikki and Jack had ever heard anyone whistle before.

Meanwhile, Ghoulina and Catman hid at the foot of the gate leading into Crag Heap Castle, watching scores of Goblins walk past them while they waited for Wishbone's signal.

Goblin Acres was a sprawling town of wooden shacks and huts, and houses made of brick and mud. All the buildings were small and built low to the ground. The town was filled with Goblins either walking about or riding a variety of big, crawling insects. A few Gnomes, Imps, and Pixies were among the crowd, either on foot or sitting in carriages drawn by giant ants. Rising straight and tall and high above the town stood the castle of Crag Heap, the lair of Hobgoblin.

"How much longer do we have to wait?" Catman asked impatiently. He clenched and unclenched his paws, claws fully extended.

"Not much longer. Although it's a long walk for him and he has to drag the backpack all the way, Bob should be there by now. Hopefully, because he's so small, nobody will pay attention to him and he will get there safely," Ghoulina told him. "The healing potion works fast, and the Wishmothers told us the Wands would work their magic quickly, too."

"But still, they have to hurry," said Catman. "Those spells won't last all day."

Ghoulina scratched Catman's head gently behind his ears, causing him to purr softly. "Be patient, my friend," she told him.

"Aw, I needed that to calm me down. Thank you."

"Anytime," Ghoulina said smiling. "The cat in you needed that."

They didn't have long to wait. They heard a loud whistle coming from deep inside Crag Heap. The whistle was so loud that it stopped the Goblins, Gnomes, Imps, and Pixies in their tracks.

As the echoes of the whistle began to fade, Ghoulina said to Catman, "Now!"

Clearing his throat, Catman raised his head, cupped his paws around his mouth, and roared louder than a tiger. His roar was spine-tingling, blood-curdling, and bone-chilling. The inhabitants of Goblin Acres stared at each other in fear, not knowing what was happening.

"Wow! Your tea and the Wishmothers' spell really gave my voice a mighty boost. Listen," Catman suddenly shouted. "Look!"

Hundreds of cats meowed and hissed and snarled as they emerged from every street and back alley in Goblin Acres. From every rooftop, window ledge, nook, and cranny came hundreds more cats of all colors, breeds, and sizes. Traffic came to a stop, and the town's residents tripped, fell, and bumped into each other as they fled to the safety of their homes. The army of cats stormed through the gate of Crag Heap and entered the castle.

Catman smiled, quite pleased with himself, and said, "You're up next, Ghoulina."

Pulling the rubber bat from her pocket, Ghoulina held it high above her head and chanted:

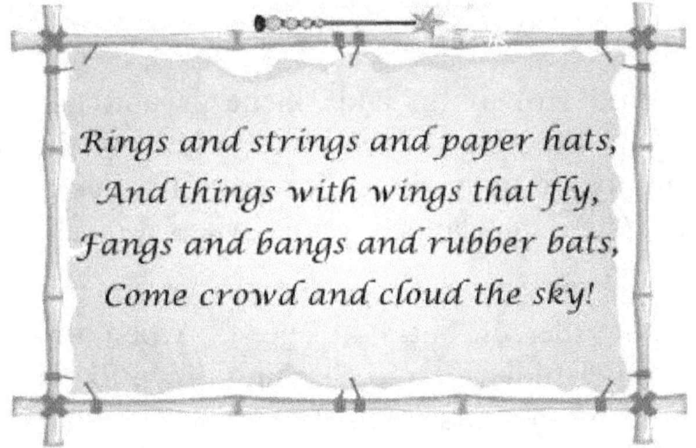

"Done!" she said, returning the rubber bat to her pocket.

Seconds later, the sky darkened as colonies of huge, black bats appeared. Hundreds of bats soared through the sky and flocked together over Goblin Acres. The flapping of their wings was so loud it sounded like a tornado. Up and down streets and alleys they flew, chasing after Goblins and Gnomes. They flew through open windows and open doors, down chimneys and up to rooftops. Imps and Pixies bumped and crashed into each other in their efforts to flee the swarm of bats.

Within moments, Goblin Acres was deserted. The bats swarmed flying through every open space they could find.

"Well, our work here is done," Ghoulina announced.

"Now what?" Catman asked.

"We wait," she told him.

Inside the cell, the transformed Jack, Nikki, and Wishbone stood near the iron-barred door and watched as hundreds of cats and bats invaded the dungeon, chasing Gnome and Goblin guards and soldiers all over the place. Pixies, Imps, and Ogres ran as fast as they could as the bats and cats chased after them. Even the two Goblins guarding the cell panicked, turned, and fled.

"I hope the cats and bats bite and scratch them all! They deserve it." Jack said.

The Silver Skeleton shook his head. "No, Jack. Only if they don't flee and decide to fight back."

"What do we do now, Wishbone?" Nikki asked.

"We have to find Hobgoblin and Ebenezer and take them to the Wishmothers," he explained. Then he took hold of the cell door and with all his mighty strength, ripped it free of its lock and hinges, and tossed it aside. The door clanged loudly when it crashed to the floor. "Let's go!"

They hurried from the cell but didn't get far when a squad of Goblin guards and Gnome soldiers came charging down the corridor, chased by a large group of cats and a colony of bats. Leading them as they fled that invasion of winged and furry creatures were Hobgoblin and Ebenezer.

"Don't let them escape!" Hobgoblin ordered his troops.

Ebenezer snarled and licked his sharp teeth.

"What do we do, Wishbone?" asked Nikki.

"We fight!" said the Silver Skeleton.

"That's all I want to know," said Jack, sticking his slingshot inside his belt.

Ebenezer howled and raced toward Jack, who quickly raised his shield. The Tasmanian Devil crashed into the shield, bounced off of it, and fell to the floor. When Ebenezer hopped back to his feet, Jack tossed his shield aside and charged forward. They crashed into each other, bashing and smashing and gnashing in a wrestling match that shook the walls of the Deep Dark Dungeon. Jack felt stronger than ever before and threw Ebenezer across the room as if the nasty beast was a stuffed toy.

Hobgoblin screeched and turned to flee. He ripped the tapestry off the wall and threw it on the floor behind him, hoping his pursuers would trip over it.

"Don't let him get away," Wishbone told Nikki. "I'll handle these other goons."

Nikki ran after Hobgoblin. She leaped over the tapestry with ease and chased him down the corridor. *I feel super strong and I'm as fast as lightning. I love it,* she thought.

Wishbone battered his way through the squads of Gnomes and Goblins. He punched and kicked them, grabbed them, and tossed them aside. They came at him, but they could not stop him. A group of Goblin guards and Gnome soldiers jumped on top of him and tried to bring him down. The Silver Skeleton stood his ground, stronger and mightier than ever before. His metal fists pounded and smashed their heads. He threw them down the corridor and up into the air, where they collided with the stone ceiling and then crashed to the floor, unconscious.

Wishbone was a whirlwind of flashing fists and kicking feet as he bashed them until they either fled or were sprawled on the ground. There was no stopping the Silver Skeleton. He was a force to be reckoned with.

Meanwhile...

Nikki caught up with Hobgoblin, grabbed him from behind by his scrawny shoulders, and slammed him into the wall. Then she spun him around and punched him in the face. He hit back with two quick punches, both of which Nikki blocked with her forearms. Then she took hold of his arms and started shaking him back and forth until he flopped in her hands like an old rag doll.

With a mighty effort, Hobgoblin squirmed and wormed his way out of her clutches, retreated a few paces, and turned to face her. He pointed a long, claw-like finger at her and said, "I cast my spell and send you to—"

"Won't work, Hobart," Nikki told him. "You can physically hurt us, but your magic is useless against us. Surrender or I'll break every bone in your body."

Hobgoblin squalled, "Never!" Then a blast of sparks shot from the tip of his finger, aimed straight at Nikki.

Nikki stood her ground as the magical sparks exploded harmlessly before reaching her. She smiled and said, "It's time to give up, Hobart."

With another screech, Hobgoblin turned and ran down a corridor.

Nikki pulled the nunchucks she'd tucked into her belt, aimed, and threw the weapon at him. The nunchucks, each wooden end attached by a chain, spun and flew down the corridor, stopping only when it crashed into the back of Hobgoblin's misshapen head. He tumbled to the floor and didn't move again.

Suddenly Nikki turned back to her natural self. Feeling a little disappointed because she liked being the Warrior Girl, she walked down the corridor, retrieved her nunchucks, grabbed Hobgoblin by his collar, and dragged him back across the floor.

Meanwhile...

The Tasmanian Devil rose to his hind legs, his jaws snapping at Jack, who deflected every blow from Ebenezer's paws, punching back with a left hook and right uppercut. Back and forth across the floor of the Deep Dark Dungeon they fought, relentlessly hammering away at each other. Jack threw another right cross to Ebenezer's jaws, but it was a fake-out. The blow never landed because Jack then sucker-punched the Tasmanian Devil with a left hook to the belly. Howling, Ebenezer fell to the floor and rolled over onto his back, groaning in pain. Taking advantage of the situation, warrior Jack jumped on top of him. The Tasmanian Devil tried biting Jack's fists and arms but succeeded only in having his teeth broken by Jack's punches.

Ebenezer yelped in pain. "I give up! I give up!" He wept like a coward.

"You bit me, you devil," said Jack. "Let's see how you like it."

Grabbing one of Ebenezer's paws, Jack bit down hard on it, hard enough to draw blood. The Tasmanian Devil yelped again, and then Jack hit him with a grand-slam, knock-out punch.

Leaping off his unconscious foe, Jack grabbed the fallen tapestry and ripped off a piece of it to tie around Ebenezer's jaws. Then he wrapped him in the rest of the tapestry, tied it shut like a sack, and stood up.

"You're lucky I didn't have any stones for my slingshot," Jack said, and kicked Ebenezer. That's when he noticed that he was wearing his own clothes again. He took off the Jack O'Lantern mask, grabbed the sack containing the Tasmanian Devil, and rejoined his friends.

"Is it over?" he asked Wishbone.

"Give me a minute, Jack," said Wishbone. He held a Goblin in each hand by their throats, bashed their heads together, and let them drop to the floor. "Now it's over."

"What's next?" asked Nikki, giving Hobgoblin a kick in the ribs for good measure and then tying him up with a piece of the old tapestry.

"Hold on," Wishbone said. He walked over to another cell door. He peered in through the iron bars, and then ripped the door off its hinges. "You can come out now, Your Honor," he said, bowing.

A moment later, a skinny and dirty little goblin in ragged clothes emerged from the cell, squinting and rubbing his eyes. "Wishbone!" he whooped happily.

"Jack, Nikki, this is Creach Gillman, the real Mayor of Goblin Acres," said Wishbone.

Nikki curtsied. "Hello, Sir," she said, picking up her backpack.

"Hi," Jack said with a proper bow.

"My thanks to you, Wishbone, and to you children, too," said Mayor Gillman. "Please excuse me. I have so much to do."

The Mayor of Goblin Acres bowed and walked away in a dignified manner.

"Where to now, Mister Wishbone?" Jack asked, returning his mask to Nikki's backpack.

"Back to Wormbelow," Wishbone replied.

"Not without us," said Catman, rushing into the dungeon.

Ghoulina joined him. "Sorry we took so long," she said. "We had to deal with everyone who didn't hide from the cats and bats, and stayed to fight us."

"Catman!" Nikki gave him a great big hug.

Jack sang out happily, "Ghoulina!"

She kneeled and opened her arms as he ran to hug her. "What took you three warriors so long?" she asked.

"Well, we *did* have to deal with these two maggots and their minions," Wishbone the Silver Skeleton told her. He took Hobgoblin from Nikki, holding him by his scrawny neck. Jack handed him the sack containing the Tasmanian Devil. "Now we can leave," he said.

Nikki was only too happy and naturally eager to leave, but when she glanced up at a narrow window and saw that it was dark outside, she grew very worried. *Oh, no! It's dark outside and it's so late,* she thought. "We're in big trouble!" she told Jack. "We just disappeared in the morning. Grandma must be worried sick by now."

"I know, right?" Jack's shoulders sunk with worry as if a huge weight had been suddenly dropped on him. "I bet my parents and every policeman in Diddlebury is looking for us. I'll be grounded until I'm thirty!"

"Me, too!"

Chapter 7

The full moon hung bright in the night sky when Nikki, Jack, their companions, and their prisoners returned to the graveyard in Celestria. Stars glittered and sparkled as Ghoulina kneeled in front of the black pumpkin and summoned The Trinity of Wishmothers.

They appeared and hovered in the air above the black pumpkin, still bound to it with iron chains. They smiled sweetly at everyone and thanked each of them for helping recover their Wands and capturing Hobgoblin and Ebenezer Rex.

"You did very well," said Minerva.

Gladiola nodded. "We are very proud of you all," she said.

"Now, if you please," said Prunella, "bring the prisoners forward."

Jack and Catman untied the tapestry in which the Tasmanian Devil was rolled up like a burrito, and let him loose. But they did not remove the cloth that tied his jaws shut, which prevented him from biting and even speaking. Ebenezer did not try to run. He knew it was all over for him. He just laid there on the ground, trembling and whimpering like a frightened dog.

Wishbone dragged Hobgoblin forward and forced him to kneel in front of the Wishmothers. He had no fight left in him; he just kneeled there, ready to beg for his life. His entire body was shaking, hands clasped together as he made his appeal to the trio of ghosts.

"Have mercy, please, I beg of you!" he cried.

"Murderers!" said Prunella.

"Traitors!" said Gladiola.

Minerva glared at Hobart T. Goblin. "Do you really think we will show you mercy?"

"I'm sorry. Forgive me. I'll be good from now on, I swear!" Hobgoblin pleaded.

"Be grateful that we will not take your lives, as you took ours," said Prunella.

Gladiola smiled, but it was not a friendly or forgiving smile. "But after this night, you will wish that we had," she told Hobart.

Hobgoblin buried his face in his hands and wept and Ebenezer whimpered.

"Ghoulina, what do you think would be the most fitting punishment for these two?" asked Minerva.

Ghoulina was in deep thought for a few seconds and then replied, "Although they deserve worse, I think shrinking them to the size of bugs would be punishment enough."

"I agree," Gladiola said. "Living in fear that every creature bigger and stronger than them wants to eat them is enough punishment."

Prunella nodded in agreement. "Make it so, Wishmother in training."

Ghoulina faced Hobgoblin and Ebenezer, raised her hands into the air, and chanted:

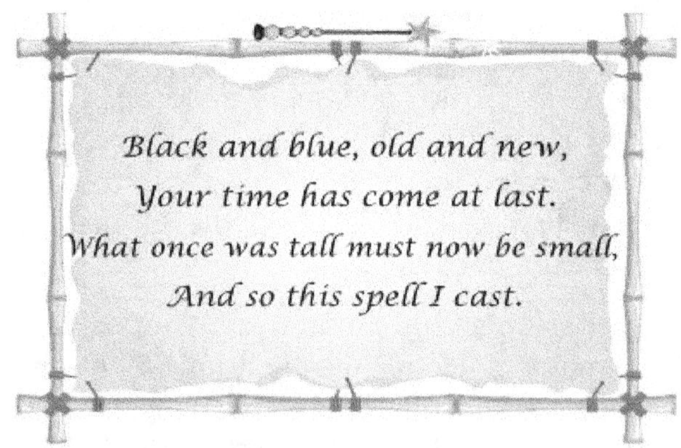

Beams of green and orange light flared from the tips of Ghoulina's fingers and floated toward Hobart and Ebenezer. The lights grew and floated over them, and with a flick of her fingers Ghoulina reduced the prisoners to the size of cockroaches.

Hobart squealed and Ebenezer squeaked as Ghoulina took a small glass jar from her skirt pocket, bent down, and placed it over them. "Don't worry," she said. "I'm not going to kill you. Later I will take you as far as I can from here. You've caused enough trouble and I don't want to see your ugly faces ever again."

"All the things you carry in your pockets, what is the jar for?" Wishbone asked, laughing.

"I collect herbs and other stuff to make potions, as you know," Ghoulina replied. "I carry jars to put slimy things in it, so I don't make a mess of my clothes."

"It makes perfect sense," Wishbone agreed. He turned his head when he heard Minerva's voice.

"Listen everyone," said Minerva, getting everyone's attention, "bring out the Wands and put them on the pumpkin."

Nikki reached inside her backpack for the plastic mask and the popcorn ball, but they were no longer in there. Instead, there were two straight and simple Wands, each beautiful, elegant, and made of gemstones. One carved from jade, the other from amethyst. Amazed and speechless, Nikki placed the Wands on the pumpkin and asked, "How could that be, Wishmothers? You said you couldn't use the Wands because Wishbone changed them, but now…"

"Because the danger is gone and the Wands have no reason to hide anymore, they have changed themselves back to their natural state," Minerva explained.

Jack stared in amazement at the Wands. "Those are really magic Wands!"

Ghoulina stepped forward, and what she held in her hands now was no longer a toy rubber bat but another exquisite Wand, this one made of black onyx. She carefully put it down on the pumpkin, next to the others.

Minerva turned to Nikki and Jack, studying them for a few seconds. Nikki felt uncomfortable and a little afraid. Jack, too, for he grabbed his cousin's hand and squeezed it tightly.

"You have no need to be afraid, my dear children," said the Wishmother.

"Indeed," Prunella agreed.

"But it's almost midnight, and I know my grandmother is worried sick," said Nikki.

"We missed Halloween, and if we're still here at midnight, we'll be stuck here for a year," said Jack, squeezing Nikki's hand even tighter.

This time, Gladiola's smile was sweet and kind. "You do not need to be concerned about that, my angels," said she. "Trust us and all will be well."

"Remember, kids," said Ghoulina, "you have one wish left. Do you wish to go home?"

Nikki looked at Jack, and Jack looked back. "Remember what we talked about back in the cell?" she asked. "Do you understand what Ghoulina is asking and what we must do, no matter what happens to us?"

"Of course, I do," he said. "This is a test. And we have to choose wisely. We can't think of ourselves and we can't be selfish."

Ghoulina smiled lovingly at the kids. "So, what do you wish for?" she asked.

Once again, Jack and Nikki looked at each other and nodded. Together they said, "We wish that the Wishmothers could be free of the black pumpkin."

Wishbone cheered and Ghoulina smiled with joy. Catman applauded and then swatted at the nosy spiders that came down from their tree on their silvery strands to see what was going on. As the spiders dangled in front of Catman's face, he glanced at the jar, and a sly smile crept over his lips.

The Wishmothers sighed with relief as the chains that bound them to the black pumpkin dissolved and vanished. The Trinity of ghosts floated down to the ground and bowed.

"Thank you, children!" they said in unison.

"Look!" Jack yelled, pointing. "The black pumpkin turned orange."

"That is because we have been set free," said Minerva.

"Your sacrifice, your unselfish choice to help us shall not go unrewarded," said Prunella.

The Wishmothers put their heads together and Gladiola whispered, "There is still time and we have our Wands."

Nikki didn't want to eavesdrop, so she took a step back and then noticed that Catman was staring at something with a smile on his face. She elbowed Jack gently to get his attention.

Catman chuckled softly and took a step forward. He kicked the jar that held Hobart T. Goblin and Ebenezer Rex. The jar tipped over and he watched the frightened prisoners try to scurry away. "Oh, how absolutely clumsy of me," he said.

"Quick. Don't let them get away!" said Wishbone, who noticed what happened but didn't pay attention to the satisfied smirk on Catman's face.

Before anyone could move, the nosy spiders quickly dropped down, snatched up the tiny Goblin and Tasmanian Devil, and carried them up to the tree on their thin strands.

Catman laughed. "I guess they were hungry," he said.

"You did that on purpose!" Ghoulina accused Catman, winking at him.

"Who? Me?" Catman said with an innocent expression on his face. "I don't think anyone will miss those nasty creatures, and besides, spiders have to eat, right?"

Minerva smiled, cleared her throat to get everyone's attention, and said, "It's time for us to use our Wands." She reached down and picked up the black onyx Wand. "Onyx for strength and for power!"

Prunella reached for the jade Wand. "Jade for prosperity and ambition!" she said.

"Amethyst for healing and perfection!" Gladiola said, picking up the amethyst Wand.

In the Wishmothers' hands, each Wand glowed with its own inner light.

"And now we can combine our powers and do as we once promised," said Prunella.

"Wishbone Jones, please step forward," said Minerva.

The Silver Skeleton moved to stand in front of the ghostly Trinity of Wishmothers.

"For your loyalty and sacrifice," Minerva told him.

The Wishmothers held out their Wands, each one touching the other, pointed them at Wishbone, and spoke in unison:

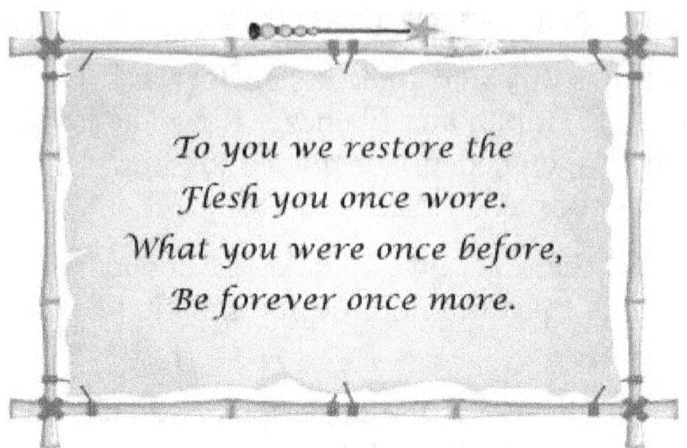

Violet-colored light wrapped itself around the silver exoskeleton that encased Wishbone's charred and broken body. Next a bright green flash of light surrounded him, and then a blanket of black smoke fell over him.

Nikki squeezed Jack's hand as the smoke and magical lights circled Wishbone's body.

A few seconds later the black smoke faded away, the green light winked out, and the shimmering violet light disappeared. Everyone watched in awe as the Silver Skeleton was replaced by a tall and handsome man in silver armor. His hand brushed his long, flowing blond hair out of his eyes when he turned toward Ghoulina with a bright smile on his face.

"Bob! You're healed," said Ghoulina with tears in her eyes.

He walked toward her and took hold of her hands. "Yes, Hannah. The Wishmothers kept their promise, but you were the one who saved my life on the battlefield." Removing his silver glove, he touched his face. "It feels so good to touch my skin and feel the warm flesh beneath it," he said with tears running down his face.

Ghoulina reached out and caressed his long, blond hair lovingly while she looked into his blue eyes. "It feels wonderful, Bob," she whispered.

Catman sat down on the ground and wept with joy. "So beautiful," he said. "I'm so happy."

Jack sniffed and wiped his nose on his sleeve. "It's like a fairy tale." He sighed and then quickly added, "I'm not crying, I'm not!" He glanced at the others, but when he saw that nobody was paying attention to him, he sniffed back his tears and wiped his nose again.

"It's perfect," Nikki said, choking back her own tears as she felt the love between Wishbone and Ghoulina.

Then, going down on one knee, Bob Jones bowed his head and kissed Ghoulina's hand.

Minerva gave them some time to enjoy their happy moment, and then she said, "And now, children, it is time for you to return to your own realm."

"But how?" asked Nikki. "Can you send us back?"

"No, we can't," said Prunella.

Gladiola pointed to Nikki's backpack and said, "But you have the blue Key Stone that brought you here, dear."

"But that stone belongs to Wishbone," said Nikki.

"Yeah, it's not ours," Jack added.

Wishbone stood and turned to Nikki and Jack. "The Key Stone is yours to keep," he told them. "Then you can use it to visit us next year."

"Oh, thank you! We will," Nikki said, hugging them both.

"But where will you find another Key Stone, Mister Wishbone?" Jack asked.

Wishbone and Ghoulina exchanged smiles. "Bob and I will share our lives together, so he can use my Key Stone," she said.

"Hannah, with those words, you made me the happiest man in Creepy Hollow," he said with a tremble in his voice.

Ghoulina flashed a beautiful smile at him and squeezed his hand.

"Don't forget your bag, Jack," Catman said. "I'm sure the Wishmothers will let you take the pumpkin home with you."

Jack's eyes lit up. "Can we, Wishmothers?" he asked.

They nodded, and Minerva said, "Of course you may, my child."

"Thank you!" said Jack. He picked up his messenger bag and the pumpkin.

"I guess this is goodbye, for now," Catman said with a sniffle.

Nikki hugged him. "Don't be sad. We'll be back," she promised him. "By the way, I've been curious to find out what else do you carry in your large pouch besides the keys to Wormbelow?"

"Catnip for Poe, the cat part of me, and chocolate for the human part of me," Catman said with a wink.

Nikki laughed and Jack stuffed the pumpkin inside his messenger bag. "Well, I guess this is goodbye," he said. He shook hands with Catman and Wishbone, and then turned to Ghoulina. "I wish I was tall enough to give you a kiss," he said to her.

Ghoulina smiled. "Well, what if I kissed you?" She leaned over and kissed him on each cheek. When she stood up, she mussed his curly hair. "Be a good boy, Jack."

Jack blushed and then grinned. "Well, I'll try. But I'm making no promises," he said.

"Good enough," Ghoulina said with a laugh.

"It's almost midnight, Nikki and Jack," said Minerva. "Bring the Key Stone here."

Oh, boy! Nikki thought. *I bet we are in big trouble.*

"We missed Trick or Treating!" Jack remembered.

"You're worried about *that?*" Nikki asked him. "Grandma and your parents are going to kill us."

"Hurry, children," said Prunella.

Nikki reached inside her backpack and pulled out the blue Stone. She pushed Jack ahead of her as they approached the Wishmothers. Their new friends followed.

"Both of you hold onto the Stone," Gladiola instructed them. "Do you remember the magic words?"

Yes, I do!" Nikki told her.

Holding the key to the Ectomagic Gate, Jack and Nikki watched as the Wishmothers laid their Wands on the Key Stone.

"Say the words, Nikki," Minerva told her.

"Snappy fingers, cracking bones," Nikki recited the magic words quickly.

They heard the snap and crackle of static electricity and the strange humming noise. Then the gateway shaped like a wheel of swirling, shimmering light opened.

"Goodbye, everybody," Nikki said, looking at their new friends one by one.

Jack waved and said, "Goodbye. See you next year."

Everyone waved goodbye as Nikki and Jack stepped through the Ectomagic Gate.

Epilogue

When Nikki and Jack emerged from the magical gate in Grandma's backyard, they were surprised to see that it was broad daylight. The sun hung in the sky, directly overhead.

We didn't miss Halloween after all! Nikki realized. "The Wishmothers sent us back in time, Jack. That's why they laid their Wands on the Key Stone and made us hold it together."

"We're time travelers," he said. "How cool is that?"

They saw Grandma Sweet rush out of the house, wearing her floral design apron over a blue house dress, and when she spotted the kids she shouted, "Nicolette Angelina Sweet and John Francis Brady!" When she used their full names like that, instead of their nicknames, it usually meant big trouble. "Where have you been for the last three hours? Lunch is on the table and it's going to get cold."

"Oh, we were playing in the woods," said Nikki, feeling bad that she told a lie. "We can't tell Grandma the truth, right?" she whispered to Jack as they hurried toward the door.

"Of course not!" he whispered back and then said out loud, "We got a pumpkin, Grandma."

 Grandma Sweet eyed the pumpkin suspiciously. "Mister Bonejingles is missing. You didn't trade my wind chime for that pumpkin, did you?"

Jack and Nikki looked at each other.

"No, we didn't. Honest, Grandma," Jack told her.

"Maybe somebody stole Mister Bonejingles," Nikki said, telling another lie and feeling bad about it.

"Maybe the wind blew him into the creek and he floated away, Grandma," said Jack. "Or maybe he just got tired of hanging there and went home." *That* was certainly the truth.

"Oh, Jack, what a fertile imagination you have," said Grandma Sweet. Then she held out her hand: in her palm sat the book of matches Nikki had taken from Jack earlier that day and then left on the front porch steps. "I know these are your matches, Jack. Am I right?"

Nikki expected Jack to lie, but he surprised her.

"Yes, Grandma," he said. "I stole them from you, Grandma. I'm sorry."

Grandma put the matches inside her apron pocket. "I should punish you both for wandering off and playing in the woods all morning. I should *really* punish you, Jack, for playing with matches. But I won't, if you promise me one thing."

"Anything, Grandma," Jack said eagerly.

"You must promise to stop playing with matches, and this time you'd better mean it," Grandma told him. "Is it a deal? Because I would hate to ground you, which means you'd miss out on Halloween this year and all that candy."

"Yes, yes, I promise, Grandma," Jack said.

"So you've finally learned your lesson?" Grandma asked.

Jack glanced at Nikki, then looked at her grandmother and nodded. "Yes, Grandma. I learned quite a few things today. I promise. I'm done playing with matches."

"I'll make sure he keeps his promise," said Nikki.

Grandma Sweet smiled sweetly. "I know you will, dear." She pointed to the pumpkin. "What are you going to do with the pumpkin, kids?" she asked.

Jack shrugged. "I don't know," he said. "Cut it open and roast the seeds, I guess."

"And then we carve it," Nikki said.

"Carve it into what?" Jack asked her.

Nikki rolled her eyes. "Into a Jack O'Lantern, silly," she laughed. "Oh, look! Kids are coming to Trick or Treat already. We better get going and put our costumes on."

"I'll go get the candy bowl," Grandma Sweet said and rushed back inside the house.

ENTER IF YOU DARE

Jack turned to the group of children. "Can I take a picture of you for my Instagram page?" he asked, taking his phone out of his pocket.

"Sure," the kids replied and posed for the picture on the steps.

"What's your costume, Nikki?" Jack asked.

"I'm going to be a Witch," Nikki giggled. "And I'm going to paint my lips blue just like Ghoulina. What's your costume?"

"Isn't that a little spooky? You have a witch costume and this year I chose a skeleton costume. Or maybe I'll use my black cat costume from last year," Jack replied, rubbing his chin thoughtfully. "But I think instead of just wearing a black furry jumpsuit, I'll put on my pirate outfit. I'll look exactly like Catman!" He winked playfully at Nikki.

"Yes, it is spooky!" Nikki agreed. "But I'm glad we went to Creepy Hollow and helped our friends."

"Me, too," Jack replied. "Let's go eat and then go Trick or Treating."

The Power of the Sapphire Wand
Creepy Hollow Adventures 2
Erika M Szabo & Joe Bonadonna

When autumn leaves fall
And the night winds call,
When the moon sheds
Ghostly light,
October comes 'round
With a whispery sound
And on Holloween night,
Creepy Hollow can be found.

Prologue

It was a warm, rainy night in late October when Angelina Strong and her husband Mike left their one-year-old daughter in the care of Angelina's mother so they could take a week's vacation in Montana. An icy-white, full moon glowed in the night sky, surrounded by dark gray clouds and only a pocketful of the brightest stars. Lightning flashed in the distance, followed by the angry growl of thunder. Ghostly winds howled in the night like lonesome wolves, scattering the wet, fallen leaves in every direction.

Angelina, Mike, and her mother stood on the front porch, sheltered from the wind and the rain. The porch had not yet been decorated for Halloween, something Angelina's mother loved doing every year.

"Thanks, Mom," Angelina said, putting her baby daughter gently into her mother's arms.

"We hope the baby won't be too much of a handful for you," Mike told his mother-in-law. "We really need this vacation, you know."

Angelina's mother smiled lovingly at the little baby she held tenderly in her arms. "How could such a little angel ever be a handful?" she said. "You know how much I love taking care of my granddaughter."

"This is very sweet of you, Mama Rose," said Mike.

"I'm the baby's grandmother, and it's my job to be sweet, and it's my job to spoil her as much as I want," his mother-in-law told him.

"Just don't spoil her *too* much, okay?" he asked.

Mama Rose smiled at him. "I promise I'll try not to."

"Oh, I can see you two are going to be best of friends, Mom—and we're going to have a spoiled little girl on our hands!" Angelina said. She looked at Mike and they started laughing.

"Now you two run along. You have a long drive to the airport," said Mama Rose.

"Yeah, and it's raining," said Mike. "The roads might be slippery."

Angelina kissed her mother. "We'll call you as soon as we arrive," she said.

"We'll be back in a week," said Mike.

"Be careful on the coastal highway," Mama Rose cautioned them. "You know how dangerous those roads overlooking the ocean can be. Have a safe trip, have fun, and stay out of trouble."

"Where's the fun in that?" Mike joked, kissing his mother-in-law on the cheek.

"Goodbye, Mom," said Angelina. "See you soon."

Angelina and Mike then ran towards their car, got inside it, and drove off.

Grandma Rose hugged the baby and glanced at the sky. "It's just you and me now," she said to her granddaughter. "Let's go watch some television before I put you to bed. Okay?"

The baby giggled and cooed with delight. Then her grandmother took her inside the house and closed and locked the front door.

The streets were indeed wet and slippery. Mike drove his car carefully, keeping to the speed limit and slowing down on turns and curves in the road. There were no people out walking around and no other cars on the streets as they reached the edge of Diddlebury. They turned down the main road that wound its way through the forest of Weeping Meadow and eventually to the coastal highway that would take them to the airport.

They drove through an old warehouse district, talking about things they planned to do and places they wanted to see in Montana. Mike stopped the car when he saw the traffic light turning yellow. Angelina looked out the driver side window and watched a young man walk towards the street corner and take a step off the sidewalk as soon as the light turned red. At that moment, a car speeding from the opposite direction ran the red light and hit the young man, who flew up into the air and then landed on the street like a rag doll.

Angelina and Mike watched in horror as the car, without slowing down, sped away. They got out of their car and ran across the street.

They found the young man unconscious and lying on the road. Blood seeped from the gash on his forehead, and his left leg and arm seemed to be broken. Angelina knelt beside him and touched his carotid artery on the side of his neck to check his pulse.

Reaching for his cell phone, Mike said, "I'll call 911."

"They won't get here in time," Angelina told him. "He's badly hurt and his heart is barely beating. If we wait for the ambulance he's going to die. I have to save him."

"But you can't, Angelina," said Mike. "You know what your mother said about using your magical powers. It's too dangerous."

"I have no choice, Mike," she said. "I can't let this man die!"

Mike sighed, nodded, and returned the cell phone to his pocket. "You'll have to wipe his memory, too, so he doesn't remember what happened."

"I know," said Angelina, rubbing her hands together and chanting strange words softly, under her breath.

Looking around, Mike saw no one. Luckily, the neighborhood was deserted. When he looked at Angelina again, he saw that her hands were glimmering with a silvery light. She was moving her hands slowly over the young man's body without touching him. The young man moaned softly as his broken arm and leg straightened. He groaned as Angelina wiped the blood from his forehead with a sweep of her hand after the gashing wound had closed.

Mike watched with amazement as Angelina's hands started to glow with a soft, golden light. She put her hands against the sides of the man's head and whispered a chant under her breath. As she moved her fingers, the young man's body rose into the air and floated towards the sidewalk. Mike watched his wife without blinking and held his breath, afraid that it would break Angelina's concentration.

He took a noisy breath when the young man's body was lowered to the ground into a sitting position and his back propped up safely against a large mailbox.

"I'm never going to get used to the magical things you can do," he said lovingly to his wife, who stood up and walked over to the sitting but still unconscious man.

"He's going to be fine," she assured Mike. "We have to go. He's going to wake up in a minute with no memory of what happened to him and I don't want him to see us."

Mike nodded and they ran back to their car, got inside, and drove away. Angelina turned in her seat and glanced out the back window. She watched the young man with a satisfied smile on her face as he stood up, shook his head in confusion, and started walking away.

"It was amazing what you did back there!" Mike squeezed Angelina's hand. "You saved a man's life. Do you want to call your Mom and tell her what happened?"

Angelina shook her head. "I don't think we have anything to worry about, and I don't want Mom to worry, either."

But Angelina *was* worried and afraid of what her magic might have unleashed.

The couple drove for almost a half hour over the winding coastal road overlooking the cliff and the ocean far below. The rain had stopped but the road was still wet and slick.

"It should take us no more than an hour to reach the airport," Mike told his wife.

Suddenly they heard the snap and crackle of static electricity, followed by a weird, humming noise. It sounded like a beehive full of angry bees. Angelina sat up straight in the passenger seat and looked through the windshield.

"Mike, what's that up ahead?" she asked.

Mike slowed the car to a crawl, lowered his side window, and stuck his head out. "I have no idea," he said. "I've never seen anything like that before."

"Neither have I," said Angelina, her voice almost a whisper. Goosebumps crawled over her arms, and the inside of her belly turned into an icy ball of fear as she watched the huge whirlpool of swirling green light hovering in the middle of the road. It looked like a vortex that stretched across the width of the road, causing Mike to step on the break and stop the car.

"Time to call your mom," said Mike.

Reaching for her cell phone, Angelina tried to call her mom, but something was wrong. She looked at her cell phone. "My battery just died," she said.

Mike pulled out his cell phone and glanced at it. "Mine's dead, too," he told her. He looked up from his phone and shouted, "Oh, no! Look!"

They watched in horror as frightening creatures leaped from the swirling light one by one.

"Wolfmen!" Angelina cried.

Mike looked at her. *"Wolfmen?"*

"Yes," said Angelina. "Werewolves who have chosen to remain werewolves for as long as they live. My mother told me that they're the servants of an evil witch."

"You mean they come from—" Mike started to say.

"Yes, they do," his wife told him. "Let's get out of here!"

"Make sure the doors are locked," said Mike. He stepped on the gas pedal, the tires spun on the slick road for a moment, and then the car took off like a bullet. Suddenly the vehicle began to hydroplane on the wet highway. Mike hit the brakes, but the car slid sideways off the road and slammed into a tree. Angelina and Mike were unhurt, thanks to the airbags, but they were stunned and shaken.

Mike and Angelina heard a growl and when they looked out the car window, they saw a giant monster, about seven feet tall, staring at them.

He wore a black vest over a ragged, red T-shirt, brown leather pants, and matching boots. His face, arms, and bald head were all scarred, as if someone had taken him apart piece by piece and then stitched him back together. He looked a lot like Frankenstein's monster, with ghostly white skin. One of his eyes was red, the other green. In his left hand he held a small, glowing purple and orange stone. In his right hand he carried a mace—a huge war club with sharp metal spikes and a head like a sledgehammer on one end.

The giant walked slowly towards the car, surrounded by his gang of Wolfmen.

"Run, Angelina! Get out and run!" said Mike. "I'll try to hold them off."

"I won't get far, and you can't fight them alone," said Angelina. She unhitched her seatbelt, jumped out of the car, and stood there, facing the monsters.

Mike popped open the trunk door, hopped out of the car, raced around to the back, and pulled out a tire iron, ready to defend himself and his wife. "Run, Angelina! Go!" he shouted.

Angelina raised her arms, but before she could utter one magic word, a pair of Wolfmen moved fast and seized her by the arms, capturing her. One cupped a hairy paw over her mouth.

"No!" Mike screamed as he rushed around to the other side and started beating the Wolfmen with the tire iron. Then two more came up behind him and threw him to the ground.

The huge monster who looked like Frankenstein stepped forward. "Don't hurt them," he told the Wolfmen in a gruff and sinister-sounding voice. "Queen Evila doesn't want them harmed. Take them through the Gate."

Mike and Angelina struggled helplessly as four of their werewolf captors dragged them into the whirlpool of shimmering green light and disappeared.

The monster and the remaining werewolves stared at the shimmering light. The black-furred Wolfman looked at his master and asked, "What do we do with the car, Mutanto?"

"Set it on fire, Howler," said the big, scarred monster.

Howler, Mutanto's second-in-command, turned to three dumb-looking werewolves who wore torn and ragged blue jeans and were standing off to one side. These Wolfmen had not taken part in the actual attack on and abduction of Angelina and Mike.

"Boo, Goo, Poo—set the car on fire," Howler told them.

"But we don't have any matches, Boss," said Boo, a red-furred Wolfman who spoke in a bitter and unhappy tone of voice.

Howler howled at Boo. "Then drive it off the road and hide it," he said.

"But we don't have driver's licenses," said Goo, a filthy-looking Wolfman with leaves and twigs and stems stuck to his matted gray fur.

"I don't even know *how* to drive," said Poo, a mangy Wolfman with brown fur that smelled so foul that he often had to roll around in the poop of other animals, just to hide his own disgusting odor.

"You three are *so* totally worthless!" growled Howler.

"Shut up, all of you!" yelled Mutanto. "Just push the car off the road and over the cliff. It'll crash into the sea and look like a real accident. And make it snappy, because we have to get back to Creepy Hollow before Evila has a fit."

Howler nodded his big, shaggy wolf's head and turned to Boo, Poo, and Goo. "Well, what are you guys waiting for? A special invitation?"

Mutanto shook his scarred head. "I wonder what those three idiots would do without us to tell them *what* to do," he moaned.

"Hurry it up there, you bumbling stooges!" Howler yelled at the three not-so-smart Wolfmen. "We have to get back to Creepy Hollow and return the dead king's Key Stone to Evila. Now shake your tails and get moving, you furry freaks!"

"I don't like this," Boo whispered to Goo and Poo. "I don't like this at all. It's not right."

Nevertheless, the three Wolfmen did as they were told, stepping all over each other's paws as they struggled to push the car away from the tree and over the cliff, where it tumbled into the sea far below.

Once that had been accomplished, the five Wolfmen stepped through the Ectomagic Gate a second before it vanished.

Chapter 1

Nikki Sweet and Jack Brady weren't related by blood and weren't really cousins. But that's how they thought of themselves, as cousins. Their parents had gone to junior high and then high school together in the town of Diddlebury, and became best friends. Although Nikki's parents had died under mysterious circumstances when she was a baby, Jack's parents were always there for her. Uncle Frank and Aunt Mary, as Nikki called them, loved her as much as they loved their son, Jack, who was a year younger than Nikki.

Jack spent a lot of time at Grandma Sweet's house when his parents were busy and, imitating Nikki, he started calling her grandmother "Grandma."

On September 26, Nikki turned thirteen. Her grandma threw her a nice party, with Jack, his parents, and a few of Nikki's friends from school. Among the many presents she received was another year of karate lessons at the local martial arts school, a gift from her grandmother. Nikki loved her martial arts instructor, and wanted to keep training, keep practicing. She had a natural talent for using nunchucks.

Nikki's thirteenth birthday was also the day that changed her life.

After the birthday party was over and Nikki was alone in her bedroom, she felt comfy and cozy in her brand-new pajamas. She sat at her desk, playing with her colorful collection of river stones. Suddenly she felt the bed beside her begin to vibrate, making her stuffed animals look as if they were dancing. The posters of rock stars and movie stars hanging on her walls began to shine with a blue light. Then her hands began to grow warm, glowing with golden light as her fingers started to move on their own. She was frightened that she couldn't control the movements of her fingers but she was fascinated by it, too. Nikki watched, feeling scared, as her fingers carefully arranged the stones in a circular pattern, and then into strange symbols within the circle.

"What's going on?" she asked herself, her body tingling all over.

A moment later, the tingling sensation went away, and then her hands stopped glowing and no longer felt warm. Everything had returned to normal, except for the river stones sitting on her desk in a perfect circle, with the strange symbols inside it.

Nikki had no idea what had just happened. She thought about going downstairs to tell her grandmother, but then decided against it. Something weird had certainly taken place, something that frightened her and which she didn't understand. She crawled into bed shaking, and pulled the cover up to her chin. Nikki thought about what happened a year ago when she and her cousin Jack had gone to Creepy Hollow with the talking wind chime whose name was Wishbone Jones, the Silver Skeleton. She recalled their battle with the evil Hobgoblin and wondered if the magic he had tried to use against her, but which she had deflected with her shield, had affected her in some way, giving her some of his magic. She wondered if Jack had experienced anything like this and made a mental note to ask him, when the time was right.

Nothing unusual happened for the next few days. Nikki studied hard, did her homework, helped Grandma around the house, and took her karate lessons. At times, she would sit on the front porch, watching the boys play baseball on Whipple Street, and thinking about what had happened on the night of her birthday party, wondering what it all meant and if it would happen again. But everything remained perfectly normal.

A few days later, Nikki volunteered to stay after school and clean the classroom's chalkboard and erasers for her teacher. Jack had detention once again for failing to turn in his homework on time, and Nikki wanted to wait for him, so they could walk home together. She had no karate class that day, so she decided it was time to confide in Jack, to tell him what happened in her room that night, and find out if anything weird like that had happened to him.

When she was finished with her cleaning, Nikki decided to water the plants that were sitting on top of the bookshelves by the windows.

That was when she noticed one of the potted plants had begun to wither and turn brown, and a few of its leaves had fallen to the floor. Setting the watering can aside, Nikki touched the dying plant and felt her body tingle, and her hands grow warm and begin to glow with the golden light again. Taken by surprise and unable to move, she had no control of her hands as they gently caressed the plant. Then slowly, the leaves of the dying plant began to turn vibrant green as the plant grew healthy and once again stood straight and tall.

Nikki's hands dropped to her sides when the plant had fully recovered, and she stumbled backwards a few steps, totally shocked by what had just happened.

Wow—I healed a dying plant! Nikki thought. *But how?*

Her thoughts were interrupted by loud, shouting voices coming from outside.

"Plenty weird! Plenty weird!"

"So weird even the teachers are scared!"

Glancing out the window, Nikki saw two boys taunting a girl about Jack's age who was dressed in black. She saw Jack throw his messenger bag on the sidewalk, lead the Goth-looking girl behind him, and raise his fists as he faced the two boys.

"You guys are just asking for trouble!" Nikki heard Jack say.

Nikki quickly grabbed her backpack and raced from the classroom to help Jack.

When Nikki ran outside, she saw the two boys facing Jack in threatening poses and staring at him with glaring eyes. The girl whimpered and took a few steps backwards.

"So what are you gonna do about it, Brady?" asked the pimple-faced bully.

"Yeah, think you're tough enough to fight us both?" said the second bully, a chubby kid with a buzzcut hair style.

Jack took one step forward, stopped, and scowled at the two boys. There was an intense expression on his face. "You guys have no idea where I've been, what I've seen, and what I've done," he told them.

Pimple-face laughed. "Is that so?"

"Yeah?" said Chubby. "What of it?"

Taking another step forward, Jack raised his fists. "You do *not* want to mess with me," he said in an angry and threatening tone of voice. "But if you're crazy enough to tangle with me, then you're going to see how crazy *I* am, and you're going to run home to your mothers, crying like a couple of babies!"

Jack's confident tone of voice and the fierce look in his blue eyes made the bullies glance at each other with fear in their eyes as Jack took one more step forward. Feeling strong and brave, Jack took another step closer to the cowering boys and howled like a coyote. He raised his arms high above his head and leaped forward, landing right in front of the bullies.

"Boo!" he shouted.

The bullies jumped. Pimple Face shrieked and backed away.

"You big bully, you scream like a girly-girl," Jack said, laughing.

The chubby boy giggled, and Pimple Face turned red and punched his buddy's arm. "This guy is nuts!" he said, trying to collect some dignity. "Let's get out of here."

"Yeah, they ain't worth it," replied Chubby, trying to muffle a laugh by covering his mouth.

They turned and ran down the street.

"That was so cool, Jack!" Nikki cried when she finally reached him. "You scared the daylights out of those two."

"Nah, it was nothing," Jack said as he blushed and turned away to hide it.

Nikki smiled when she saw the quick glance Jack shot at the Goth girl who walked closer to him.

"You are my hero, Jack. Thank you for defending me," she said with a smile. "They've been tormenting me whenever they can catch me alone, because of the way I dress."

Jack looked at her and his face turned red again. "Aw, gee, you're welcome," he said and thought, *I faced spooks, evil crows and shadows, a Tasmanian Devil, and the Hobgoblin himself in Creepy*

Hollow last year, so two ordinary bullies weren't going to frighten me.

"I'm so proud of you, little cousin," Nikki said as she stepped closer to Jack.

"Do we have to hug?" Jack asked playfully, taking a step back.

"Nope." Nikki laughed and asked, "Who is your friend?"

"Oh," Jack said. "This is my friend, Peggy Ward. She's new here at school."

"Everyone calls me 'Plenty Weird,'" said Peggy. "Except for Jack." She smiled at him and once again, he blushed.

"And I won't call you that, either," said Nikki. She shook hands with Peggy, admiring her outfit of black tights, skirt, boots, shirt, and jacket. Her black hair was long and done up in pigtails. Peggy's skin was pale, but healthy-looking. *She looks a lot like Ghoulina,* Nikki thought, *and I bet that's the main reason Jack likes her.*

Ever since their return from Creepy Hollow, Jack had started wearing black jeans, T-shirts, and hiking boots, trying to look as Goth as he could. His parents had even let him grow his curly black hair down to his shoulders. Nikki, however, still liked wearing yellow T-shirts, blue jeans with the cuffs rolled up, and running shoes. The only thing different about her was that she often wore her long, auburn hair in a ponytail, and she had grown to be the same height as Jack; although older than him by a year, he had always been taller than her.

"Well, I have to get home now," said Peggy. "Thanks again, Jack. I'll see you in school tomorrow. It was nice meeting you, Nikki."

"It was nice meeting you, too," Nikki replied.

Peggy Ward smiled at Jack and Nikki, then turned and skipped down the street in the opposite direction the two bullies had gone.

"You were very brave, Jack," said Nikki.

"It was nothing," he said. "I always knew that those two are cowards. It's about time someone let those punks know they don't really scare anybody."

"I bet they will think twice before they try to bully anyone else," Nikki said. She then continued, "Grandma made oatmeal cookies today. Want to come over?"

"You kidding?" Jack laughed, picking up his messenger bag filled with school books. "Let's go!" he said.

They crossed the street at the corner and headed towards Whipple Street to Grandma Sweet's house.

While Jack called his mother on his cell phone and told her where he was going, Nikki tried to figure out how to tell Jack what happened in her bedroom the night of her birthday, and then again today in the classroom.

Walking beside Jack, deep in her thoughts, Nikki noticed a robin lying on the curbside grass. The poor bird was struggling to get up and fly away, but couldn't.

Jack spotted the bird, too. "Looks like he's got a broken wing," he said, slipping his cell phone back into his pocket.

Kneeling down, Nikki looked closely at the injured robin. Its wing was indeed broken.

"What are we going to do, Nikki?" asked Jack.

"I don't know," she replied.

Nikki suddenly felt the tingling sensation come over her again, and her hands began to grow warm. But this time she was in control, and as her hands began to glow with the golden light, she reached for the robin and gently picked it up. The robin didn't struggle as Nikki cupped her hands around its trembling body. The frightened bird seemed to sense that Nikki was going to help.

"Whoa!" said Jack. "What's happening?"

"I don't really know," said Nikki. "This is the third time this has happened to me, but this is the first time I'm in control of my hands."

Jack's blue eyes almost bulged out of their sockets. *What?*

"Hush," said Nikki as her warm and golden-glowing hands lovingly stroked the robin and its broken wing. "I'll tell you everything on the way to Grandma's."

A few moments later, the robin chirped, flapped its wings, and flew from Nikki's hands. The small bird circled the sky three times above Nikki as if thanking her before it turned and headed towards the forest of Weeping Meadow. The tingling sensation stopped, and Nikki's hands returned to normal.

"Wow! You healed that bird," Jack said. "You can do magic!" Then he stopped and gave Nikki a long, thoughtful look. "It *was* magic, wasn't it?"

Nikki nodded and said, "I think so. But I don't understand how that could be. Has anything weird like that happened to you since we returned from Creepy Hollow?"

"Nope," he said. "I just feel more confident. You know? I would love to go back there again for Halloween."

Nikki had never said a word about Creepy Hollow to Grandma, as if her grandmother would ever believe such a wild story. Jack had never told his parents, either.

"I'd like to visit our friends there again, too," said Nikki.

Over the past year, since their adventures in Creepy Hollow, their relationship had changed. Jack now had a great admiration for Nikki, while she came to realize that he was a lot more than just a doofus. While Nikki sensed that Jack was somewhat in awe of her, she also saw that he was a little bit jealous of her, too, and it bothered her.

"Well, I have no idea what's going on," she told him. "It all started the night of my birthday party."

"Have you told Grandma about any of this?" Jack wanted to know.

"Not yet," Nikki replied. "But I think I'm going to have to tell her, after all this."

Jack nodded and chewed his bottom lip. "When?"

"I don't know," Nikki admitted. She paused thoughtfully, her forehead wrinkled in a frown, and then she snapped her fingers. "Look, Halloween is this coming Sunday, right?"

"Yep! October thirty-first, as always," Jack said with a smart-aleck grin.

Nikki punched his shoulder playfully. "You're coming over to spend the weekend with us, right?" she asked.

"You bet!" Jack said. "Mom and Dad are going out of town for the Halloween weekend. Now this is supposed to be a surprise, but they're taking us all to Disneyworld during Christmas vacation."

"Awesome!" Nikki said. "Now look, I want you with me when I tell Grandma everything that happened to us last year. I'll tell her Friday, as soon as you come over."

"Sounds like a plan," said Jack. "I just hope she believes us."

Nikki sighed. "I do too, Jack. I do too."

Chapter 2

Meanwhile in another realm…

Bob "Wishbone" Jones and his wife Hannah, the Healing Witch, lived in the village of Springdale, which was near the spirit realm of Celestria and the graveyard known as Wormbelow. Hannah, who preferred to be called Ghoulina, was a vegetarian ghoul who ate only cooked vegetables. She and Wishbone had been married nearly a year and had been blessed with a baby girl named Ava, who was almost three months old. While Wishbone was a warrior, a member of the Order of the Silver Knights, he was a carpenter by trade. Ghoulina divided her time between caring for their daughter and studying to become a Wishmother. Although she was an expert at casting spells, she would not receive her magic Wand until she had completed her training under the tutelage of the Trinity of Wishmothers, who dwelled in Celestria. The Jones family lived in a small but lovely cottage that was built of blue stone and gray mortar, had comfortable rooms, a fireplace, and a library filled with books.

One day in October while Wishbone was tending to his garden, the town gossip strolled past the cottage, stopped, and leaned on the white picket fence. He was a tall, grungy-looking man, with bad teeth and dirty fingernails. No one knew his real name, so everyone called him Tattler because he liked to spread rumors and make up stories. He was a bitter man and jealous of everyone who had magical powers.

He thought that spreading gossip and making up stories would make him popular but all it did was cause people to avoid him and even cross to the other side of the street when they saw him coming. Wishbone was one of the few villagers who tolerated him.

"Say, Wishbone, have you heard about Farmer Brown's oldest daughter running away with a musician? Her father is furious and I bet he will disown her. He's a rich man, you know," he blabbed.

Wishbone looked up, brushed his long blonde hair from his eyes, and frowned. "No, Tattler," he said. "I haven't and I don't want to hear about it."

"Well," Tattler said. "I just thought you might be curious."

"I'm not, and you shouldn't stick your nose into other people's business," said Wishbone.

Tattler rubbed his dirty face and changed the subject. "So how's your lovely wife and your brand-new baby girl?" he asked.

"My family is fine, thank you," Wishbone replied. "Now, if you don't mind, I must ask you to be on your way. I have a lot of work to do today."

Tattler took it as an insult and said indignantly, "Well then, I'll be going. I was just trying to be friendly and a good neighbor."

"I know you were and I'm sorry for cutting you short," Wishbone said to Tattler, trying to be as nice as possible. "But today I don't have time for a chat. I must get back to work."

"Say hello to Hannah for me," said Tattler.

"I will," Wishbone replied.

Tattler nodded and then he turned and walked away.

Watching Tattler turn a corner and disappear from sight, Wishbone shook his head. He didn't like nor trust him because he was not only a troublemaker but a known thief, as well.

Wishbone went back to work but a short while later he heard his daughter, Ava, crying, and before he could put his rake down, the baby's cry turned into a loud scream. The house began to shake, the windows rattled, and even the flowers trembled. The neighbors' dogs began to howl, cats screeched, and flocks of startled birds flew from the trees.

Dropping his rake to the ground, Wishbone ran for the back door and into the house.

Inside the cottage, pictures and paintings swung back and forth, bouncing off the walls. Dishes clattered in the china cabinet and crashed to the floor. The walls trembled and floorboards vibrated under his feet.

As Wishbone raced towards the nursery, suddenly the baby's screams stopped and the house stopped shaking. Wishbone stepped into the nursery, which was painted pink and black, and saw Ghoulina sitting in the rocking chair and cuddling their beautiful baby in her arms.

"Hannah, what happened this time?" Wishbone asked, wiping sweat from his brow.

Ghoulina, dressed in a black and purple gown, and wearing blue lipstick, smiled at her husband. "Ava saw a snake on the window sill and it frightened her," she explained.

"What? A snake? Where is it now?" Wishbone asked with great concern.

"Oh, I grabbed it and threw it out the window as far away as I could," Ghoulina replied.

Wishbone sighed and leaned back against a wall. "Wow, Ava's magic is already powerful."

"She's coming into her magic far too early and she's too young to understand or control it, Bob," said Ghoulina.

The young parents realized that their daughter had a rare magical gift called *Vocalocity*, the ability to use her voice as a sonic weapon, even when the baby was only a few days old. Whenever baby Ava cried because she was hungry or needed her diaper changed, her voice sent out a gentle ripple of vibrations. But when she was angry or frightened, her voice became very loud and powerful. Wishbone and Ghoulina were the only ones who could quiet her, which made finding a babysitter nearly impossible. And only Wishbone and Ghoulina were immune from the power of Ava's Vocalocity, although it did give both of them goosebumps and made them nervous and sweaty.

"Hey, Wishbone," they heard their neighbor's voice.

Wishbone walked to the window, pulled the pink curtain aside, and looked out. He saw their neighbor, a stocky man wearing a straw hat, leaning on the fence.

"Can I help you, Martin?" Wishbone asked.

"You've got to do something about your daughter," Martin said angrily. "Every time she cries I feel nervous and my dogs go crazy. Today my cat got so frazzled that she scratched me." He showed his bloody arm to Wishbone.

"I'm so sorry, Martin," Wishbone apologized. "But you know we can't do anything until she's old enough to learn how to control her powers."

"I know, I know," Martin replied. "Just keep her quiet when you can."

"We will, I promise," Wishbone told him. With a weary sigh he closed the curtain and turned to Ghoulina. "I wonder why Ava's voice affects every living thing, but the bat that got in the house last week wasn't affected," he said.

"I'm not sure," Ghoulina told him. "But probably because bats make high-pitched sounds and listen to the returning echoes to build up a sonic map of their surroundings in their brain. Maybe their echolocation system is a similar frequency to Ava's voice and it doesn't affect them."

"Makes sense to me," said Wishbone.

Ghoulina smiled at the baby in her arms. "Look at her, she's sleeping like a baby," she said with a soft laugh. She looked at her husband then, with concern in her eyes. "That snake looked sinister and when I grabbed it…it felt dirty and slimy. I saw it slither away and disappear behind the shack."

Wishbone bent down to kiss his wife and baby. "It's long gone by now, and after feeling Ava's power I doubt that it will ever come back. You just rest while I go finish the flowerbed," he said, closing the window and walking out of the room.

Ghoulina smiled and started humming a lullaby to her baby.

Chapter 3

Bleakvale was a barren, desolate country north and east of Celestria and the village of Springdale. The sky above the land was always gray and cloudy, shutting out most of the sun's light. There were no trees, and very little vegetation grew there, only what the residents needed to eat. It was a sad place, and its people were an unhappy lot living under the thumb of Evila, the Grim Witch—the Queen of Bleakvale Coven.

Evila was a beautiful, yet cruel, power-hungry and calculating woman. About thirteen years ago she murdered the King of Willow Haven and turned his kingdom into a wasteland. She enslaved the good witches of Weeping Willow and absorbed their magical power the way a vampire sucks blood from its human prey. Dark desires burned in her cold heart as she renewed her quest to find and consume as much magical power as she could, and that's all she cared about. After she came to power, she named the castle Dreadful Hall.

Queen Evila, dressed in a long crimson gown, watched with a menacing glare of her dark eyes, which matched her raven-black hair, as the snake slithered across the stone floor, crawling towards her. Guarding their white-skinned Queen stood the monstrous Mutanto and his werewolf henchman, Howler. Behind them cowered the three dull-witted Wolfmen: Boo, Goo, and Poo. They watched as the snake reached Evila's red shoes, stopped, and coiled its body before her.

"Cute snake," Boo snickered.

"Cute? How can it be cute? It's a slithering, ugly rope," growled Goo.

"Watch out you guys! It might be poisonous," Poo warned the others as he took a step back.

Evila glared at Mutanto, her red lips forming a thin line. "Must those three cowardly idiots stand here in my royal presence?" she demanded.

"They'll not befoul your chambers again, Your Majesty," said Mutanto and then jutted his chin at Howler.

Howler got the silent message and growled at the three Wolfmen. "Get back to the basement where you belong and wait for further orders, you knuckleheads!" He held his breath in disgust as the stench of the trio hit his nose. "And take a bath, Poo. You stink like roadkill!" he instructed.

"But I took a bath in March—and it's only October!" Poo protested weekly.

"Get out of my sight," Howler growled, feeling frustrated.

The trio of werewolves hurried towards the door, trampling each other.

"She scares me," Poo whispered.

"Me, too," Goo replied, pushing Boo aside.

"Don't push me!" Boo hissed, conking Goo on the head.

Goo growled, ready for a fight, but when they heard Howler's booming voice, *"Out!"* they scurried out the door.

Evila rolled her eyes and asked Howler, "Can't you find better help than those idiots?"

"They're loyal and follow my orders blindly, Your Majesty," Howler told her.

"Well, it's your choice," Evila said. She reached down and picked up the snake that was coiled up by her feet and held it at eye level. "So, my lovely little Slither has returned," she said, kissing the serpent's head. "And what have you found out? What news have you brought me? Is everything I've heard true?"

The serpent hissed, "Put me down, Your Majesty, and I will tell you."

With an impatient sigh, Evila bent down and set Slither on the floor. She watched as the snake began to change its shape, transforming itself into a tall, scraggly man.

"Your Majesty," he said, bowing to his queen.

"Well, Slither—or shall I call you what everyone else calls you?" she asked.

"You may call me whatever you wish, my Queen," said the dirty, disheveled-looking man.

"What have you learned, Tattler?" she asked.

Only Queen Evila and her most faithful servants knew that the gossip of Springdale, Tattler, was a shapeshifter. Turning himself into a serpent was his only power, his only magical talent. But unlike the Wolfmen, who were also shapeshifters and chose to stay in wolf form, Tattler had no desire to remain a serpent permanently. He had bigger dreams than that.

"What you have heard is true, Your Majesty," Tattler said. "The baby possesses magic that has not been seen in Creepy Hollow for more than a hundred years. She is strong and powerful, and she could be very useful to you."

"Excellent!" said Evila. "How shall it be done? What do you suggest?"

"Bats are not affected by her, my Queen. So, here is what I think should be done…," said Tattler, and then he told her his plan.

When he had finished speaking, Evila rubbed her hands together. Feeling excited, she turned to Mutanto and Howler. "See to our prisoners. Tell them they will soon have company. Then prepare for the arrival of our new guest."

"As you command, my Queen," said Mutanto.

Howler bowed and smiled with glee. "As you wish, Your Majesty."

Mutanto turned on his heels and left.

Howler motioned to Tattler to follow him and said, "You earned your reward, Tattler. Come on, I saved a few juicy rats for you in the dungeon."

Tattler's eyes lit up, and he followed Howler like an obedient dog. "Good. I'm starving!" he mumbled as a drop of drool rolled down on his grimy chin. "The rats in the towns and in the fields are skinny and hard to digest, but in the castle they grow fat and lazy and are easy to hunt."

Evila rolled her eyes in disgust and murmured under her breath, *Patience, Evila, patience. You must tolerate the useful help, no matter how gross they are.*

Later that night, Evila stood on the castle's balcony. She folded her hands across her chest, bowed her head, and began to hum a strange melody, a song without words. A few seconds later she raised her head, stared at the sky, and chanted:

A cold wind stirred and whirled through the courtyard below.

Acting as her guards, Boo, Goo, and Poo, standing off to one side, shook their heads and exchanged fearful looks.

"I don't like this one bit," said Boo, the red-furred Wolfman.

"Me, neither," said Goo, the one with gray, matted fur.

"She scares me a lot," said Poo, the stinky Wolfman with mangy, brown fur.

Evila spun around and glared at them. "Silence, you fools!" she hissed. The trio shrunk back and turned silent. Satisfied, Evila pointed her gnarly, twisted Wand at the sky. Then she opened her mouth and slowly exhaled clouds of black dust, ash, and soot into the air. *"Fityfirity!"*

A moment later, a large, dark shadow with wings appeared in the night sky.

Meanwhile, back in Creepy Hollow, Catman, whose real name was Otto, went to visit Wishbone and Ghoulina. The cat-like man in colorful outfit was the caretaker of the cemetery of Celestria and carried the keys of Wormbelow in his pouch that hung from his belt.

He had been away on a special mission for the three good witches known as the Trinity of Wishmothers, the ghostly guardians of Celestria. After he reported back to the Wishmothers, he hurried over to his friends' house to tell them what he had learned. What Catman had discovered was of the greatest importance not only to Wishbone and Ghoulina, but to everyone else living in Creepy Hollow as well.

They were sitting at the kitchen table, talking softly while baby Ava was sleeping quietly in the nursery.

"You're sure that Evila is on the move again?" Wishbone asked his old friend.

Catman mewed softly and replied, "There's no doubt about it. She's restless and bored, and is making plans that will affect us all, if she succeeds."

"So, you're saying that she's planning to conquer and destroy all the lands of Creepy Hollow, and enslave their people," Ghoulina said in a tightly-controlled voice. As a new mother, she was greatly concerned about what this would mean for her daughter.

"Yes, I'm afraid so," Catman told her. "The Wishmothers have other agents in the field, hoping to find out more. They're hoping that the Nine Guardians, the good Witches of Willow Haven, will come out of hiding and help."

"There may be only a few warriors of the Order of Silver Knights still alive," said Wishbone, "but they will join in the fight, if it comes to that."

"Unfortunately, I think it will," whispered Catman.

"What else have you learned?" Ghoulina asked him.

"Your town gossip, Tattler, is another one of Evila's spies," said Catman. "He's a shapeshifter who can turn himself into a serpent that Evila calls Slither."

Wishbone slammed his palm upon the table. "I knew that filthy scoundrel was more than he appeared to be!" he said in a loud voice.

"Keep your voice down, Bob," Ghoulina said, laying a hand on Wishbone's. "We don't want to wake the baby."

"I have more to tell you," Catman spoke in a soft voice. "The Wishmothers believe that *our* queen still lives, but has long been in hiding."

Wishbone and Ghoulina exchanged looks of astonishment and hope. "Queen Leandra? Still alive?" Wishbone asked.

Catman nodded. "Yes, we believe so," he said.

Wishbone shook his head. "But how did the Wishmothers find out?" he asked.

"Either Queen Leandra or perhaps her daughter used magic, which the Wishmothers sensed and recognized as Royal Magic," Catman replied. "Maybe Evila sensed it, too. Remember, no one really knows what happened to the queen and her daughter. So it's possible they escaped and found a safe place to hide."

"Where are they, then?" asked Ghoulina. "Where have they been all these years?"

"The Royal Family has been living almost under our very noses," Catman told her. "And you won't believe who they are."

"What do you mean?" Wishbone asked.

The loud sound of breaking glass followed by the powerful screams of baby Ava Jones interrupted them, and Catman covered his ears with his paws.

"Ava!" Ghoulina cried, leaping from her chair and rushing from the kitchen. Wishbone and Catman quickly followed her to the nursery.

"No, no, no!" Wishbone shouted in anger when they reached the baby's room and saw a huge bat holding their baby in its claws as it flew towards the broken window. Wishbone jumped as fast as he could but couldn't reach the bat.

"My baby!" Ghoulina cried out in horror, falling to her knees.

Catman roared like a lion and leaped into the air, but he wasn't quick enough, either. The giant bat escaped through the broken window and flew off into the night.

"I tried," Catman said, wiping tears from his eyes. "I'm sorry I couldn't catch it."

"We both failed," Wishbone told him, kneeling to comfort his wife, who was trembling and weeping. Then it dawned on him: "Tattler came to visit the other day, and then shortly after that Ava was frightened by a serpent on her windowsill. Catman, you said that Tattler is a shapeshifter. He must have turned into a snake and frightened Ava. It all makes sense now."

"This is Evila's work—I know it!" Catman said. "But what does she want with your baby?"

Ghoulina's voice was touched by anger and grief. "Ava's gift—her Vocalocity. That must be what she wants. She wants to absorb her power," she said.

"This is way over our heads. We need help," said Catman. "We need to go to the Trinity of Wishmothers."

Chapter 4

Grandma Sweet was a beautiful woman in in her early 60s. She had golden hair with hardly any gray in it, and there were very few wrinkles on her face. Tall, full-figured and strong-looking, she was a force to be reckoned with. But there was kindness in her blue eyes, gentleness in her manner, and a maternal, nurturing attitude about her. She had a loving heart, a warm smile. She also knew a thing or two about magic, as well, and she *sensed* that Nikki had been using magic. Grandma dreaded the unavoidable, when her granddaughter turned thirteen. She knew that according to Nikki's birthright, the powers she inherited must have manifested themselves already.

It was the Friday before Halloween when she decided it was time to have *the talk* with Nikki. Jack's parents had already gone away for the weekend, and she didn't mind that Jack was there because he was part of the family and would eventually find out the truth, anyway. It was best to tell them both the truth.

After supper, once Nikki and Jack had washed and put away the dishes, Grandma called them into the living room and told them to make themselves comfortable.

"What's up, Grandma?" asked Jack. "We haven't done anything wrong…have we?"

Grandma smiled. "No, Jack," she said. "You two have been very good lately, and I'm proud of you both. But I have important things to tell you, things that concern Nikki and will, no doubt, concern you, too."

"Important things about me?" Nikki asked. "What sort of things?"

There was a look in Grandma's eyes the kids didn't understand. "I don't want to beat around the bush, so I'm going to ask you to be straightforward and honest with me when you answer my questions. Will you do that for me?"

"Of course, I will, Grandma," Nikki told her.

"Me, too! I promise," said Jack.

"Good!" said Grandma. She looked at them both, and then settled her gaze on Nikki. "Has anything out of the ordinary been happening to you since you turned thirteen? Things being out of your control? Strange things that scared you but didn't hurt you?"

Nikki and Jack looked at each other. This was the night *they* had planned to tell Grandma about their adventures in Creepy Hollow last year, and now Grandma was asking Nikki strange questions.

"You mean things like magic?" Nikki asked.

This took Grandma by surprise, but she tried not to show it. "Yes, exactly," she said.

So Nikki told her about the river stones and how they had moved and arranged themselves in strange patterns the night of her birthday party. Then she told her grandmother about how she had accidentally saved a dying plant at school, just by touching it. "My hands turned very warm and I didn't know why," she said, looking at her grandmother with great concern and worry.

"Tell her about the robin, Nikki!" Jack said with excitement in his voice.

"Oh, yes," said Nikki. "Jack and I found a robin with a broken wing on our way home from school the other day. When I picked it up, my hands turned warm again and then they started to glow. It didn't scare me as much as it did the first time, and when I touched the bird's broken wing, it straightened and the bird flew away."

"Nikki healed the bird just like *that!*" Jack said, snapping his fingers for dramatic effect.

Their grandmother was not surprised. She had expected something like this to happen when Nikki came of age: in fact, she had been waiting for it to happen. "Now pay attention, Nikki, because I'm going to tell you about that, and about our family. Things I kept hidden from you for your own safety, things I knew I'd have to tell you about one day. Today is that day."

"Like what, Grandma?" Nikki asked.

"Well, for one, you were born with a great gift of magic, a healing gift—a gift you inherited from your dear mother," Grandma said slowly and carefully.

"My…my mother?" Nikki asked. "What do you mean?"

"Where our family comes from, magical powers are passed down from mother to child," Grandma explained. "Males can inherit the same gift of magic, but only from their mothers, not their fathers, and only if their mother is a witch."

Jack stared at Grandma Sweet. "Do *you* have magical powers?" he asked her.

"Why…yes, yes I do," she told him. "I once belonged to the Weeping Willow Coven, which was destroyed by evil forces."

"I'm sorry. Why was your Coven named Weeping Willow?" inquired Nikki.

"The sacred willow tree protects small animals and birds by giving them a hiding place in its thick branches. The fallen leaves of the willow nourish the soil of the Earth. It was our symbol because my Coven cared for the land and all living things."

"That's so cool, Grandma! Where is this place?" asked Jack. "I've never seen you use any magic."

"That's because, for reasons you will learn tonight, I never once used magic since we came here," Grandma Sweet told him.

"So where *did* we come from?" Nikki asked.

"Before I tell you that, I want you to promise me one thing, both of you," said Grandma. "I want you to promise me that you will never use magic again unless I give you permission, and you will never speak to anyone about it."

"Cross my heart, I'll tell no one," Jack promised.

Nikki frowned. "I promise, too, Grandma," she said. "But why?"

"Because it's dangerous. *Very* dangerous," Grandma told her. "Understand?"

"Yes, Grandma, I understand…I think," said Nikki.

"Good! Now listen," said Grandma. She took a deep breath and slowly exhaled. "Our family comes from a world called Creepy Hollow. We…" She fell silent when she saw Nikki and Jack look at each other in amazement. "What's wrong, kids?"

"Well, Grandma," Nikki said hesitantly. "We know all about Creepy Hollow."

This time, Grandma was taken by surprise. "How…how did you ever find out about Creepy Hollow?"

"We're sorry we never told you, Grandma," Jack apologized. "We wanted to, but just didn't know when or how to tell you."

"But we did decide to tell you tonight," said Nikki. "Honestly, we did."

Grandma stared at the kids, as amazed by what she had heard as they were to hear that she possessed the gift of magic, just like Nikki. "Before I go on, I think you'd better tell me what you know about Creepy Hollow, and I think you'd better start at the beginning," she said.

So Grandma Sweet settled back and listened as Nikki and Jack took turns telling her all about their adventures in Creepy Hollow last year.

Meanwhile, back in Creepy Hollow…

In a special cage in the basement of Dreadful Hall, Mike and Angelina Strong had been prisoners of Evila ever since that night, twelve years ago, when they were captured by Mutanto and his gang of Wolfmen and taken back to her realm of Bleakvale. The ceiling, floor, and four walls of the cage were thick and made of Wizard's Glass, with black drapes inside it that could be closed to give the couple some privacy. This prison cell was also protected by spells and enchantments, and no one except Evila could work any magic inside of it. But without the special key or knowing the spell that unlocked the cage, no living thing could get in or out.

Angelina and her husband had been provided with all the comforts of a home, except freedom. They had a luxurious bed, couch, chairs, table, and a bathroom. Although there was no television reception in Creepy Hollow, Evila's magic provided electricity for them to have a television, Blu-Ray player, and a large assortment of DVDs and Blu-Ray discs. They even had an extensive library of books, CDs, and a CD player…everything stolen from stores on Earth. However, the magical glass prison prevented Angelina from ever using her magical gift of healing. But for all the comforts provided them, those four walls in which they were confined made a prison, nonetheless. The only visitors they ever had were Evila and her minions, when the Grim Witch came to *feed* on them.

Every day the three dull-witted Wolfmen known as Boo, Goo, and Poo took their turn at guarding the prisoners. At the moment, they were squatting on the floor of the large chamber that housed the enchanted cage, but were more interested in their board game than they were in guarding the two prisoners.

Poo, the stinky Wolfman with the mangy brown-fur, reached for the little wooden boat that was his game piece. "I move five spaces," he said.

"You have to roll the dice first," said Goo, brushing leaves from his matted gray fur.

"Okay. Gimme the dice," Poo told him.

"It's not your turn!" yelled Boo, the unhappy Wolfman with red fur. He punched Poo in the chest. "Idiot!"

"Whose turn is it?" asked Poo.

"It's my turn," Boo replied.

"Then after him it's *my* turn," said Goo.

Poo scratched his smelly, brown fur. "So when is it my turn?" he asked.

"After you take another bath," Boo told Poo. "You still stink."

They were interrupted when the outer door swung open and Evila entered the chamber. Boo, Goo, and Poo leaped to their feet and bowed to their queen.

"Out of my way, you mindless mutts!" Evila said as she walked past the Wolfmen, holding her breath until she had walked far enough away from Poo. In her right arm she carried a wiggling bundle wrapped in a purple blanket. In her left hand she held her Wand, which was a gnarly and twisted tree branch, all covered with gray and green moss. The Grim Witch then pointed the Wand at the glass cage, the lock made a *clicking* sound, and then the front wall slid down into the floor. With a happy and victorious smile on her face, Evila entered the cage.

"Come to feed again so soon?" asked Mike Strong. Bone-thin and gray-haired, with his handsome face spoiled by wrinkles, he lay sprawled on the couch, reading a book. He looked too tired and worn out to even make an attempt to sit up.

Evila was over ninety years old, but because of the youth and magic she had stolen from other prisoners over the years, she remained beautiful and as young-looking as someone in their 30s. For the past twelve years the Grim Witch of Bleakvale Coven had been slowly draining Mike's strength and energy, and Angelina's magical powers, as if they were human batteries. However, she was well aware that she couldn't feed off her prisoners as if she were some kind of greedy vampire. Not for too long, no matter how careful she was. Sooner or later they would die, just as all Evila's previous captives had died after she drained their magic too fast.

"Don't worry, I won't be enjoying the taste of your dwindling energy much longer," Evila told him, walking over to the bed where Angelina lay, half asleep. She was in worse shape than her husband. Her hair was almost totally gray and her body was thin and frail. Although she and Mike weren't even 35 years old, they looked twice as old.

"You mean you're finished with us at last?" Mike asked. "So no doubt you'll be putting us out of our misery." Even if he tried, he was too weak to argue, fight, or even curse Evila. The Grim Witch held too much power over him and his wife.

Evila didn't answer as she stood next to the bed and stared at Angelina. "I have a little surprise for you," she said.

The Grim Witch handed the bundle to Angelina, who opened the purple blanket. Inside she found a baby, about three months old and dressed in a cute little black outfit, fast asleep.

"Whose baby is this?" Angelina asked, cradling the infant in her arms. *My own daughter would be thirteen years old by now!* Her broken heart shattered into even more pieces. Tears filled her eyes, but she didn't have the strength to weep. She had cried herself out long ago.

"Her name is Ava," said Evila. "Everything she needs shall be provided."

Angelina had a blank expression on her face as she stared at Evila. Then she frowned and glared at the witch. "You're going to feed on her, aren't you?" she said. "You're going to use her like a battery the same way you've used my husband and me all these years!"

Evila showed neither anger nor outrage. She showed no emotion at all. "I will, eventually, when Ava's old enough," she explained. "She has a remarkable talent and possesses a magical power unheard of for over a century. It's called Vocalocity. Let's wake her up and see what she can do."

The Grim Witch gently touched baby Ava's forehead with the tip of her gnarly Wand.

Little Ava's turquoise eyes opened wide, and then she started screaming at the top of her lungs. Evila cringed. The three Wolfmen howled in pain. Mike yelled and covered his ears with his hands as the glass walls shook and the floor started to vibrate under their feet.

"Interesting, isn't it?" asked Evila. "The baby has come into her magic years earlier than normal. She can use her gift in this room of Wizard's Glass, but can't do much damage."

Still covering his ears, Mike said, "Yes, it's very interesting."

Only Angelina Strong remained unaffected by the power of Ava's voice.

"See what I mean?" Evila said to her. "But don't worry. Your husband will get used to it, and once the door to this cage is closed again, no one but you will hear her cries and screams. So I'd advise you to keep her as quiet and as happy as you can."

Angelina held baby Ava in her arms, talking softly to her in a soothing voice and gently caressing her cheek. Ava's big eyes turned and looked into Angelina's, and a sweet little smile slowly spread across her face. When Angelina started humming a lullaby, Ava cooed and wiggled her tiny fingers.

Ava's eyes slowly closed and soon she was fast asleep.

"It seems you can tame the brat just like her mother," Evila said.

Mike removed his hands from his ears and shook his head. "Who's the baby's mother?" he asked.

"You wouldn't know her or her husband," Evila replied.

"So what more do you want from us?" Angelina asked.

"I want you to care for her as if she were your own daughter," Evila told her.

Angelina smiled at the baby in her arms, and once again she thought of the daughter she and Mike had left in the care of her mother, twelve years ago. "You know I will," she said. "But what do you intend to do with her?"

"Oh, I have plans," Evila replied. "But for now, I intend to keep doing what I have been doing each month since the night you were brought here: I intend to *feed*—which is all you earth-born witches are good for. I've had a few of you here before I found you, but sadly, they died so quickly. But you...you are strong, as if you are of royal bloodline…which is unlikely. Or is it? I wonder…"

After all these years, she still hasn't figured out who I am! Angelina thought.

"Even you non-magical humans have energy I can use," the Grim Witch said to Mike. She raised her Wand and touched his forehead with the tip of it.

Mike gasped and fell back onto the couch.

Chapter 5

The Past Revealed

"Once upon a time, more than twelve years ago, King Einar and Queen Leandra ruled over all the lands of Willow Haven, where everyone lived in peace and in harmony with nature," Grandma Sweet began, and when she knew she had Nikki's and Jack's complete attention, she continued. "The good witches of the Weeping Willow Coven helped to ensure that the crops grew strong, and all the livestock, pets, and other animals were always in good health. They also used their healing magic and spells of protection to aid the peaceful residents of nearby lands, such as Dwarf Hill, Mermaid Landing, and Elf Harbor, who had no covens of good witches to watch over them."

"Wow! I want to be a good witch, Grandma!" Jack said dreamily.

Grandma smiled and said, "You *could* be a wizard, but only a girl can be a witch." She paused to take a breath before continuing. "Evila, the Grim Witch, and her wicked witches of Bleakvale Coven were not fond of trees, plants, flowers, crops, and most other things that grew from the soil. They ate only the poisonous mushrooms and bitter moss that grew in dark caves, and they found insects a delicacy, most especially spiders, ants, and grasshoppers. Evila was a jealous and power-hungry queen, and she set her mind on conquering the lands of nearby realms. So she raised an army of Ogres, Goblins, and Gnomes, marched down from the north, and launched a surprise attack upon Willow Haven. The army destroyed everything—homes, shops, and other buildings, as well as plants and trees—and then they poisoned the soil and turned the kingdom into a barren wasteland. Caught off guard, the witches of the Weeping Willow Coven were powerless to stop them. Evila and her minions then killed most of the people and imprisoned the good witches, except for those who fled into hiding, seeking refuge with the neighboring lands they once helped."

"That's awful! Didn't the good witches know them?" asked Nikki. "Why didn't they fight Evila?"

"It is not that simple, Nikki," Grandma replied with sadness in her voice. "The Weeping Willow Coven lived in peace for so long that they didn't expect the vicious attack. Evila then murdered King Einar and stole his Key Stone, one of the only Stones that can open an Ectomagic Gate to Earth at any time during the year. Since then, Evila and her minions are able to visit Earth whenever they wish, to cause destruction, floods, famine, and draught—and to hunt for anyone who possesses the gift of magic. Queen Leandra managed to escape to Earth with her fourteen-year-old daughter and go into hiding. The queen had to do what she could to save them both from Evila, the Grim Witch."

"I wonder where Queen Leandra and her daughter are. I would love to help them," Nikki looked at her grandmother with a flash of determination in her eyes.

"Me, too," Jack said. "We could help them to get their kingdom back."

Grandma looked at the children with tears glistening in her eyes. "I will tell you something that will come as a surprise to both of you. I changed my name to Rose Sweet and your mother's name to Angelina," she said, turning to Nikki, who had disbelief in her eyes. "I was hoping to avoid detection and keep us both safe from the Grim Witch."

Jack sat on the couch, stunned and amazed, and nearly speechless. But he couldn't remain quiet for long. "You mean *you* are the queen, Grandma?" he asked with wide-eyed innocence and astonishment.

"I *was* a queen, a long time ago, Jack," she said. "But now there is no queen or king. Willow Haven has been all but destroyed by the Grim Witch."

Nikki didn't know what to make of what she had just heard. *Wow! My grandmother is Queen Leandra of Willow Haven, in Creepy Hollow,* she thought. *That explains how I had come to have magical powers. Where our family comes from, magical powers are passed down from mother to child, that's what Grandma had said earlier. My mother was a witch and now I'm a witch, too—and the youngest member of her Royal Bloodline.*

"What did you do when you came here, Grandma?" Nikki asked.

Queen Leandra, who would always be Grandma to Nikki and Jack, smiled affectionately. "Well, certain friends of our family who did not possess magic came to Earth to live, long ago," she explained. "When your mother and I arrived here, I contacted them, and they loaned us money and helped us acquire what documents we needed to make a life here. I bought this house, and became an herbalist and midwife. But I never used my magic, not even once."

Nikki understood the reasons for that. "What about my Mom?" she asked.

"I enrolled your mother in the local junior high school, where she became friends with your father and your parents, too, Jack," Grandma Leandra replied.

Jack smiled and his face lit up with pride. "Did Mom and Dad know Nikki's Mom was a witch?" he asked.

"No, I thought it best that they should not know, for their own protection," his grandmother told him. "But Angelina *did* tell Mike when they got engaged, and she swore him to secrecy."

Although he was a little disappointed and somewhat jealous of the fact that he wasn't born to a Royal Family and had no magical powers of his own, Jack was nonetheless proud that Nikki and Grandma had confided in him.

"Did Mom ever work magic after you came here to live?" Nikki asked.

"No, she didn't," Leandra answered. "Her powers were activated when we still lived in Willow Haven, and I managed to instruct and train her a little before we had to leave. Sadly, she never received her Wand, but she always knew that if she worked magic here, it might alert Evila and her minions."

Jack snapped his fingers. "Hey! Evila is 'alive' spelled backwards!" he said.

"Yes, Jack," said his royal grandmother. "And evil is 'live' spell backwards, too."

"Evil Evila, live, alive." Jack played with the words.

"Stop that, Jack," Nikki snapped at him. "We have more important things to discuss." She turned to her grandmother and asked, "What happened that night when my parents died?"

Queen Leandra put on a sweater over her rose-colored dress, took a sip of her tea, and said, "It was raining quite heavily. Your mother and father were driving along the coastal highway on their way to the airport when their car plunged off the cliff and into the sea. It took the police almost a week to find the car and bring it up from the bottom of the bay. According to the police, the car skidded off the road and hit a tree before going over the cliff. Shortly after that, I officially adopted you and had your last name changed from Strong to Sweet."

Nikki wiped tears from her eyes and went to sit next to her grandmother, to snuggle up close to her. "What was my Mom's *real* name, Grandma?" she asked.

"It was Opal, my dear," her grandmother told her. "Opal."

Jack had tears in his eyes, too. "But what about their bodies?" he asked.

Grandma Leandra shook her head sadly. "Both the driver and the passenger doors were open, so they may have tried to swim free. But the police divers never found their bodies."

They sat in silence for a while, deep in thought.

Nikki then gasped when she realized that she had used magic three times, and though twice she had no control over it, just the fact that she had *used* magic might be enough to alert Evila to her presence. "What's going to happen, Grandma, now that I've used my magic?" she asked.

Leandra sighed heavily, her eyes dark with worry. "I honestly don't know," she admitted. "Hopefully, the magic you used was not powerful enough to alert Evila."

This was all so complicated, but Jack and Nikki were smart kids and they understood everything Grandma Leandra had told them. And while they were worried, they weren't afraid. Their adventures last year in Creepy Hollow had toughened them up, and they knew that their regal and magical grandmother was there to protect them with her magic, if she had to.

"What about the Trinity of Wishmothers, Grandma?" Nikki asked. "Didn't they help fight Evila and her army? Couldn't they save Willow Haven?"

Shaking her head, Queen Leandra explained, "There was only one Wishmother in those days, the Seer Witch, as she was known. When you told me the names of those Wishmothers I knew who they were: three witches from Weeping Willow Coven who fled into hiding and took refuge in the great cemetery of Celestria. I am happy to hear they survived and became the guardians of all the spirits dwelling there. But it grieves me to hear about how that Hobgoblin had them murdered."

"They're very nice ladies," Jack said.

"They're ghosts, Jack," Nikki told him.

"Yeah, I know!" he said. "But they're still nice ladies.

Nikki grinned. "Yes, they are," she agreed.

"Come now, kids," their grandmother told them. "Put on your pajamas and get ready for bed. Then we can talk some more. Serious conversations always go down better with milk and cookies."

Nikki and Jack did not need to be told twice. They ran upstairs as fast as they could. Queen Leandra went into the kitchen, thinking about their conversation, her family history. She was worried, concerned for her grandchildren and afraid of what the future might bring.

Chapter 6

Dressed in pajamas, with their bare feet rubbing the cool, ceramic tile of the kitchen floor, Nikki and Jack sat at the table with their grandmother, Her Royal Majesty, Queen Leandra. They enjoyed their milk and cookies while continuing with the conversation they had started earlier.

"What if my magic alerted the Grim Witch to my presence?" asked Nikki. "Would she come here to get me?"

Grandma Leandra smiled to hide her concern. She tried hard to keep the concern out of her voice when she replied, "Oh, don't worry about that, dear. First, Evila may be long dead. And second, I doubt the magic you used was powerful enough to attract her attention."

Jack dunked a chocolate chip cookie in his glass of milk, chewed it quickly and then swallowed. "Well maybe we should go to Creepy Hollow to find out, and maybe we get some help from our friends," he suggested. "This is the right time of the year to open an Ectomagic Gate, right?"

Smiling fondly at the boy whom she loved as if he were really her grandson, Leandra reached inside her dress and brought out a small, sapphire pendant shaped like a heart, which hung from a silver chain around her neck.

"This is my Key Stone," she told the kids. "It is one of the only two Stones that can open a Gate any time of the year. The other belonged to King Einar, my husband and your grandfather, Nikki. Evila took it after she murdered him. But with my Key Stone, I can protect you both, if it ever comes to that."

"But how, Grandma?" Nikki asked. "It's only a Key Stone."

"It's much more than that," Leandra told her. "It's my Sapphire Wand, too. You see, only the Key Stones of the king and queen are also their Wands. This is a family secret, and while Evila can use your grandfather's Key Stone to open a Gate, she doesn't know that it's also his Wand, and even if she knew, she can never use it. Only those who are related by blood can."

Suddenly, they heard a strange noise, a humming sound mixed with the crackle of static electricity. Nikki knew immediately what that noise was. She peered through the kitchen window overlooking the back yard and saw a swirling, whirling vortex of shimmering green light forming and opening outside.

"It's an Ectomagic Gate!" she cried out.

Glancing out the window, Grandma Leandra and Jack saw the Gate materializing in the back yard.

A dark frown appeared on Leandra's face as she recognized the source of the magic power. "Someone is using Einar's Key Stone—and not for a friendly visit. Go hide in the attic," she said, clutching at her sapphire pendant.

Nikki opened her mouth to protest, but her Grandma Leandra gave her a stern look and yelled, "Now!"

Nikki and Jack had never been yelled at by their grandmother, and knew they must obey. They ran from the kitchen and headed towards the attic. Leandra rose to her feet, removed the silver chain from around her neck, and held the sapphire pendant tightly in one hand. She stood by the window, watching and waiting.

Seconds later, she saw two familiar figures—a pair of creatures she had not seen since fleeing Creepy Hollow twelve years ago.

The monstrous Mutanto and his werewolf henchman, Howler, emerged from the Gate. With them was a pack of Wolfmen, snarling and growling and baring their fangs. They stood there in silence for a moment, staring at the house.

"I know you're watching! Come out!" Mutanto shouted in his deep, gravelly voice.

Howler narrowed his eyes and licked his sharp fangs.

Leandra emerged from the house holding the sapphire pendant in her hand. Unafraid, she walked down the back-porch stairs and into the yard to confront Mutanto and his Wolfmen.

"How dare you trespass on my property?" she said. "What do you want here?"

"You know what we want," said Mutanto, "and we are taking her with us."

"Be gone!" shouted Leandra, "or you shall face my wrath!"

Mutanto laughed. "You have no power over us, old woman. Take her, boys," he said.

While Mutanto and Howler stood back, close to the Gate, the pack of Wolfmen started grunting and snorting as they slowly walked towards Leandra. She held out her pendant and whispered a spell. The Key Stone turned into a slim, three-sided Wand made of pure sapphire.

Howling in unison, the Wolfmen attacked.

"I want them taken alive!" shouted Mutanto.

Leandra flicked her Wand and a shaft of silver light shot out of it, striking the first Wolfman and turning the creature into smoke. Another blast of silvery light from Leandra's Wand turned a second Wolfman into a pile of smoldering ashes. When a third Wolfman drew close enough, she made him explode into a cloud of dust. But then the other six were upon her, grabbing her and trying to knock the Wand out of her hand.

Nikki and Jack watched in horror from the small attic window. "Jack, we have to help grandma!" Nikki cried out.

"But she said—oh, never mind about that now. Let's hurry!" Jack replied, feeling scared but determined.

Leandra fought bravely, but one of the Wolfmen managed to grab the Wand. It burned his paw and he stumbled backward, yowling in pain. Another werewolf clawed her shoulder, causing her to fall upon the lawn.

The back door flew open as Nikki and Jack raced out of the house.

"Grandma!" they cried out at the same time.

"Take them all!" Mutanto ordered his gang.

Suddenly, a second Ectomagic Gate appeared in the back yard. This one churned and blazed with turquoise light. Wishbone Jones and his wife Ghoulina raced from the Gate, ready to do battle.

The Wolfmen all froze and spun around, unsure of what to do next.

Nikki and Jack kneeled beside their grandmother.

"Use your healing magic, Nikki!" cried Jack, his voice filled with fear and panic.

"What else do you think I'm trying to do?" Nikki answered him, placing her hands-on Leandra's shoulder. Her hands began to grow warm and started to glow with golden light.

Jack stood up and grabbed a shovel that was lying near the porch, ready to defend Nikki and their wounded grandmother.

"Kill these two!" Mutanto told his Wolfmen, pointing at Wishbone and Ghoulina.

With a chorus of howls, the werewolves charged forward.

Ghoulina raised her hands, pointed her tightly-closed fists at the oncoming Wolfmen, and chanted:

There was a brilliant flash of turquoise light, and all at once the Wolfmen ready to pounce on Wishbone and Ghoulina were transformed back into men—pale and naked men who suddenly lost their werewolfish courage. They whined and wailed in fear, turned and raced back towards their Gate, where they leaped through it like a pack of cowardly rats.

Wishbone and Ghoulina turned to face Mutanto and Howler.

"You ain't seen the last of us!" Mutanto shouted.

Howler whimpered like a frightened puppy as he and Mutanto escaped through their Ectomagic Gate. The portal winked shut a second later.

With Jack's and Nikki's help, Leandra stood up, her wound completely healed.

"Are you okay, Grandma?" asked Nikki.

"Thanks to you, I am," Grandma Leandra replied. "Luckily I was only clawed. Had I been bitten, you couldn't have healed me. There is no cure for a werewolf bite."

Jack's heart stopped pounding when Wishbone and Ghoulina joined them.

"Your Majesty," said Wishbone as he and Ghoulina bowed to Queen Leandra.

Nikki watched her beloved grandmother smiling warmly at their rescuers. "My grandmother is a queen. She's a *queen* and she's called *Your Majesty*. Wow!" she whispered to Jack.

"I know, right?" Jack replied with a dreamy expression on his face.

They looked at each other for a moment, but then, knowing that the danger was over, they ran to greet their old friends.

Leandra cleared her throat to get their attention, and when everyone looked at her she said, "I'm grateful for both of your help."

"I'm glad we arrived in time, Your Majesty," Ghoulina replied.

"How did you know we were under attack?" Leandra asked her.

"Just as Nikki's use of her powers alerted Evila to the presence of a witch living here, it also alerted the Wishmothers," Ghoulina explained. "But unlike Evila, the Wishmothers recognized Nikki's magic for what it is: the magic of Willow Haven's Royal Family."

"If Evila could sense Nikki's growing but still weak power, then she must have grown even more powerful over the years," said Grandma.

"Indeed she has," Wishbone told her.

Nikki and Jack looked at each other. This was all so incredible.

"Where's Catman?" asked Jack.

"He stayed in Creepy Hollow to keep watch on our foes," Ghoulina answered. Her silver eyes studied Jack from his head to his boots, admiring his all-black outfit. "I like your new clothes, Jack. They fit you well."

Jack blushed. "Thank you," he said.

Ghoulina smiled at Nikki, and then bowed her head. "I see that you have the healing magic," she said.

Nikki nodded. "Looks like I do," she said. "It started on my thirteenth birthday."

"Let's go inside and talk," Leandra told everyone.

They hurried into the house, made sure all the doors and windows were locked, and then Leandra cast a powerful spell of protection over her home. Then she remembered that Jack's parents expected a call from them; she dialed and assured them that everything was alright. Jack said a quick hello to his parents and afterwards, everyone gathered in the kitchen.

Nikki asked Wishbone, "When you were the wind chime Grandma found hanging from the porch roof, did you know she was Queen Leandra?"

"No," answered the blond-haired, handsome Silver Knight. "I was just a wind chime then, remember? And that's all your grandmother thought I was."

"And we were both your age when Evila destroyed Willow Haven," Ghoulina explained. "Neither of us ever saw your royal grandmother before tonight."

Jack looked at Wishbone. "So you never spoke to Grandma?" he asked.

Wishbone shook his head. "I couldn't talk or even move. I was in a magical trance, a spell cast by Hobgoblin."

"Then how were you able to talk to us last Halloween?" Nikki asked.

"It was all because of you, Nikki," Wishbone explained.

Nikki's eyes went as wide as saucers. "Me?" she said.

Before Wishbone could answer, Jack snapped his fingers again. "I get it!" he said. "Nikki found your Key Stone in the creek. When she touched it, the magical powers she was born with must have triggered something that broke the spell that Hobgoblin cast on you!"

"Brilliant deduction, Jack," Wishbone told him. "Although I didn't know it at the time, that's exactly what happened. Nikki didn't *use* her powers, not like she used them to heal your grandmother's wounds tonight. But it was her magical blood, her Royal Blood that activated my Key Stone." He smiled at Nikki. "I always knew there was something special about you, Nikki—and you, too, Jack."

Nikki and Jack grinned and gave each other a fist bump.

"Evila must have sensed Nikki's powers when she consciously used them to heal a wounded bird the other day," said Leandra. "So the Grim Witch sent Mutanto and his thugs here, to capture her for whatever evil purpose she has in mind."

"That's only part of it, and part of the reason we came here," said Wishbone. "We need your help, Your Majesty."

"Of course, I will do whatever is in my power," said Queen Leandra. "Tell us what's going on."

Wishbone and Ghoulina then told Leandra and the kids about their baby daughter, Ava, and how she had been kidnapped by Evila and her minions.

"You have a baby—and that evil queen took her from you?" Nikki said, starting to cry.

Jack clenched his fists in outrage. But he put one arm around Nikki and hugged her. "Let's go rescue Ava and make that Evila pay!" he said with angry determination.

"And so we shall," Wishbone told him.

"I am so sorry," Leandra told Wishbone and Ghoulina. "I know how frightened and worried you both are."

Wishbone nodded, and Ghoulina said, "Thank you. We know of your own pain and the grief you have suffered and endured over the years."

The Queen gave Ghoulina a long thoughtful look. She sensed there was more Ghoulina and Wishbone had to say.

"Catman was at our house the night Ava was kidnapped," Ghoulina explained. "Afterwards, he went out and started searching, looking for answers to who might have done such a thing. My husband and I went to stay in Wormbelow, with the Wishmothers. Catman has friends he enlisted as spies and secret agents, and they found out that Evila had stolen our baby, for what reason, we do not yet know. But we do know that she is planning to wage war again."

"Then what are we standing around here for?" asked Jack. "Let's go!"

"Yes," said Leandra, and after a thoughtful pause she continued. "Ghoulina, both you and Nikki have Key Stones, and I have mine."

"What do you propose, Your Majesty?" Ghoulina asked, clutching her turquoise Key Stone in one hand.

"We open three Ectomagic Gates, each to a different destination, but we go through mine to reach Celestria and the Trinity of Wishmothers," said Leandra. "The lingering, Ectomagic traces of three Gates will confuse our enemies, and mine will be the most difficult for them to use in order to pick up our trail."

"But Grandma, I forgot the magic words I used last year to open a Gate," Nikki said.

"You don't need to use magic words anymore to open a Gate, dear," Grandma Leandra told her. "Now that your magical powers have begun to manifest, all you need to do is think of where you want to go, to *wish* for a Gate to open, and so it will happen."

Wishbone coughed and cleared his throat. "There is one other thing, Your Majesty," he said. He cleared his throat again. "Catman captured three of Evila's Wolfmen, and after a very brief interrogation, found out that your daughter and her husband are still alive."

This news surprised Leandra so much that she sat down in one of the kitchen chairs, heart pounding and hands shaking. "My Angelina! My Opal, still alive after all these years?"

Nikki shouted, "My Mom and Dad are *alive!*"

"Yes, they are," Ghoulina told them. "They've been prisoners of Evila for the past twelve years. We don't know why. Those Wolfmen didn't know why, either."

Nikki and her grandmother started crying, and they hugged each other. Leandra then realized that, for some urgent reason, her daughter must have used powerful magic the night she and her husband Mike were driving along the coastal highway. That magic had alerted Evila to her presence.

Jack held back his tears and clenched his fists. "Evila is going to pay for this!" he said.

Chapter 7

The Grim Witch was in a terrible mood, furious and frustrated, but not defeated. In her anger, Evila threw books across her chamber, smashed a mirror hanging on a wall, and kicked chairs and rugs out of her way.

Standing off to one side were the twelve wicked witches of the Bleakvale Coven, known as the Silent Sisters. Each one was small and shrouded in gray, with hoods and veils to hide their faces. They never spoke, never even moved a step unless Evila told them to do so. They were allowed to use their magical powers only when she needed them. Long ago Evila had drained their energy, which helped her to stay young. She took their Wands and merged them with her own gnarled and twisted, moss-covered Wand. The Sisters stood there like mindless zombies, totally enslaved to the Queen of Bleakvale and her dark magic.

"What do you mean—you *failed* in your mission?" Evila asked the giant Mutanto, after he reported back to her.

"Just that, my Queen," Mutanto replied. "We went to Earth to kidnap the witch, just as you ordered us to do. But we found two witches, not just the one we were sent to bring back here."

Evila raised her left eyebrow. "*Two* witches?" she said.

"Yes, Your Majesty," answered the black-furred werewolf named Howler. "One was a little girl and the other an elderly woman. The child's grandmother, I think she was."

"There was a little boy with them, too," said Mutanto. "But he didn't use any magic against us. I think he's just an ordinary human."

"Interesting," said Evila. Thoughts and ideas rolled around inside her head like marbles in a bucket. "Did you recognize this woman?"

Mutanto shook his head. "No," he said. "Howler and I were standing too far away to see clearly."

"But Howler, you have the sharp eyes of a wolf," Evila told the Wolfman.

"I'm sorry, my Queen, but it was kind of dark outside, too," he said.

The Grim Witch clenched her fists and almost screamed with frustration. "You're lucky I have such a good nature and don't turn you both into dust," she said, glaring at Mutanto and Howler. "Is there anything else you observed? Anything more you can tell me?"

"The old witch had some kind of Wand, and she used it to destroy three strong werewolves," Mutanto said.

"What kind of Wand?" Evila wanted to know.

Howler growled softly, angry with himself for having failed. "We didn't see that, either," he said. "As we said, it was dark, and things were happening too fast."

This time, Evila *did* scream with frustration. "Excuses! Always excuses!" she shouted. "Why am I cursed to deal with such morons?"

Mutanto hung his big, monstrous head in shame. "But the old lady *was* clawed by one of our Wolfmen before they were rescued by that Wishbone Jones and his wife Ghoulina."

"What?" Evila said with surprise. "They know about those two witches?"

"Most certainly, Your Majesty," Howler told her. "I don't know how *much* they know about them, or if they have guessed your plans and went seeking aid to help rescue their baby. But Ghoulina cast a spell that turned the rest of my Wolfpack back into men."

"And with the Silver Knight present, plus those three witches, we chose to leave and come back here to tell you," said Mutanto. "Ghoulina is quite powerful, even without a Wand."

"There is one other thing you may find interesting," Howler said to Evila. "The young witch has the gift of healing. Before we returned here she healed the old woman."

Now that *is most interesting,* Evila thought, her fingers stroking the petals of a black rose set in a glass vase on the table next to her. "We cannot delay, not after this. No doubt the witches returned to Creepy Hollow with Wishbone and Ghoulina. We have to act, and soon!"

The two doors leading to her chamber swung open at that moment as a pair of Goblin guards ushered in Slither, the shape-changing serpent, as well as the three Wolfmen dressed in ragged old blue jeans: Boo, Goo, and Poo. Slither transformed himself with a swirl of motion and once again became Tattler, the gossip of Springdale. He and the three werewolves bowed to Evila.

"Where did you find these three junkyard dogs?" she asked Tattler.

"They were wandering around in the forest near Celestria," Tattler replied. "They got lost on their way back here."

"We went to spy on Willow Haven, as you commanded us to do, Your Majesty," explained Boo, the red-furred Wolfman. "But nothing is going on there, besides a handful of wretched and starving people living among the ruins."

"Then we went to Celestria, as you told us to do, Your Majesty," said Goo, the Wolfman with gray, matted fur. "But we couldn't get into the great cemetery because a powerful spell guards it against unwanted visitors."

"Spell?" giggled Poo, the foul-smelling Wolfman with filthy, mangy brown fur. "So help me, I can't even spell 'cemetery!'"

Howler slapped Poo on the back of his wolf head. "Shut up, you lunk-head!"

"I'm no lunk-head and you're a control freak!" Poo murmured under his breath.

"What are you mumbling about?" Howler growled, raising his paw to slap Poo again.

"*All* of you shut up!" Evila yelled, which made everyone freeze. She grabbed the glass vase and threw it on the stone floor, where it shattered into a hundred pieces.

Boo, Goo, and Poo hung their heads and shrunk back in fear.

Evila groaned with frustration. "Tattler, Mutanto, Howler: prepare our forces for war." She glared at the other three Wolfmen. "I don't know why I put up with you morons. Boo and Goo, get back in the basement where you belong and keep an eye on our prisoners. As for you, Poo...go take a bath. I do *not* want you stinking up my chamber ever again!"

———⸺⸰⸰⸰⸰⸰

Down in the dark, dank basement of Dreadful Hall, in a small chamber where Boo, Goo, and Poo slept when they weren't on guard duty or off running errands for Evila, they talked quietly and privately amongst themselves. Boo lay sprawled on a hair-covered black couch, Goo paced the floor like a caged animal, and Poo sat in a large bathtub, doing the best he could do to wash the stink and dirt from his brown fur.

Boo lit a scented candle to mask Poo's stench. "I don't know about you guys, but I've felt weird ever since we returned from trying to spy on Celestria. It's like my brain was tampered with by some kind of magic."

"Me, too," said Goo, trying to comb his matted gray fur. "It's a good thing that crazy Tattler or Slither, or whatever he calls himself, found us when he did, otherwise we'd probably still be out there, lost in the woods."

"I'm not so sure we were lost," said Boo.

"What do you mean?" asked Goo.

Flicking a piece of white lint from his red fur, Boo replied, "We had no trouble getting to Willow Haven and then finding our way to Celestria, so I don't understand how we could have gotten lost on the way back."

"Guess we took a wrong turn somewhere," said Poo, lathering his stinky, mangy fur with lavender soap.

"That's just it," Boo told him. "It's a direct route from Bleakvale to Willow Haven, a direct route from there to Celestria, and a straight shot from there to back here again. There are no twists and turns in the road."

"I guess so," said Poo.

"You know what I think? You want me to tell you what I think? Well here's what I think," said Goo, not bothering to wait for the others to answer his questions. "I think something happened to us when we reached Celestria, something we can't remember. What that is, I don't know. But that's what I think."

"That's some good thinking, Goo," said Poo, scrubbing his arm pits.

"That's *exactly* how I feel," said Boo. "You wanna know something?"

Goo nodded his shaggy head. "What's that?" he asked.

"I don't think I wanna be a werewolf anymore," said Boo.

"I *never* wanted to be werewolf," said Goo. "But what can we do? Evila turned us into werewolves and only turns us back into men when it suits her needs. She has power over us."

Poo nodded and scrubbed his wolf's face. "I don't think she likes us, either," he said. "I don't like her. I *never* liked her."

"I'm afraid of her," said Boo. "And I never liked what she's been doing to that young couple locked in that glass cage. Now she's gone and stolen a baby. A baby, for mercy's sake!"

"She's gone too far, that's for sure," said Goo.

"How far is that?" Poo asked, using a long-handled brush to wash his back.

The other Wolfmen ignored him.

Goo started cleaning his claws with a nail file. "Do you think she knows that we're really brothers?" he asked.

"Of course she does, you goofball!" Boo told him. "She knows our True Names, and that's what gives her power over us."

"That makes sense, brother," said Goo. "And it's enough to scare the fur right off my hide. We have to get out of here and away from her before the war starts and it's too late to leave. I don't wanna have anything to do with Evila anymore."

Boo stared at the candle's bright yellow flame for a few minutes. "I thank our lucky stars we never had to kill or hurt anyone," he said.

"You said it, brother," Goo told him. "So what are we gonna do?"

"I have no idea," said Boo. "Let me think."

"Do I still stink?" Poo asked indignantly. "But I'm using scented soap!"

"Wash the soapsuds out of your ears!" Boo growled. "I said *think.*"

"Oh, okay," Poo replied and splashed water in his ears.

Chapter 8

Celestria, the Realm of Spirits, was a vast land that included the graveyard known as Wormbelow. Here the souls of the dead dwelled in peace, sailing back and forth across a night sky painted with dark clouds. Shadows lurked everywhere beneath the light of a full moon barely seen through a veil of a dreary mist. Ghosts that were bluish-gray or silvery-white in color spent their time chilling out by graves and mausoleums or visiting with one another. Spider webs stretched from branch to branch and tree to tree, swaying as if they were dancing to the music of a gentle breeze. Bright Jack O'Lanterns hung from the trees, where strings of glowing, orange and purple lights twinkled in the darkness of night.

Queen Leandra's blue, Ectomagic Gate spun open with a whisper of exhaled air. Then she, Nikki, Jack, Wishbone, and Ghoulina arrived a second later in the beautiful cemetery of Wormbelow. Another second later, the Gate whirled shut.

"We must now close the Gates we opened, Nikki," said Ghoulina. "Hold the Key Stone in your hand, close your eyes, think hard on what you want, and then wish for it. Ready?"

Nikki nodded and did as she was instructed. "Steady."

Ghoulina shut her eyes and said, "Go!"

A moment later, they opened their eyes again.

"Done!" Nikki announced.

"*Well* done, I must say," said Leandra, smiling at Nikki.

Nikki beamed with excitement and happiness. "Look!" she said, pointing.

"It's Catman and the Wishmothers!" cried Jack.

Still barefooted and in their pajamas, the two cousins ran towards their friends.

Catman rose from where he was sitting on the steps of the great, house-like mausoleum where the bodies of the three Wishmothers had been laid to rest. He purred softly as he embraced Nikki and Jack, not bothering to wipe away the tears of joy from his eyes. Then he turned to Leandra and knelt on one knee.

"It's a great honor to meet you at last, Your Majesty," he said. "I'm known as Catman and I'm here to serve you, if you'll have me."

"Gladly and with gratitude," Leandra told him.

The Trinity of Wishmothers stood on the landing, in front of the doors to their mausoleum. Their silver eyes, like Ghoulina's, sparkled in the moonlight. The ghosts each wore an elegant gown, flowing cape, and a weird-looking hat, each one a different color. No longer chained to the black pumpkin in which the wicked Hobgoblin had imprisoned them after his henchman, the Tasmanian Devil named Ebenezer Rex, murdered them the previous year, the Wishmothers were once again free to move around. But they could never leave Celestria, the Realm of Spirits.

"Welcome back, children!" said tall and willowy Prunella Pickles.

Gladiola Scales curtsied and said in her Southern accent, "Well, I do declare! It's *so* wonderful to see the two of you again."

"Although I wish we had met again under better circumstances," said Minerva Terrapin, whose chubby figure and warm smile reminded Jack of a kindly aunt.

When Wishbone, Ghoulina, and Grandma reached the mausoleum, the three Wishmothers bowed their heads, genuflected, and said in unison:

"Welcome back to Celestria, Queen Leandra!"

"Oh, my dear old friends, it is so good to see you, and I am so sorry for what that Hobgoblin and his henchman did to you," Leandra said with a sad smile.

"I thank the suns and stars of Creepy Hollow for your safe return, my Queen," said Prunella.

Gladiola curtsied again and said, "I am *so* delighted to see you again, Your Majesty."

"And we are here to serve you, Queen Leandra," said Minerva.

"It's good to be home and with old friends again," said the Queen.

"How much do you know, Your Majesty?" Catman asked, feeling as if he'd known her all his life, having heard so much about her from Jack and Nikki.

"I know that Evila and the Silent Sisters of Bleakvale Coven are plotting war against all the realms of Creepy Hollow," she said. "I know that my daughter and her husband are alive and have been Evila's prisoners for the past twelve years, and I know that she has kidnapped Wishbone's and Ghoulina's baby daughter. And I also know that we *will* rescue them all, and then Evila will finally pay for all her crimes!"

Nikki and Jack looked at each other, their eyes wide with amazement. They had never seen their grandmother like this, so regal, so commanding, and so powerfully determined.

Wishbone turned to Catman. "What more have you found out?" he asked.

"What I have to tell you is going to upset you all, but first, let me explain how we found out what we now know," Catman replied.

Stroking his long whiskers, Catman told them how his agents had captured the three Wolfmen lurking around the borders of Celestria. The werewolves were brought to the Wishmothers, who questioned them at great length. When they were finished, the Wishmothers wiped away the memory of the interrogation from the minds of their prisoners, and released them into the custody of Catman and his agents. The Wolfmen were then escorted to the borders of Celestria and allowed to return to Dreadful Hall, and to their mistress, Evila.

"The Wolfmen are an odd trio, not very smart, and I sensed that deep inside them they have good hearts. But they're weak and were easily deceived and enslaved by Evila," Catman explained. "They are a ragged and mangy trio, and one of them smells like a sewer. I got the feeling that they fear and don't like Evila, and don't want to be werewolves anymore. They're called Boo, Goo, and Poo, although those are not their True Names."

Nikki giggled at the sound of those names. "What *are* their real names?" she asked.

"Brian, George, and Peter," Catman replied. "That's how Evila enslaved them, by using the power of their True Names against them."

"What about Nikki's parents? What about Wishbone's and Ghoulina's baby?" Jack wanted to know. "Why did Evila kidnap them? What's she doing to them?"

Catman hesitated for a few moments, thinking of how to answer Jack. Finally, he said, "There's no easy way to say this. So here goes. For the past twelve years Evila has been feeding off of Angelina and Mike, stealing her magic and his human strength, and they are almost spent. But now she has found a new source of power to drain—little Ava. The power of her magical gift, her *Vocalocity*, will keep Evila young and beautiful for another fifty years, at least."

"Oh, those poor children," said Queen Leandra, holding back her tears.

Nikki and Jack said nothing, just broke down, cried, and hugged their grandmother.

"Curse her!" shouted Ghoulina. "I will destroy her and her power once and for all!" Then she started weeping, and Wishbone wrapped his arms around her.

In a voice cracking with anger and worry, Wishbone asked of the Wishmothers, "Do you have a plan? Tell us what to do."

"War is inevitable," said Prunella.

"But we do have a plan," said Gladiola.

Minerva nodded and turned to Queen Leandra. "The Seer Witch foretold of your return, Your Majesty, and she sent out the call to the nine remaining members of Weeping Willow Coven. They will meet you in Starvale and help you heal the destroyed realm of Willow Haven. Then the great bell shall be rung to call back all those who fled in fear of Evila."

Leandra nodded. "This I can and shall do," she said. "I fear I may be too old to do battle, but I swear I will fight with all the powers I have."

"What about us?" Wishbone asked.

"You have two tasks to perform before you confront Evila and her minions," Gladiola said to the Silver Knight.

"First, you must travel to the Lair of Moriah to retrieve the sword she used in battle, before evil corrupted her heart and body," Prunella explained. "Then you must venture into the Valley of Lost Souls to find the Crystal Heart. With this in your possession, Ghoulina, your healing powers will increase ten-fold. You must use it to help Queen Leandra cleanse the barren lands of Bleakvale and make it as beautiful and healthy as it once was."

"Word has been sent to the last of your Order of Silver Knights," Minerva told Wishbone. "They will join you on the hilltop overlooking the barren plain of Bleakvale."

"What about our baby and Nikki's parents?" asked Ghoulina.

"Yes," said Wishbone. "How do we rescue them? How do we save them?"

"Leave that to us," Gladiola told him.

"Even though we cannot leave Celestria, there is still much we can do," Prunella said with a sly wink.

"Messenger birds have been sent out, and you will find certain allies along the way who will know what to do and how to save your daughter, and Nikki's parents," said Minerva.

"What about us?" Nikki asked.

"Yeah," said Jack. "What do we do?"

Minerva said, "Nikki, you are of Royal Blood and now that you are coming into your magic, you shall assist Ghoulina along the way. But Jack, this is a dangerous quest, and because you have no magical talents you must remain behind, here with us."

Jack was furious. "No offense, but I will *not* stay behind with you and leave my friends to go off without me!" he shouted. "They need me, and after everything that happened to us fighting Hobgoblin last year, you know I can fight. You have no right to keep me here!"

"Jack, please, listen to me," Leandra told him. "We each have a job to do, and your job is to remain here and help the Wishmothers."

"No, Grandma," Jack told her. "I'm sorry to disobey you but this time I have to. I deserve the right to go. I *earned* that right!"

"Everything your teachers tell you goes in one ear and out the other," Nikki told Jack. "But now you *must* listen to Grandma!"

"No, Nikki!" he argued. "I have to go and protect you."

Wishbone then said, "I will protect Ghoulina."

"And I will protect them all!" Catman said.

Queen Leandra cast a hopeless glance at the Wishmothers, sighed, and then nodded slowly. Although she could have exercised her royal power and ordered Jack to stay behind, she just didn't have the heart to do it.

"This goes against my better judgment, Jack," she said, "but I trust in the power of the Wishmothers and now seek their counsel. Whatever they decide, I will agree to—but just this once. Understand?"

"Yes, Grandma, I do," said Jack, hoping the Wishmothers would decide he should go along with Nikki and their friends.

The Trinity then turned to each other and bowed their heads until their foreheads touched. They conferred in silence, telepathically. When at last they were done, they turned to Jack.

"You are correct, Jack," Prunella said, once she and the other Wishmothers had finished. "We have no right to keep you here and we have no power to do so."

"Therefore," said Gladiola, "we will once again grant you three wishes, to help you during the journey. But you must use all three wishes wisely this time. Do you understand?"

Jack nodded solemnly, but could not hide the smile on his face. "Yes, I do."

"Very well," said Minerva. "You may go, Jack. But you and Nikki cannot go while still wearing your pajamas." From inside her cape she produced her black onyx Wand and waved it over the heads of Nikki and Jack.

As if by magic, which naturally it was, Nikki and Jack found themselves in the warrior outfits they wore for a short time on their last visit. Nikki smoothed her tunic, tied her hair in a headband, and adjusted the blue Key Stone hanging by a chain around her neck. Jack was very pleased as well. They both looked different from their normal selves and felt stronger and more confident.

I'm Zinja, the Warrior Girl again! Nikki thought. "Wow, this is awesome! Thank you, Wishmothers!"

"Totally!" Jack agreed, dressed in the same warrior clothes he wore when he and Nikki fought Hobgoblin and the Tasmanian Devil.

"I like the color," Catman remarked, brushing lint from his favorite vest.

Prunella said to Jack and Nikki, "Now, I think you must each have a weapon, but *not* swords or knives. What would you like?"

Nikki didn't have to think twice. She was, after all, taking karate classes. "Nunchucks!" she said. "Can I have the nunchucks again?"

"Certainly," Prunella said. She pulled her jade Wand from inside her robe, waved it over Nikki's head, and the nunchucks magically appeared in Nikki's hand.

Jack frowned thoughtfully. "Where's my slingshot? Last time I was here I had a slingshot, which I never got to use!"

"You know your mom and dad don't want you playing with a slingshot anymore, not after you broke their front window last summer," Nikki told him.

"*That* was a one-time accident!" Jack persisted. "You know I can hit anything I aim at."

Queen Leandra said, "Under the circumstances, and the fact that we are in Creepy Hollow and we're far away from home, I say...let Jack have his slingshot."

"Very well, then," said Prunella. Waving her Wand over Jack's head, a slingshot appeared, tucked inside his leather belt.

"I think Jack needs his shield, too," Catman told the Wishmothers.

"Right you are!" Minerva told him.

With a wave of her Wand, a large round and pointy shield suddenly appeared, strapped to Jack's right arm.

"But I don't want a shield this time!" Jack whined. "How am I going to use my slingshot? I need my arms and hands free. Besides, this shield is *heavy.*"

"Stop complaining, Jack!" said Nikki.

Catman picked up a rock and threw it at Jack, who raised the shield to protect himself by instinct. The rock hit the shield and bounced away.

"What did you do that for?" Jack complained.

"To show you why you need the shield," Catman told him. "You can carry it on your back, the way many warriors in olden times used to do."

Jack looked at the shield and thought about what Catman had told him. "Ha! I guess we can use it as an umbrella or a picnic table," he said.

"Yup, a good shield has many uses," Catman said with a laugh. He helped Jack strap the shield to his back.

"There are two last things we can do," said Gladiola. "First, I can cast a Warding Spell to protect Jack and Nikki from any bad magic. But there will still be physical dangers along the way and you must be always on your guard. I can also cast a Cloaking Spell that will conceal you from Evila and her minions. But keep in mind, my friends...once you reach the Realm of the Grim Witch, those spells will vanish."

Everyone understood and everyone was ready to leave. Then Jack thought about what he could use one of the wishes for and snapped his fingers.

"I wish that baby Ava, Aunt Angelina, and Uncle Mike were free!" he said.

He waited, but there was no sound of the bell-like *Ding* that had announced the granting of his wish, as he had heard last year.

"What happened?" asked Jack. "How come my wish didn't come true?"

Minerva smiled kindly upon him. "I'm sorry, Jack," she said. "But Evila's magic is too strong and we have no power to grant wishes where her realm is concerned. If it were that easy, baby Ava and Nikki's parents would have been set free the moment we learned they were Evila's prisoners."

Jack shook his head and thought: *Why can't anything ever be easy for once?*

"You children will be okay," Grandma Leandra told Nikki and Jack. "You're under the protection of the Wishmothers and in a grand company of companions. I know this is dangerous and scary, and we're all taking chances, but just do your jobs, listen to Catman, Wishbone, and Ghoulina, and you'll be fine. You'll make me proud— not that I am not already proud of you two."

"Are you leaving now, Grandma?" Nikki asked. "I wish you were coming with us."

"I do, too," said Leandra. "But I have a very important job to do. I must go meet with my sisters of the Weeping Willow Coven and use our power to heal and rebuild Willow Haven. I *will* join up with you as soon as I can."

"Promise?" asked Jack.

"Cross my heart," his grandmother told him. "I trust in the Great Power of this Universe, which is the Power of Good, and everything's going to turn out fine."

"I believe you, Grandma!" said Nikki.

Leandra then kneeled in front of Nikki and took hold of her hands. "You are of Royal Blood," she told her. "You are the granddaughter of a king and queen, and the daughter of a princess. Always remember that. And now you must prove yourself. You were born to do what now you must do—save Creepy Hollow from the forces of evil."

"Oh, Grandma!" Nikki said. She broke down in tears and hugged her grandmother.

Jack tugged on Grandma Leandra's sleeve. "What about me?" he asked.

While the Queen kept one arm wrapped around Nikki, she turned to Jack. "Dearest Jack, my darling boy," she said. "You may not be of Royal Blood, and you may not be of *my* blood, but you are of my heart and I love you as if you my very own grandson. You, too, are important and have a job to do. I see that now. You were born for this, as well. Fate has chosen you to be a guardian and a warrior, and from this day on, by the power vested in me as Queen of Willow Haven, I declare that you and your parents *are* of Royal Blood."

"I love you, Grandma!" Jack said, embracing her as he started to cry.

Catman purred with joy, his eyes filling with tears. Wishbone and Ghoulina also had tears in their eyes when they said farewell to Queen Leandra and wished her good luck. Even the ghostly Wishmothers had ghostly tear drops in their eyes.

"Now, before I leave I must choose more suitable clothes for my journey than this old dress and sweater," said Leandra. With a wave of her pendant it turned into her Sapphire Wand, and with a flick of the wrist her clothes changed.

"Wow! You look beautiful, Grandma!" said Nikki.

"A royal lady in royal blue with a jeweled crown," Ghoulina said to Wishbone. "We have a Queen again!"

"Grandma is a queen! Can you believe it?" Jack whispered to Nikki.

"It's like a dream," Nikki said. "But it's not a dream. We're in Celestria, my grandmother is a queen and we're warriors."

"Don't forget that you're a princess," said Jack with a wink.

Leandra looked at Nikki and Jack and said, "I'll see you all real soon!" She closed her eyes and a split-second later, she vanished.

"Teleportation!" Nikki realized.

"A rare gift," said Prunella.

Gladiola nodded. "A very special talent, indeed," she said.

"Not even the Grim Witch has such a gift," said Minerva.

Catman, Wishbone, and Ghoulina gathered around Nikki and Jack, and they received the blessing of the Wishmothers.

"Well now," said Jack. "When do we eat? When do we leave? And where do we go first?"

Chapter 9

Early the next morning, Nikki, Jack, Ghoulina, and Wishbone set out from Celestria, heading east towards the Borgo Bridge spanning Darkwater River. Catman and Wishbone led the way, with Nikki behind them, and Ghoulina and Jack brought up the rear. It was a warm and pleasant morning, but gray clouds covered the sky as far as the eye could see. A strange and eerie, dark amber light had spread for miles and miles in all directions. The light was unlike any light Nikki and Jack had ever seen.

They had to skirt around the edges of Mungo Swamp, a large bayou of dark, yucky, filthy, and foul-smelling water. Dead trees lined the banks on the far side of the marsh, where weeds and brown grass stretched for miles to the north. There were no signs of birds, ducks, frogs, or any other living thing. The entire area was silent and deserted, and the dirty swamp water as still as if it were frozen over in winter.

"This place stinks!" said Nikki, holding her nose.

"It used to be a beautiful meadow with a crystal-clear lake in the middle, when the good witches were in power. Evila's dark magic turned it into this foul-smelling swamp," Wishbone told her. "Thankfully, we can't smell it in Celestria or Springdale."

"Thank the stars for that!" said Catman.

Jack and Ghoulina chatted as they walked along together, talking about her marriage to Wishbone, the birth of their daughter Ava, and the fear and worry she had for her baby. But he could see that discussing Ava was making Ghoulina sad.

To help take her mind off her worry and all kinds of gloomy thoughts, Jack changed the subject and asked, "Where did you grow up, Ghoulina."

Ghoulina's silver eyes studied the sky, as if watching for some sign of good or bad tidings. "In Ghoul Stone," she replied.

"You mean *Gall* Stone, don't you?" he asked.

"Goodness no, Jack!" she replied. "Ghoul Stone is the name of my village. It lies way behind us, far to the west, beyond Red Crow Forest and Gremlinville."

Jack remembered passing Gremlinville during his and Nikki's adventures in Creepy Hollow last year, and he shuddered at the memory of the scary Red Crow Forest. "Then you left to study to become a Wishmother?" he asked.

"No, first I studied to be a Healing Witch. But enough about me. I'm curious why you started wearing black clothes. Last year you preferred colorful T-shirts, but now even your socks are black. Why the sudden change?" she asked Jack

Jack blushed. "Well, you see, there's this new girl at school—Peggy Ward," he told her. "She dresses like you and is just as pretty as you, too."

In spite of her sadness and the fear for her baby daughter's life, Ghoulina laughed softly. "Why, thank you, Jack!" she said. "That's very sweet of you. Tell me more about Peggy Ward."

"Um, she's real smart and very nice, but she's also shy and quiet," he said. "I made friends with her right away, but she's always being picked on by bullies. They call her 'Plenty Weird,' because of the way she dresses. I stick up for her. I'm not afraid of those creeps."

"Good for you, Jack!" said Ghoulina. She put her arm around him as they continued walking across the bridge. "You like this girl, don't you?"

Jack hesitated a moment. "Well, yeah. Sure. I guess so."

"Does she like you?" Ghoulina asked.

"Sort of...I think," said Jack. "I like hanging with her. Sometimes I'd rather hang out with her than with Nikki."

"Then you must *really* like her," Ghoulina said.

Jack blushed again. "I guess I do."

As they walked along, Nikki turned her head and saw Jack looking for rocks and stones he could use in his slingshot. Searching the ground, he'd picked up a few stones, studying them and weighing them in his hand. Some he tossed aside and others he would place inside the leather pouch hanging from his belt, next to his slingshot.

"Since when did *you* start collecting rocks?" Nikki asked, still holding her nose. "That's *my* hobby, Jack."

Jack tied his pouch shut. "Don't worry. I'm not taking over your hobby. I need stones because I can't put marshmallows in my slingshot," he told her. "This is serious business."

"Oh, yes," Nikki teased. "We're warriors now. You know, I can barely recognize us because even our faces have changed. You're not the chubby kid anymore who whined like a spoiled brat last year when you got tired of walking."

Jack was about to reply with a snarky remark when the filthy and stinky water of the swamp started bubbling and churning and swirling around. Disgusting odors rose into the air with even more disgusting puffs of marsh gas. The friends stopped in their tracks, wondering what was happening.

Trying to breathe through her mouth, Nikki said, "I've never seen anything like this before. Luckily we don't have swamps like this."

"Looks like someone flushed a toilet," said Jack.

"Smells like it, too!" said Catman.

And then, from below the scummy surface of the swamp there rose an ugly and even more putrid-smelling creature—a huge monster with tentacles growing out of its back. It had arms with claws and piercing yellow eyes, but its lower body was hidden in the murky water. Its teeth looked small but sharp in its huge mouth. The creature floated towards the edge of the swamp and bellowed in anger.

"What in the name of the stars?" Wishbone said.

"Everyone, get back!" Ghoulina shouted.

The five companions quickly moved away from the edge of the swamp.

"Who dares to touch my things and steal them from me?" the Thing growled in a voice that sounded like it had a chest cold and was all congested.

"We touched nothing of yours," Wishbone told the swamp creature.

"*Everything* around here belongs to me!" roared the Thing.

Jack stepped forward. "I'm very sorry, Mister," he said. "I didn't know the rocks belonged to you. Here, I'll put them back where I found them."

As Jack reached into his pouch, the Thing shouted, "Sorry? *Sorry?* Well it's too late for that, you little thieving brat!"

"My cousin is *not* a thief!" yelled Nikki.

"Ah, another brat!" the creature said. It belched swamp gas and then bellowed again. "Maybe I'll save you both for appetizers. I am quite hungry."

"You do and I'll give you one mean case of indigestion!" said Jack.

"And I'll make you so sick to your stomach, you'll throw up!" Nikki shouted.

Quick as a sparrow flying from one tree to another, the Thing's sticky tentacle stretched out, grabbed Jack by his belt and lifted him into the air.

"Help!" cried Jack. "I can't get to my slingshot!"

Nikki rushed forward, swinging her nunchucks over her head. "You leave my cousin alone, you smelly old goon!" she said. When she hit the Thing in its belly with her nunchucks, the weapon sprung back as if it hit a rock.

Then the Thing laughed as its other tentacle stretched out, grabbed Nikki, and lifted her into the air, too.

"Help us!" she cried. "This Thing smells so bad, I'm going to pass out or throw up!"

The swamp monster pulled Jack and Nikki close to its mouth and sharp teeth.

"Let them go!" shouted Catman, rushing forward to save the kids.

"Put them down, I order you!" Wishbone roared.

Catman kicked and scratched the Thing with his boots and claws, but its stone-hard hide broke off a few of his nails and he didn't hurt the creature.

Wishbone punched the Thing again and again, but it was like hitting dirty, slippery armor.

The monster just laughed at them. "Nobody is allowed to steal from me!" it bellowed. "And I'll show you what happens to fools who dare to cross my borders!"

"It's no use!" Ghoulina shouted to Wishbone and Catman. "You can't hurt it!"

Still holding Nikki and Jack in its sticky tentacles, the creature knocked Catman aside easily. When Wishbone threw another punch at the Thing, the fiend sent him sprawling, too.

"It's time for dinner!" said the Thing, his huge mouth starting to drool.

The tentacles slithered from the Thing's body like snakes, one wrapping itself around Wishbone and the other around Catman. The swamp fiend picked them up and eyed them hungrily.

Catman scratched and tried to pull the Thing's tentacle that was coiled around his waist, but his efforts proved useless. "Get this cursed thing off me!" he wailed.

"Ghoulina—it's up to you, honey! We can't defeat this thing!" yelled Wishbone, struggling in vain to unwind the tentacle wrapped around him.

"That's enough!" Ghoulina yelled, her silver eyes flashing, red, yellow, and silver again. "You're no creature of Nature—you're a spawn of dark magic and evil!"

Raising her arms into the air, she chanted:

Black and purple sparks exploded from Ghoulina's fingertips and flew straight at the creature, hitting it right between its yellow eyes. The monster wailed in pain and dropped Jack, Nikki, Wishbone and Catman to the ground, where they almost tumbled into the swamp.

The creature shrieked as its body started to dry up, crumble, and fall apart like a sand castle. With a final cry, its body broke apart into a thousand pieces and fell back into the swamp. The area surrounding Mungo Swamp grew silent again, and its filthy, bubbling, and bad-smelling water became as still as the surface of a dirty mirror.

"Is everyone all right?" asked Ghoulina, rushing over to Wishbone and their friends.

"I'm okay," Nikki told her, brushing dirt and leaves from her clothes.

Jack flicked moss from his sleeve. "Me, too," he said.

"I'm fine, my nails will grow back in a few days," said Catman, picking leaves off his clothes. "Thanks, Ghoulina."

Wishbone nodded and wiped mud from his arm. "What *was* that Thing?" he asked.

Ghoulina shook her head. "I've never seen anything like it before," she said. "But I bet it was something created from the spillage or fallout of Evila's poisonous magic."

"Evila has a lot to answer for—spoiling and corrupting Nature like that," said Wishbone.

"And that's just a sample of what her bad magic has done to this part of Creepy Hollow," said Ghoulina.

"We'll get even with her!" Jack said fiercely.

"Well, let's get out of here, first," said Catman, his nose twitching at the nasty stench of the swamp. "This smell makes me nauseous."

"I agree," said Wishbone. "We're not very far from the Borgo Bridge. We can be there and across Darkwater River probably within an hour."

Chapter 10

About an hour later the five friends reached the Borgo Bridge, which would take them to the opposite bank of Darkwater River. Catman and Wishbone once again led the way, with Nikki, Jack and Ghoulina bringing up the rear. As they crossed the old bridge, Nikki wondered if her grandmother had a chance to meet the last remaining members of her coven. Even though her grandmother was the mighty Queen Leandra, Nikki worried about her. She knew her as an ordinary, older woman and still couldn't wrap her mind around the fact that her sweet grandmother was a queen and a strong warrior. *She's a powerful witch*, Nikki thought, reassuring herself. *Once she reunites with the Nine Guardians of the Weeping Willow Coven, they will begin to heal and rebuild the Realm of Willow Haven. I must keep faith and hope that Grandma will be okay.* Nikki had no thoughts for her own safety; her main concern was for her grandmother.

When they had finally crossed the Borgo Bridge and reached the other side of Darkwater River, Catman called a halt.

"We'll rest here a few minutes," he said.

Nikki remembered that last year they traveled west from Celestria, and then turned north. This time they were heading east, in the opposite direction; their final destination, Bleakvale, was located to the northeast of Borgo Bridge.

Wishbone said, "All right, now listen up, everyone. We're going to be passing through Gloomy Gulch soon, and there are a couple of things you need to know, first."

"What's a gulch?" asked Jack.

"It's a narrow ravine marking the course of a fast stream," Nikki replied.

"I knew that," said Jack.

"Yeah, right," said Nikki, rolling her eyes.

Jack gave her an angry look but didn't say a word.

Catman smiled under his whiskers. *I love it when the cousins tease each other*, he thought. *Their bickering and teasing always challenges them to come up with great ideas.* He said out loud, "But the stream in Gloomy Gulch is now nothing more than a small creek flowing through the Hills of Glum."

"But we have to watch out for Creeps," said Wishbone.

"Oh, we have plenty of guys like that at school," said Jack. "They're all bullies, and I hate bullies."

"I don't think Wishbone's talking about *those* kinds of creeps, Jack," said Nikki.

"Says who?" said Jack.

Nikki tapped her chest. "Says me!"

"Nikki's right, Jack," Catman told him. "The Creeps here aren't really dangerous and can't hurt you. But they *will* eat your clothes. They're like the moths in your world. They love to eat clothes, especially those made of wool."

Nikki and Jack looked at each other and started laughing.

"Go ahead and laugh. Some of your clothes are made of wool," Wishbone told them. "You won't find it so funny when they eat all your clothes and leave you out here stark naked."

"I guess that *is* kind of creepy," Jack admitted.

"So what do we do to keep them away?" asked Nikki.

"I can cast a Spell if they attack us," said Ghoulina.

"Sorry, honey," said Wishbone. "There is no magic in Creepy Hollow that can affect them. So everyone find a stick or a branch to fight them off with."

"I have my slingshot!" Jack said.

Nikki nodded and said, "And I have my nunchucks!"

Catman purred. "Those'll work," he said. "And I have my paws and some of my sharp nails are still intact."

Wishbone searched and found a branch as big as a baseball bat. Ghoulina picked up a slightly smaller branch from some old oak tree.

Without another word Catman led his four companions into Gloomy Gulch.

On both sides of Gloomy Gulch, the Hills of Glum rose tall and steep, towering a hundred feet high above their heads.

"The Creeps live in those caves in the hills," Catman told them.

The creek itself was so narrow and shallow that it didn't have enough water in it for any fish larger than minnows. But the water was clear and Jack could see the minnows swimming around.

They were almost a quarter of the way through Gloomy Gulch when they heard what sounded like large cats scratching the sides of a living room couch.

"Quiet, now," said Wishbone. He pointed to a gang of strange creatures that came creeping and crawling down out of the caves in the hills.

"Creeps?" Jack asked, noticing that the creatures resembled bright pink salamanders but were as large as a grown pig. They had the heads and faces of men and women, and four small, turtle-like feet. Their two arms were short and muscular, but looked very strong.

"Creeps," said Catman. "I think—" He didn't have a chance to finish his sentence because one Creep jumped on his back, wrapped its arms around him, and took a huge bite from the shoulder of his vest. Then the creature hopped off his shoulder and scrambled back towards the caves. "Curse that filthy little sneak! This is a new vest!"

Another Creep jumped on Nikki, knocked her down and started chewing on one leg of her leather pants. But the leather was tough and the slimy creature started spitting and crawling up her leg.

"You don't like leather, huh? You're going for the wool shirt," Nikki grumbled and tried to kick the Creep off her leg, but its claws held on firmly. "Get this creepy Creep off me!" she shouted.

Jack put a stone inside the pocket of his slingshot, pulled back on it, took aim, and fired. The stone flew fast and struck the Creep on the head. It squealed, let go of Nikki's pant leg, and rolled over, dazed and unable to move. Nikki jumped to her feet and started using her nunchucks, twirling the weapon over her head, around her back, and switching it from hand to hand. She whacked and thwacked the Creeps while Catman punched and kicked nasty creatures left and right, bowling them over or sending them tumbling through the air.

Three pig-sized Creeps suddenly attacked Ghoulina, knocking her to the ground this time, and then started chewing on her black and purple gown.

"I could use a little help here!" she yelled.

Jack raced over to her and kicked one Creep as if it were a soccer ball—kicked it right across the ravine. Then he dropped his slingshot, grabbed the other two by their necks, and bashed their heads together until they went limp. He tossed the Creeps aside and helped Ghoulina to her feet.

"Thanks, Jack," she said.

Picking up his slingshot, Jack bowed to her. "My pleasure, Missus Jones," he said with a grin. When another Creep wriggled towards them, he put a large stone in his slingshot, aimed, and fired, sending the ugly beast off into dreamland with a big bruise on its forehead.

Two Creeps then picked up handfuls of rocks and stones and started throwing them at Jack and Nikki.

"Hey!" Jack shouted. Thinking quickly, he removed the shield from his back and used it to protect Nikki and himself from the rocks. When the two Creeps stopped to pick up more rocks, Jack threw his shield at them as if he was throwing a Frisbee. Through luck, magic, or skill, Jack's shield whacked one of the Creeps on the head, knocking it senseless. The other one ran away to hide.

"Good job, Jack!" Nikki told him.

Jack grinned at her. "Thanks," he said. Then he gathered up more stones and went back to work using his slingshot.

Meanwhile, Wishbone swung his branch like a baseball bat, clubbing Creeps left and right, swatting them aside as if he was at the batting cage, practicing for an upcoming game. But then two rather fat Creeps jumped on his back and knocked him off balance. Wishbone fell flat on his face while the Creeps broke a few of their sharp teeth trying to bite through the shoulders of his silver breastplate. Nikki ran to help

Wishbone, giving the first Creep a hard karate chop to the back of its neck, and it rolled off Wishbone, totally unconscious. When the second Creep turned to her, Nikki swung her nunchucks in the air and conked the foul beasty on the head with her weapon. The Creep hissed and then fainted.

"Thanks, Nikki," said Wishbone. "I'll go help Catman. You go stand with Ghoulina."

"What about Jack?" she asked.

Wishbone smiled. "I think Jack's doing all right by himself. Look!"

Nikki turned and saw Jack shooting stones rapidly from his slingshot, hitting four out of five Creeps every time. Seeing how Wishbone and Catman fought back to back, Nikki rushed over to Ghoulina and they fought back to back, too. Nikki used her nunchucks and karate kicks, and Ghoulina used her oak branch. Together they smashed and bashed every Creep that attacked them and tried to take a bite out of their clothes.

When Jack's pouch was empty he started picking up stones from the creek bed. His slingshot made snapping sounds as rocks and pebbles whizzed through the air, thumping almost every Creep he aimed for. He knocked Creeps down one by one, as if they were targets at a shooting gallery.

Finally, the Creeps had enough and they retreated, slithering back to their caves and carrying their wounded with them, clutched tightly in their jaws.

When it was all over, Wishbone asked, "Is everyone okay?"

"This dress is ruined!" Ghoulina said. "But it's nothing compared to what I'm going to do when I get my hands on Evila! Her dark magic made these creepy crawlers, too."

The five companions stopped to catch their breaths and quench their thirsts from the small canteens of water they each carried.

Jack walked over to where his shield was lying on the ground, picked it up, and slung it across his back. "I guess my shield came in handy, after all," he said.

"Told you so," said Catman, kneeling to sample the water in the creek. "This is safe to drink," he announced, "and it tastes good, too!"

"Great!" Wishbone said. "We can refill our canteens."

At that moment they heard a rumbling sound. The ground trembled and the ravine itself started to shake.

"*Now* what?" Jack wanted to know.

Catman glanced ahead, his keen cat-eyes searching the ravine. "Everyone stay quiet and don't move," he said. "I'll handle this."

Moments later, a small herd of wild horses thundered down the ravine towards the five companions. There was a lovely white mare, three beautiful chestnut-brown mares, and a handsome black stallion with a snow-colored crescent on his forehead.

Trailing behind the horses, stumbling and wobbling on uncertain legs was a cute, cinnamon-colored, male foal.

Nikki and Jack watched Catman bow to the horses as they slowed to a halt. Then Catman and the stallion walked towards each other.

"What's Catman doing?" asked Jack.

"He's going to talk with them," Ghoulina told him.

"*Talk* to them?" Nikki asked with amazement and excitement, and a little disbelief in her voice. "Can the horses talk back?"

"Of course," Wishbone replied. "These are the Wild Horses of Scarlet Canyon. They can only speak with those who have the Gift."

"What sort of gift?" Jack wanted to know.

"The gift of being able to communicate with animals," Ghoulina answered. "It's a very rare talent. Catman is the only one I know who has the Gift."

"These horses have never been broken and don't know the feel of wearing a saddle," Wishbone explained. "They won't tolerate such a thing. They choose who will be honored to sit on their backs." He bowed to the stallion and continued, "Thank you for helping us."

Catman translated what Wishbone said and then translated his reply to Wishbone, "You're welcome. We move faster than you on your two short legs and we can hardly wait to see the evil witch gone. Then my herd could unite again."

Wishbone bowed again and turned to walk back to Ghoulina. Catman and the stallion talked for a short time, nodded to each other, and then Catman turned to his friends. "Jack, come here, please."

Jack glanced at Nikki, at Ghoulina, and at Wishbone. He was a little uncertain, but nevertheless, unafraid. When Nikki and his friends nodded reassuringly, he walked towards Catman.

"Jack, this is Domino," said Catman, introducing him to the stallion. "He wants to know if you have the Gift. He can sense that you do."

"Hello, Jack," said Domino. "Can you understand me?"

Goosebumps crawled all over Jack's body. He almost took a step backwards, but collected himself and remained standing where he was. He couldn't believe that he understood the stallion perfectly. *I have the Gift!* He was proud and honored beyond words.

"Yes, yes, I can understand you, Mister Domino," he said.

"Excellent!" said Domino, neighing with pleasure. "But please, just call me Domino. We're all friends here."

"When Evila destroyed Willow Haven, she tried to enslave the horses of Scarlet Canyon, make them pull wagons and coaches, and carry her warriors into battle," Catman told Jack. "But the horses refused, and then the herds scattered all over Creepy Hollow in order to avoid being turned into Evila's draft animals."

Domino turned his huge head and nodded to one of the mares. "Fiona, come here, please," he said.

The beautiful white mare walked towards Jack and Catman. The little colt nickered softly and followed the mare, his long legs still weak and wobbly. The foal stumbled and almost fell down.

"Hi, Jack," spoke Fiona. "This is my son. He is too young to talk yet, but he will learn. As you can see, he is still a bit uncertain on his legs and lacks the confidence he needs to walk and gallop and trot with the rest of us."

"He was born only a few days ago," said Domino. "We didn't find a good name for him yet. Would you like to give him a name, Jack?"

"Me? Why…why, I'd be honored!" said Jack. He looked at the cinnamon-colored colt and felt sad for the young horse. *Let's see, what would be the perfect name for him? A name to give him the confidence he needs?* Jack thought long and hard, and finally came up with the perfect name. "Champ," he said. "I like that name." He turned to the colt. "Do *you* like it?" he asked.

Champ whinnied with pleasure, stumbled over to Jack and nuzzled his shoulder.

"He likes you," Fiona neighed softly.

Jack stroked Champ's nose and neck. He fell in love with the foal at once. "And I like him, too!" he said.

Catman called the others over to meet the herd. "Domino and his herd know that we serve the Wishmothers and Queen Leandra," he told his companions. "They have agreed to carry us along on our journey."

"That's great! Tell them thank you," said Nikki, knowing she could not speak with the horses the way Catman and Jack could. She envied her cousin, but was also very proud of him. *He has the Gift!* Nikki thought and then said, "Jack, finally you won't be complaining about having to walk everywhere we go."

"Who's complaining?" Jack asked her. "That was *last* year, Nikki. This is *this* year!"

Nikki laughed. "I have never ridden a horse before and I don't think Jack has either, so we don't know what to do," she admitted.

"It's easy," Wishbone told her. "You just mount up on the left and hang on. I'll help you both, if you need it. But with the Wild Horses, you have nothing to worry about."

Jack, Catman, Domino, and Fiona talked amongst themselves for a few minutes. When they were finished, Catman turned to his friends.

"Wishbone, you will ride Domino," he said. "Nikki, you, Ghoulina, and I will ride the three mares."

"What about Fiona and her foal?" Ghoulina asked.

"Champ is too small to ride, as you no doubt can see," Jack said. "And he'll have a hard time keeping up with us. So until he grows more confident and steady on his legs, I'm going to ride Fiona and carry Champ on my lap."

"Sounds good to me!" said Nikki, impressed by how Jack stepped up to take charge.

Jack mounted Fiona, and Wishbone gently gathered Champ in his arms and set him on Jack's lap before he mounted Domino. The colt neighed with pleasure and snuggled up against Jack.

Because of her long gown, Ghoulina had a hard time mounting her horse. "I should have worn different clothes for this outing," she mumbled and with a snap of her fingers, she turned her long dress into loose-fitting trousers. "That's better," she said.

Wishbone glanced at her admiringly. Ghoulina had a thought. She murmured a spell and touched Catman's shoulder, repairing his torn jacket.

Catman smoothed the flawlessly restored jacket and purred, "Thank you, my dear! It was very nice of you."

"You're welcome, "Ghoulina replied, smiling with a twinkle in her eyes. "I can't let a snappy dresser like you wear torn clothes."

Catman purred shyly and said, "We should go. Let's not waste time."

Jack grinned at him. "Let's ride, we're burning daylight!" he said.

"Burning daylight?" Catman asked.

Seeing the puzzled expression on Catman's face, Jack said. "Never mind, it's just an expression for not wasting time."

"Then we're saying the same thing but with different words."

"Right," Jack nodded, feeling a little embarrassed.

Chapter 11

They rode the Wild Horses of Scarlet Canyon for almost an hour before Ghoulina called a halt.

"What's wrong, honey?" Wishbone asked his wife.

"We need to rest a little. I'm not used to riding on horseback and my backside and legs are killing me," Ghoulina told him.

Nikki sighed as she slid off the mare's back. "My thigh muscles are on fire, too," she said.

Wishbone smiled sympathetically. "Yes, it takes a little getting used to. Try to relax and adjust to the rhythm of the horses."

Everyone dismounted, and Wishbone gathered little Champ in his arms and set him down. The cinnamon colt started prancing around on unsteady legs, stumbling only once. Jack knew all Champ needed was a little encouragement.

"Come on, Champ! You can do it!" Jack called out.

The colt neighed happily and wobbled over to Jack, brushing up against him and stomping the ground with one front hoof. Fiona, Champ's mother, trotted over to Jack and nudged him with her nose.

"That's it, Jack," said the white mare. "He'll get the hang of it. Just keep talking to him and he'll soon be talking as much as you do!"

Jack laughed, Champ nibbled on his arm, and he hugged the colt.

Nikki and Ghoulina sat on the soft grass. "Jack certainly loves that little horse," said Nikki. "He's always liked animals, but I've never seen him like this before, and I certainly had no idea he could talk to animals."

"He has a natural way of bonding with animals. His Gift just needed to be triggered," said Ghoulina. "He understands them, feels what they feel, and cares for them. The Gift in him is strong, like the magic in you, Nikki."

"I think he's really going to impress that new girl in school when we get back home," Nikki told her. "She reminds us of you."

"Oh, Peggy Ward," said Ghoulina. "Yes, he told me all about her. He has a big crush on her. I think he's in love."

"Ghoulina, you told us a little about the Seer Witch, the last time we were here," said Nikki. "Grandma told us that she was the only Wishmother, at one time. What happened to her? Who is she? *Where* is she?"

"The Seer Witch is a strange and mysterious spirit, who came here from another world, like you and Jack did," Ghoulina explained. "She's anywhere and everywhere she wants to be."

"You mean she's like a ghost?" Nikki asked.

Ghoulina shook her head. "No, dear, she's something more, and something quite different," she said. "When the good witches you know as the Trinity of Wishmothers went into hiding after Evila destroyed Willow Haven, the Seer Witch gave them the power to grant wishes to all those who are in need and deserve such a gift."

"Will the Seer Witch come here to help us?" Nikki asked.

"Only if she wants to," Ghoulina told her. "As I said, she's strange and mysterious, and I have no idea where she is right now."

"Well, I'd like to meet her one day," said Nikki.

"Perhaps you will," said Ghoulina. "Her name is Julianna."

After a short rest, they mounted the horses and set out again. They rode at a decent pace while Jack kept up a non-stop flow of chatter, telling Champ all sorts of stories and talking about all kinds of things.

They rode north and then east for about another hour, through fields of tall, green grass, passing through lush meadows, and splashing across small creeks.

Finally, they drew to a halt in a vast plain, at the entrance to a great structure built of stone. It looked like an ancient tomb, for it had no windows and only one small entrance.

"Here we are. This is Moriah's place," Wishbone announced. He dismounted, walked over to Jack, and gently slid the young horse from his lap. While the other mares grazed, Fiona happily watched her son prance around, and Domino whickered with pride. He walked over to the five friends.

"The entrance is too small for us," Domino told Catman and Jack. "We shall wait here and graze until you return." Then he turned and joined his small herd.

"So who's this Moriah and what's her story?" asked Jack.

While Catman and Ghoulina made torches by using her and Wishbone's branches and then wrapping one end of each with moss and vines and weeds, Wishbone explained:

"Moriah was one of the two Sapphire Knights, a very special order of warriors created by Queen Leandra to be the Royal Family's personal guard," he said. "But Moriah was swayed by the power of Evila's magic and swore allegiance to her. When Moriah was finally captured by the other Sapphire Knight, Queen Leandra punished her by casting a spell over her and banishing her to this place."

"Moriah can never leave here unless she apologizes for her treachery, and renews her oath of service and loyalty to Queen Leandra," Catman said.

"What about her sword?" Jack asked.

"Moriah's sword wasn't taken from her because she was brought to trial before the great battle," Wishbone replied. "Moriah never fought in that battle and never killed anyone. Thus, Queen Leandra was lenient with her, allowing her to keep her sword, hoping that one day she would ask for forgiveness and redeem herself."

"Is it a magic sword?" Nikki asked.

"In a way it is," said Wishbone. "You see, the swords of the Sapphire Knights were enchanted by Queen Leandra, I guess you could say."

"I get it," said Jack. "But what happened to the other Sapphire Knight?"

"He was slain defending the King, and his sword was destroyed," said Catman.

"Let me understand this," said Nikki. "So, Moriah is the only survivor and there is only one sword left, and because her sword was enchanted by my grandmother when she was queen, we need the sword to defeat Evila and her minions."

"Exactly," said Wishbone. "If Moriah gives us her sword willingly, then that will count as the first step on the road of redemption."

"What if she refuses to give it to us?" asked Ghoulina.

Catman growled as he picked up two rocks and began scraping them against each other. "Then we must take it from her," he said. When the rocks finally caused a spark to flare, he used it to light the torches.

Jack set his hand upon his slingshot. "So what are we waiting for?" he asked.

Leaving the Wild Horses outside, the five companions entered the darkness of the tomb-like building.

The structure did indeed resemble a tomb, being dark, dank, and dusty. It smelled musty, too. Cobwebs graced every nook and cranny, and shadows lurked in every corner. The stone floor was littered with the bones of small animals, and there were slimy spider-like webs still clinging to them.

Nikki guessed the truth about those bones. "If Moriah can't leave here, how does she manage to find things to eat?" she asked.

"The spell that was cast upon her allows her to emit a sweet odor that attracts unsuspecting animals," Wishbone replied.

Jack sniffed the musty air. "I don't smell anything," he said.

"You would if you were a rabbit, a squirrel, or a badger," Catman told him.

"Yuck!" said Ghoulina. "She's definitely *not* a vegetarian!"

"That's quite correct, young lady," a woman's voice echoed from the darkness. "I am anything *but* a vegetarian."

Then, from out of the shadows emerged Moriah.

Nikki and Jack moved back three steps as the cold fingers of fear ran up and down their spines.

"Wow!" Jack managed to say.

Moriah had a beautiful human head with long black hair, piercing eyes, and pale skin. But her body was turned into a red scorpion, her hands into claws and from her lower back protruded a deadly stinger.

"What do you want here?" Moriah demanded, crawling closer to her uninvited guests.

"We came for your sword," Wishbone told her. "It's time to hand it over to those who have need of it and can best use it."

Moriah's laugh was the cackle of an evil witch. "Is that so?" she asked. "Well, none of you shall have it and none of you shall ever leave here!"

Then she spun a thick strand of silken thread from her saliva and threw it at Catman. The sticky rope began wrapping itself around him. Everyone shouted as he was pulled towards Moriah. With the roar of a lion, Catman used his torch to burn the silvery rope and set himself free. But before he could get away Moriah lashed out with her powerful arm and sent him crashing into one of the stone walls. He slid down the wall and plopped down on the floor, dazed and bruised.

"Otto!" Wishbone shouted, using Catman's real name. He balled his fists and ran to help his friend, but Moriah kicked him with another one of her legs, and he flew through the air to land with a thud at the feet of his wife.

"Bob!" Ghoulina yelled, kneeling to check how badly he was hurt.

Slowly the Scorpion Woman advanced closer to her. Her long tail with its sharp stinger lifted and curled in the air.

Jack knew Moriah was about to sting his friends, so he raced towards them and turned his back to the Scorpion Woman, so that when the stinger struck it slammed into his shield.

Moriah screeched with pain and anger, and started to back away.

Jack turned around, grabbed his slingshot, and placed a large stone in its leather pocket. Nikki grabbed her nunchucks with one hand and pulled the Key Stone from her pocket, clutching it tightly in one hand. Somehow, it gave her courage.

When Ghoulina saw that her husband was not badly hurt, she rose to her feet and turned to face Moriah. Her silver eyes flashed red, then yellow, and then silver again. "Enough!" she cried. "Now watch and listen, Nikki," she said.

Raising her hands into the air, she chanted:

Moriah screamed as her own silken webbing wrapped her in a silver cocoon. But she kept moving forwards, hissing and shouting curses.

Jack took aim with his slingshot and let the stone fly. It hit Moriah in the center of her forehead, causing her to lose her balance and fall onto her back. When the Scorpion Woman started to get up, Nikki rushed towards her and whacked her on the head with her nunchucks. Moriah fell back again and this time she did not try to get up.

Nikki kneeled beside her, still clutching her Key Stone. "Now you listen to me, Moriah," she said in a stern and very mature voice. "If you don't give us the sword we'll tie you up like a sack of potatoes and leave, and you'll never get another chance to make up for all the bad things you did!"

"No, please—no!" Moriah begged.

"She's not so tough," said Jack. "She's just a bully."

"Tell me this, Moriah," said Nikki. "If you had the chance to redeem yourself, to beg for forgiveness and say you're sorry for having betrayed Queen Leandra...would you do that?"

"Oh, yes! Yes, I would," said Moriah. "I was wrong and weak, and Evila used her power over me. I made a huge mistake and am so sorry for what I've done. But I am trapped here and must remain a thing of evil forever, because Queen Leandra is long dead. There is no hope for me!"

And then she started to weep.

"There is hope and a chance for you to regain the honor you lost," Nikki told her. "Swear on your name and on your word of honor to become a loyal subject again, because Queen Leandra of Willow Haven has returned!"

"The Queen? *Alive?*" asked the Spider Woman.

Nikki nodded. "Yes! I am her granddaughter, and I promise that if you give us your sword so we may defeat Evila once and for all, I will plead your case and help you all I can."

Moriah raised her head as Catman, Ghoulina, Jack, and Wishbone approached her. She stared at Wishbone. "You are a Knight of the Silver Order," she said. "The Silver Knights, I know, are incapable of telling lies. So, tell me...is this all true?"

Wishbone bowed his head and then looked at Moriah. "It is the truth, Moriah," he said. "Queen Leandra lives, and she has returned to Creepy Hollow. Now your chance has come at last, to reclaim your name and honor and become a Sapphire Knight once more!"

"Long live the Queen!" Moriah shouted in joy, and fresh tears filled her eyes. "Then take the sword—it is yours to use until I have earned the right to use it again in service to Queen Leandra."

From out of the shadows, floating in mid-air, there appeared a great sword sheathed in a dark blue scabbard. Wishbone reached out, took the weapon, and removed it from its sheath. The long sword glowed in the darkness, and it was forged of strong, sapphire-blue steel. Testing its weight and balance by swinging it over his head and waving it from side to side, Wishbone replaced it in its sheath and buckled it to his belt.

"Thank you, Moriah," he said. "When we have defeated Evila and accomplished all we set out to do, Queen Leandra will remove the spell and free you from this place."

"Promise?" Moriah asked hopefully.

Wishbone smiled. "Silver Knights never lie," he told her.

Ghoulina smiled lovingly at him, and then snapped her fingers.

The cocoon holding Moriah prisoner vanished with a popping sound, and she rose to her feet. "Please, do not forget about me!" she begged.

"We won't forget," said Jack. "And I'm sorry I hit you with a stone, but you almost killed my friends. You understand, don't you?"

"Yes, yes, I do," said Moriah. "I am sorry, too."

"Don't worry. Everything will turn out all right, Moriah," Nikki said in a kind voice. "Cross my heart, you have my word."

The companions thanked Moriah, said their farewells, and walked back towards the entrance to her lair.

"Nikki, Jack, I am very proud of you both," said Ghoulina.

"Me, too," said Wishbone.

Catman purred. "Me, three!" he said.

Nikki and Jack grinned, giving each other a high-five.

Chapter 12

Nikki, Jack, and their three companions rode the Wild Horses of Scarlet Canyon for another hour, using a nice and easy gait so Champ could trot alongside them, strengthening his muscles.

"You're doing fine, Champ!" Jack encouraged him from Fiona's back. "Pretty soon you'll be galloping just like a grown-up horse!"

Champ whinnied happily, keeping pace with his mother and father.

"I have a feeling the first word he speaks will be your name, Jack," Fiona told him.

"But shouldn't it be 'Mama' or 'Papa?'" asked Jack.

Fiona neighed and shook her head. "Not necessarily," she said. "Horses are different from people, you know. We do things differently. The first word I spoke was 'water,' after I drank from a clear mountain spring."

"The first word I ever said was 'run,'" said Champ's father, Domino.

"You see, Jack," said Catman, who was riding one of the mares, "although people and horses are different, we are all alike in many ways. We all have parents and family and friends whom we love and spend time with."

Nikki, having adjusted to the rhythm and movements of her horse, felt more comfortable riding. She moved closer to Catman and Jack. "What are you talking about?" she asked. "All I can hear is neighing, huffing, and grunting sounds."

"We're talking about how families are equally important to people and animals," Catman said.

"That is so true. Horses and people have been connected for a long time. Horses played a huge role in the history of our world," Nikki replied. "They have always been our friends and helpers. We couldn't have built our civilizations without them."

"And dogs, too," said Wishbone, who was riding Domino.

"Don't forget cats!" said Catman. "Cats are important."

"Yes, they are," Nikki agreed. She turned to Jack and said, "I wish I had the Gift so I could talk to the horses, too."

"Well," said Jack, "they can understand you, and there are other ways of communicating with them. Besides, *you* have the gift of magic."

"And her talent is growing all the time," said Ghoulina. "Nikki was a big help when we had to deal with Moriah." She smiled at Nikki. "I'm very proud of you," she told her.

Blushing, Nikki said, "Thank you."

They continued riding along, passing a low range of hills. Nikki talked about her favorite school subjects—history, math, geography, and reading—and discussed her karate classes and how much she enjoyed that. She knew that Wishbone and Ghoulina were sad and worried about their baby daughter, Ava, and she hoped her stories would at least cheer them up a little. In the meantime, Catman exchanged stories with Fiona and Domino, while Jack talked non-stop to Champ, praising and encouraging the young colt, hoping he would soon start talking.

As they drew near to a fork in the road, Catman's ears stood erect and turned toward the faint sound coming from the side. "Do you guys hear that?" he asked.

Wishbone called for a halt. "Hear what?" he asked.

"It sounds like a baby crying," said Fiona.

"Fiona said it sounds like a baby crying," Jack told the others. "I hear it, too."

Thinking of her baby daughter, Ghoulina glanced around. "Quiet," she whispered. "It's coming from around the bend, where the hills turn off to the right."

"I can hear it now, too!" said Nikki.

Domino nodded his great head and looked at Jack. "Not a baby. It sounds more like a—"

The stallion never had a chance to finish what he was saying, for Jack swung down from Fiona and raced ahead on foot. Little Champ took off after him, trotting as fast as his young legs could carry him.

"Jack! Wait!" yelled Catman.

Then the others followed Jack, down to the fork in the road where the hills curved gently to the right. There they reined in the horses and came to a halt. Champ decided to rest, so he kneeled next to his mother.

"Oh, my!" said Nikki. "Giant skeletons!"

Ghoulina shook her head sadly. "Dragon bones," she told her.

Indeed they were, the bones of two huge dragons, all bleached white from being exposed to the sun for years.

Jack reached the huge skeletons and found a male dragonet, a baby dragon, lying there beside the bones, crying and wiping his tears with his leathery wings. The dragonet was roughly the size of a small cat. His hide had a sickly yellow color and Jack saw blisters all over his small body. He looked at Jack with his sad green eyes, thumped the ground with his long tail, and clawed the dirt.

"Hello, my name is Jack," he said, sitting down in front of the young dragon. "Can you talk? Can you understand me?"

The little dragon wiped his tears. "Yes, I do," he said.

"Why are you crying?" asked Jack.

"It's my parents' Sadiversary," replied the dragon.

Jack frowned. "What's a *Sadiversary?*" he asked.

"It's like an anniversary, but not a happy one," the dragonet told him. "For us dragons, a Sadiversary marks another year since the death of our loved ones."

"Oh, I'm very sorry," said Jack. "How long ago did your parents die?"

"Almost thirteen years ago," said the dragonet.

Nikki cautiously approached them, not wanting to frighten the baby dragon.

"Hello!" the dragon greeted her.

"I can understand you! I have the Gift!" she said.

"This is my cousin Nikki," Jack told the dragon.

The dragon nodded. "Hello, Nikki," he said. "I'm sorry to disappoint you, but you don't possess the Gift. Dragons can speak to and be understood by humans, animals, and magical creatures, too."

"Oh," said Nikki, sounding a little disappointed.

Jack said to the dragon, "You said your parents died almost thirteen years ago. So, what happened to them?"

The little dragon frowned and his green eyes darkened. Wisps of white smoke floated out of his nostrils. "The Grim Witch murdered them!" he cried.

The dragon went on to tell them how Evila had plotted to enslave the great dragons who once dwelled in the northern realm of Dragon's Den. Her plan was to use her magic powers to force the dragons to serve her, to fight for her, to burn the towns and villages of anyone who got in her way. The race of dragons, being a peace-loving species, fled south, across the Gonji Ocean. The dragonet's parents were the last to leave their realm, moving slowly because they had a brand-new baby with them. So it was that when they stopped to rest one night, Evila and her minions caught up with them and killed them.

"My mom hid me in a cave, and she and dad tried to fight off Evila and her gang of witches and Wolfmen, but the Grim Witch was too powerful," said the dragon. "I'm pretty sure she doesn't know about me."

"Well, *we* know *all* about Evila," Jack said.

"You do?" asked the dragon.

"Yes," said Nikki. "We're on a mission for the Wishmothers—a mission to destroy Evila and rescue my parents and my friends' baby."

"Oh, wow!" said the dragon. "Can I come with you? Maybe I can help? I've been so lonely all these years, and it will be fifty years before I reach my full size and I can fly across the ocean to search for the other dragons. I still can't fly very far. I'm only thirteen years old and I'm not that strong."

"Sure!" said Jack. "I don't see why not, and you won't be alone anymore. Right, Nikki?"

"Right-O, Jack!" Nikki agreed. "And I'm thirteen years old, too!" she told the dragon.

"Oh, thank you!" said the dragon. He flapped his wings, rose into the air and flew over to Jack, landing on his shoulder. "I hope you don't mind, Jack."

"Not at all," Jack told him.

"Looks like you have a new friend," Nikki said to Jack.

Jack smiled, scratched the dragon behind his tiny ears, and stood up. "Come on, our friends are waiting for us," he said.

Together they walked back to where their companions waited for them. The dragonet perched on Jack's shoulder like a parrot on a pirate.

Champ, the young colt, rose to his feet and ran to Jack. When he saw the dragon on Jack's shoulder, Champ whickered happily, bucking and prancing about with great joy.

"This is Champ," Jack told the dragon.

"Hello, Champ," said the dragon.

The little foal neighed happily, jumped straight into the air, kicked backwards with his hind legs, and then settled on his hooves again.

Jack introduced everyone to the dragon, and the dragon said hello to everyone.

"What's his name, Jack?" asked Catman.

"I don't know," Jack said with a shrug of his shoulders.

"Everyone has a name," said Wishbone.

Ghoulina turned to the little dragon. "What's your name, little one?" she asked.

"Oh, my parents didn't have a chance to name me, they called me by my baby name, Kicsisarkany," said the dragon. "Can you find a good name for me, Jack? Dragons are named on their second birthday, but I've been all alone. There was nobody to find a good name for me."

Jack thought about it for a while.

"Come on, Jack," said Nikki. "We don't have all day!"

"I'm thinking! I'm thinking!" said Jack.

Then, just as Jack turned his head, the dragon sneezed and tiny sparks flew from his mouth. "Oh, I'm *so* sorry!" he said.

Jack turned to his friends and smiled. Both his eyebrows were singed. "Oops, remind me next time not to stand too close to this little rascal. Sparky," he said, wiping the snot off his forehead. "I'm going to call him Sparky."

The little dragon clapped his wings and said, "Sparky, I like that!" Then he bowed his head. "Sorry about the eyebrows."

"No biggie," Jack said. "They'll grow back."

About half an hour later the companions decided to rest and let the horses graze. While Catman, Ghoulina, and Wishbone sat together with their backs against a large boulder, Nikki and Jack went off on their own. Nikki watched Sparky fly around in circles, flapping his wings. Jack sprawled out on the grass with Champ next to him as he tried to teach the colt a few more words.

"Can you say my name, Champ?" asked Jack.

The colt neighed and shook his head.

"Well, then," said Jack. "Are you hungry?"

Champ whinnied and nodded.

"At least he understands you," Nikki said to Jack. "And that's a good start."

"I'm a little hungry, too," said Sparky, still flying in circles over Nikki's head.

"What do you like to eat?" she asked.

Sparky settled down on the ground beside her. "Oh, I like bats and rats and lizards," he told her. "I eat snakes, too. I like snakes the most."

"Yuck," Nikki told Sparky, "I'm sorry, but we don't have any bats, rats, or lizards."

"That's okay," Sparky told her. "I can eat grass. But what I really need is dragon's milk. Dragon babies need dragon's milk at least twice to develop immunity against diseases. I was too young when my parents were killed. My mother only had a chance to feed me once, that's why my skin is blistered and looks sickly yellow. It's supposed to be green, and my horns won't grow, either." He choked on his tears.

Jack suddenly jumped to his feet, startling Champ. "My wishes!" he said. "I *so* totally forgot about the three wishes the Wishmothers gave me!"

Ghoulina, Wishbone, and Catman joined the kids.

"What sort of wish are you going to make?" asked Catman.

"I could wish for Champ to talk," Jack replied with a wink.

Wishbone frowned. "I don't think that's necessary, Jack," he said. "Champ will talk when he's good and ready."

"And don't forget, Jack," said Ghoulina, "you promised you wouldn't waste any of these wishes on silly things, like you did last year."

"That's right, Jack," Nikki told him. "Don't make a selfish wish. You should wish instead…" Nikki looked at the scrawny little dragon.

Jack rolled his eyes at Nikki. "Don't you think I know that? I was just teasing," he said, laughing. He closed his eyes for a second, opened them again and said, "I wish I had a bucket of dragon's milk!"

Ding!

A bucket filled with a thick, silvery liquid materialized suddenly on the grass.

"Dragon milk!" Sparky shouted out joyfully. He flew over to the bucket, landed on its rim, and started drinking. He looked up and said, "This is *so* good! Jack, you saved my life," and then kept on drinking until the bucket was empty. Once he was finished, Sparky flew a short distance away from the others, landed, and squatted on the ground.

Nikki clapped her hands. "That's what I wanted to tell you, Jack, but it seems like we had the same thought!" she said. "An unselfish wish—and a wish that was wished to help someone else."

After a few minutes, Sparky flew back to land on Jack's shoulder, nuzzling his neck. "Thanks, Jack!" he said.

Everyone was amazed at the drastic change of Sparky's appearance. His hide turned to a healthy green color and the blisters were gone.

"My horns are starting to grow, look!" Sparky flew off Jack's shoulder and started jumping up and down on the ground excitedly and sneezing balls of small flames all around him.

Jack stepped on the dry grass, stomping out the fires, and smiled at the happy little dragon. "Yes, you have and I'm happy for you, but enough of the excitement for now. You're going to burn down the land."

Sparky calmed down and settled on Jack's shoulder. Jack turned and noticed a number of little silver balls, about the size of marbles, lying on the grass where Sparky had squatted. He walked over there and picked one up. Nikki and their friends joined him.

"Look!" Jack said. "Silver dragon poop!" He picked up one of the silver balls and noticed that it was hard and had no smell at all. Then he started gathering up the silver balls and stuffing them into the pouch hanging from his belt. He looked up at Nikki, grinned mischievously, and tossed a silver ball at her. She leaned away from the flying ball, which bounced off her leather shirt and landed on the ground.

"You're disgusting, Jack," she scolded him. "That's *poop*, for Pete's sake!"

"Not just any poop—this is *dragon* poop!" Jack told her

Nikki shook her finger at him. "Poop is poop, no matter whose poop it is," she said.

"But this is *silver* poop, Nikki," said Jack.

Catman meowed, Wishbone groaned, Ghoulina laughed out loud, and Sparky sneezed a bunch of sparks.

"Poop!" yelled Champ.

"Champ, you just said your first word!" Jack said, wrapping his arms around the colt's neck and giving him a big hug. "That's awesome!"

"That's not quite the first word I ever expected to hear him say," said Fiona.

Domino neighed, as if laughing. "Me, neither!" he said.

"I hope he doesn't go around saying it all the time," said Fiona.

"Well, it's not really offensive language," Domino told her. "Relax. Everyone poops."

With a sigh of frustration, Nikki said, "You know, Jack, you're nuts!"

Jack grinned. "There's a method to my nuttiness," he said.

Ghoulina bent down and picked up the silver ball Jack had thrown at Nikki. "Jack is right," she said. "This is solid silver and very valuable. These are called Dragon Rocks, and they are found nowhere else in this part of Creepy Hollow. If nobody touches them within a day or so, they eventually dissolve and melt into the ground." She tossed the Rock into the air, caught it before it fell to the ground, and put it in her pocket. "I'm keeping this one for good luck," she said.

Remembering what happened at Grandma's house the night Evila's minions attacked, Jack winked at everyone, picked up the rest of the Dragon Rocks, and stuffed them in his pouch.

"Knowing Jack, he'd pick those up even if they *weren't* made of silver," Nikki said. "He's always picking things up. I mean, he's a *boy*, and boys—"

"Will be boys," Ghoulina finished Nikki's sentence. Deep in thought for a minute, she said. "You know, Nikki, it's about time for people to stop saying that. People always said that as an excuse when boys were given more value in society and a lot less strict rules than girls. They thought that a woman's only job was to raise children and take care of their families because they don't have as much capability of learning and thinking as males. Those old times are long gone and women proved it time and time again that they're equally capable of learning and doing everything."

"That is so true, Ghoulina. I'm never going to say that again," Nikki said.

Although Ghoulina smiled, her pretty white face was darkened by the shadow of fear and worry, and there was sadness in her silver eyes.

Nikki knew Ghoulina was thinking about her baby daughter, and she took hold of the Goth witch's hand. "Don't worry, Ghoulina," she said. "We'll save Ava, and we'll save my parents, too. We'll save everyone in Creepy Hollow."

Chapter 13

Deep in the basement of Dreadful Hall, Evila the Grim Witch met with the monstrous Mutanto and his werewolf henchman, Howler.

"Is everything set to go?" she asked.

Mutanto nodded. "Yes, Your Majesty," he replied.

"Is my army prepared to march at my command?" she asked.

"Our Goblin and Gnome warriors are standing ready. We are waiting for your orders, my Queen," Mutanto told her.

"My Wolfmen drool and sharpen their fangs and claws, Your Majesty," Howler said to Evila. "And we have a platoon of forty Ogres all armed and ready to fight."

Evila rubbed the palms of her hands together. "Excellent! Soon I will send word and you and Howler can order our troops to march, Mutanto," she said.

"Where do we attack first?" asked the scar-faced giant.

"We'll take a shortcut straight through the ruins of Willow Haven, and then we'll cross the Violet River and attack Dwarf Hill."

Howler wailed with glee and licked his fangs. "They'll never see us coming," he said.

"Exactly!" said Evila. "From there we'll march against Elf Harbor and Mermaid Landing. Nothing shall stand in our way."

"What about the baby's parents...that Wishbone Jones and his wife, Ghoulina?" Wishbone asked. "Surely they'll try to save her."

At that moment Slither, the sneaky snake, wriggled into the chamber and transformed itself into Tattler, the gossipy shape-changer. He smiled arrogantly at Mutanto and Howler.

"And then there are those two witches—the kid and the old lady, plus that bratty little boy who Wishbone and Ghoulina stopped these two from kidnapping," he said, pointing at Mutanto and Howler. The scarred giant glared at Tattler. Howler growled. Tattler ignored them and said, "What about them? I don't even know where they're at or what they're up to."

"Do you really think they scare me?" Evila asked. "Let them come. I'll make sure they never leave!" She cracked her knuckles and said, "Mutanto and Howler, go and get everything ready. Wait for my orders, and then we go to war!"

Mutanto and Howler glared at Tattler, bowed to Evila, and then left.

As Evila and Tattler walked towards the cage of Wizard's Glass that held Nikki's parents and baby Ava Jones prisoner, she glanced at the three Wolfmen on guard duty. They were sitting at a table in a corner, playing cards. They quickly rose to their feet and bowed to their queen.

"You three guys are so totally useless," Tattler told them.

The Grim Witch sighed and shook her head in disgust.

When she reached the glass cage, she stared at her captives. "Twelve years they've been locked in there, and once a week I steel magic and energy from them," she said in a soft tone of voice. "I'm surprised they lasted this long. But they won't last much longer, that's for sure. Well, the baby will supply me with what I need, when she's old enough. She's the only important one. Soon I can dispose of Angelina and her husband."

Mike Strong was lying on the bed, still resting after Evila had stolen more of his body's energy. He sat up and glared when he saw the Grim Witch. His wife, Angelina, was sitting up in bed, rocking baby Ava in her arms. The infant was calm and quiet, and smiling at Angelina. *She treats that baby as if it was her own child*, Evila thought.

Evila slid open a small panel in the wall facing her, which allowed her to speak with her prisoners. "So sweet...the perfect scene of domestic bliss," she said. "The baby seems quite content, Angelina. She hasn't cried or screamed once since we put her in your arms."

"Ava is a good baby," Angelina said in a weak voice. "She isn't afraid of Mike and me. She knows she's safe with us." She sighed and smiled at the baby. "It has been many years since I held a baby in my arms, not since I held my…" She couldn't finish her sentence, for she started to cry. Baby Ava reached up and touched the tears on Angelina's cheek, as if to comfort her. Angelina gathered what strength she had and then said, "Ava is not even afraid of *you*, Evila—not as long as she's with us."

"In another year, she *will* be afraid of me. *Very* afraid," said the Grim Witch.

Rising slowly from the bed, Mike walked towards the glass wall of their prison cell. "If I could reach through this wall and get my hands on you, Evila," he said, "I'd—"

"You'd *what?*" Evila asked him. "Choke the life out of me?"

Tattler laughed at Mike. "If you did that, then you'd rot in here forever!" he said.

"You should know by now that Wizard's Glass is unbreakable, and only the Grim Witch can work magic inside of it," said Mutanto. "But don't worry, folks. It will all be over soon. Changes are coming."

Evila and Tattler turned and walked over to the table where Boo, Goo, and Poo were sitting and playing cards. Queen Evila grabbed the table and flung it across the chamber, scattering cards everywhere. The three Wolfman jumped out of their seats, standing and trembling as Evila gave them the evil eye. Poo hid the cards he was holding behind his back.

"I don't pay you idiots to sit around all day having fun!" Evila snapped at them. "You're supposed to be guarding the prisoners!"

"Excuse us, Your Majesty," said Boo, "but we *are* guarding the prisoners. We keep our eyes on them all day long."

"You call that *guard duty?*" Tattler asked him.

Goo nodded. "But they can't escape because the cage is made of magic crystal and the door can only be opened from the outside," he said.

"I know that, you fool!" Evila said. She turned to Poo. "You smell as if you finally took a bath. But what are you hiding behind your back?"

"Four aces," said Poo, showing her his cards.

Evila screamed with frustration. "Why am I cursed to deal with such morons!" she said, knocking the cards out of Poo's hand. "Now listen, you fools. Soon we march to war, but you three aren't coming."

"We're not?" asked Boo.

"No, you're not," replied the Grim Witch. "I want you to stay here and keep watch on our guests over there. And if I don't like what I see when I come back, I'm going to shave off your fur and lock you in barrels filled with ice. Plus, I'm leaving Tattler in charge. Understand?"

Tattler smiled at the werewolf brothers. "I'll be right outside the door," he told them.

The three goofy Wolfmen nodded in silence.

Without another word, Evila and Tattler turned and left, closing and locking the outer door behind them.

When she was gone, Boo said, "At least we don't have to go fight and kill—or *be* killed. I wouldn't like that one bit. No sir. But if I were a violent werewolf, I'd rip that Tattler guy's lungs out. I hate him!"

"That settles it then. I don't want to be a werewolf anymore," said Goo. "We have to somehow get out of here and hide some place where Evila can never find us."

"I want to be human again, too," said Poo. "And if we can figure out where to go, somewhere safe, I'd like to take Angelina, Mike, and the baby with us, so they can be safe, too."

Boo and Goo looked at their brother, surprised that he said something that wasn't dumb or silly. They were even more surprised by the fact that they agreed with him.

Meanwhile in Willow Haven, Her Majesty, Queen Leandra worried about Nikki and Jack, even though she knew they were in good hands. Wishbone, Ghoulina, and Catman would look after them, and the Trinity of Wishmothers would keep them as safe as they could. But she knew she had to set aside her fears and concerns for the time being because she had much work to do.

She sped up time in parts of Creepy Hollow that Evila and her army had destroyed but then moved on and didn't control anymore. Although Evila was strong from the energy she drained from the witches and Leandra's daughter, she was not strong and powerful enough to control a large land such as Creepy Hollow, only a small part of it.

Waving her Sapphire Wand high over her head in a circle, the queen created a rainbow of dazzling colors to appear in the sky over her realm of Willow Haven. The power of her Sapphire Wand began to heal the forests, rivers and meadows of her kingdom.

The Wishmothers called the Nine Guardians of Weeping Willow Coven to assist and with their combined effort, the trees, flowers, and grass had started growing again. Crops sprouted from the good earth of farmlands, the creeks and rivers ran with fresh, clean water, and the birds, squirrels, foxes, and other animals began to return. Word had been sent to all those who had fled Willow Haven after Evila had destroyed their land. They were returning by the hundreds, to rebuild their homes and lives.

Surrounding the base of the great hill called Crown Top was the town of Starvale, the heart and soul of Willow Haven. Once it was a desolated area of burned houses and broken buildings made of wood and stone, but no longer. Leandra, with her nine sister witches and the help of many good men, raised the town from the ashes of its grave and began the rebuilding of Starvale. The last of the Order of the Silver Knights had come home to defend their realm and serve their queen. The twelve Silver Knights and a militia of strong men would face the Grim Witch's army of Gnomes and Goblins, Ogres and Wolfmen. The Nine Guardians and Queen Leandra herself would stand against Evila and the twelve Silent Sisters—the witches of Bleakvale Coven.

Queen Leandra stood alone at the base of Crown Top Hill while the Nine Guardians in blue robes assisted in the rebuilding of Willow Haven. Then she pointed her Sapphire Wand at the ruins of the royal castle perched atop the hill like a broken crown on the skull of a long-dead king.

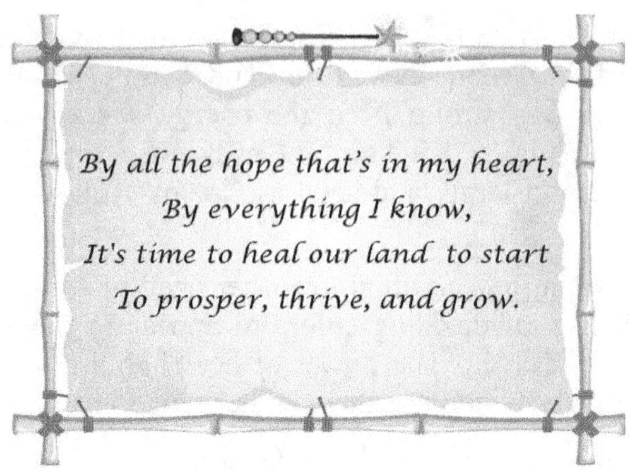

With a wave of her Sapphire Wand, the Queen of Willow Haven cast a bright blue light over the ruins of Crown Top Hill. With the sounds of whispers and softly blowing winds, the blue light settled over the castle ruins, and slowly bricks and mortar, wooden beams and marble pillars, and walls made of blue stone rose from the ruins and began to piece themselves together. The outer walls of the castle took on a golden glow, the color of the rising sun. A great silver bell also rose from the desolation and destruction, rising high into the air and hovering there until it settled itself once again on the roof of Crown Top Castle.

Queen Leandra felt strong enough to take up her crown and the responsibilities that go with it, and once again reign over her lands and all her people. The healing and rebuilding was almost finished.

"Your Majesty," said a voice from behind her.

The queen turned and lowered her Sapphire Wand as her Nine Guardians approached her. Each of the good witches wore a robe that was of a different shade of blue, and each held a large, ivory-colored Wand. One Guardian stepped forward and bowed.

"Has there been any word of my grandchildren and their friends?" asked Queen Leandra. "Are they safe?"

The Guardian nodded. "The Wishmothers have reported that Evila has no idea of their whereabouts and is quite unaware of what they are doing, and what they have accomplished, Your Majesty."

Thank you Mother Nature! Leandra thought and then asked, "How soon before we can march against Bleakvale?"

"Very soon, Your Majesty," the Guardian replied. "Your grandchildren and their companions have one more quest to fulfill before they head for Bleakvale. The owls of the forests are watching, and the birds will tell us when it's time."

"And then the silver bell will be rung, summoning all able-bodied people and every creature to march to the defense of Willow Haven," said Queen Leandra.

"Yes, Your Majesty," spoke the Guardian.

"What about my daughter and her husband, and the baby, Ava Jones?" Leandra asked, hoping against all hope.

"They are alive and still prisoners of the Grim Witch," the Guardian replied. "But we have a plan to rescue them. Word has already been sent, seeking out those who can help us."

"What sort of plan?" asked Leandra.

"It involves those spirits who dwell in the Valley of Lost Souls," said the Guardian.

The Guardian outlined her plan, and as the queen listened, her heart began to burn with renewed hope.

"May the sun and stars of Creepy Hollow look down upon us with favor and bless this plan," said Leandra.

The Guardians each bowed their heads as Leandra raised her Sapphire Wand again, pointed it at the sky, and saw the sun reflecting brightly off it. In the very center of Starvale, in a vast and brand-new garden of grass and flowers of many colors, a tall and majestic weeping willow began to grow where only cold rocks and barren soil had been before.

Finally, the great bell began to ring, summoning all those loyal to Queen Leandra who were willing to fight for Willow Haven. She began to weep with joy and with the hope that soon her family would be back in her embrace again, happy, healthy, and unharmed.

Queen Leandra turned the flow of time back to normal.

Chapter 14

Nikki and Jack rode their Wild Horses side by side, following Catman, Wishbone, and Ghoulina, who were in the lead. They were almost near to their destination.

Once again, Jack carried Champ across his lap, while Sparky the dragon flapped his wings, flying around to search for things to eat.

Jack rubbed the colt's nose. "Can you say my name, Champ?" he asked.

"Champ," said the colt.

"No, that's your name," Jack told him. "My name is 'Jack.'"

"Jack," the colt repeated.

"Yes, that's right!" Jack shouted. "That's awesome, Champ!"

"I'm so proud of you, Jack," said Nikki. "You're going to be a great dad one day."

Jack smiled with pride and continued teaching Champ to speak.

Sparky flew circles around Nikki's and Jack's heads, and then sneezed. A bunch of sparks sprayed from his nose.

"You're supposed to cover your nose and mouth whenever you sneeze, Sparky," Nikki told him.

"He would burn his front legs, Nikki," Jack told her. "How's he going to cover his mouth and nose?"

"He can use one of his wings," said Nikki.

"But he's *flying,* Nikki!" said jack. "If he did that, he'd crash and he'd burn his wing, too."

"A snake!" Sparky shouted.

Champ let out a happy neigh and yelled, "Snake!"

The little dragon nose-dived and swooped down on a good-sized rattlesnake slithering through the grass a few yards ahead of Jack and Nikki. The dragon rose into the air with the wriggling snake in its teeth, bit the snake's head off, spit it out, and then swallowed the still wiggling body whole.

"Dragon diet. It's disgusting, but at least he knows not to eat the poisonous head," said Nikki.

"Disgusting to you but a delicacy for him," Ghoulina laughed.

Sparky settled back on Jack's shoulder as they continued riding along. A short time later, Catman called a halt and told everyone to dismount. They had reached a wide plain of dry land, and up ahead was the pass leading to the Valley of Lost Souls. The valley was surrounded by a range of low-rising hills and towering mountains, and somewhere beyond the entrance was the Crystal Heart, which Ghoulina needed so she could help Queen Leandra defeat Evila, heal the land of Bleakvale, and exile all evil creatures from Creepy Hollow.

"We'll leave the horses here and enter the valley on foot," Catman said after everyone had gathered around him.

"Let's rest a few minutes before we continue," said Wishbone.

The Wild Horses went off to find some grass to nibble on. Domino and Fiona took their son Champ with them. He was quite steady and more confident on his legs now, and with Jack's help, was quickly learning to talk.

"Let me tell you a little about what we may encounter once we enter the valley," Catman said to his companions after the horses had cantered off in search of food. "About ten years ago an ordinary rat named Gnarly did a favor for Evila the Grim Witch, who rewarded him by turning him into a six-foot-tall rat, who could walk upright like a man. Gnarly declared himself the King of Rats and erected an invisible, magic barrier over the entire valley to keep all the inhabitants trapped inside. Anyone who entered the valley could never leave."

"So why is it called the Valley of Lost Souls?" Jack wanted to know.

"Because after the war with Evila and the destruction of Willow Haven, the spirits of twelve Silver Knights killed in battle got lost on their way to Celestria," Wishbone explained. "The Warrior Spirits ended up in this valley and were trapped here."

"Couldn't the Wishmothers free them?" asked Nikki.

"No. The spirits can only be set free by Queen Leandra—or by one of her descendants," Ghoulina told her. "Only you, Nikki, have the power to destroy the barrier and free the Ghost Warriors so they can find their way to Celestria at last."

"Me?" said Nikki.

"You," said Ghoulina. "And I will show you how."

Jack chewed on a fingernail and asked, "What about the Rat King?"

Catman grinned and crossed his arms over his chest. "I'll deal with him," he said. "After all, he's nothing but a big fat rat. But I'm part cat!"

Nikki and Jack laughed and applauded.

"Come now, Nikki," said Ghoulina. "Let's take down this magic barrier."

Nikki and Ghoulina led the way, followed by Jack, Wishbone, and Catman. Sparky flew over to join them, landing on Jack's shoulder.

"I'm coming, too!" said the young dragon.

When they reached the entrance to the Valley of Lost Souls, they could see the forest lying surrounded by tall mountains. But it was like looking through a dirty window, all hazy and blurry. Jack reached out and felt the solid, invisible barrier.

"That's some barrier, isn't it?" said Wishbone.

"It's the best there is!" Catman said with a laugh.

"Yep," Jack agreed. "It looks like the smudgy school windows back home, when kids press their noses and sticky hands on the glass. But it feels like solid stone. I can *wish* it away, if you want. I still have two wishes."

"No, Jack," said Ghoulina. "Save them. We might need them later. This is easy and it's something Nikki has to learn how to do."

Jack shrugged his shoulders. "Okay," he said. "You see? I'm not being selfish!"

"You'll make a fine warrior, Jack," Wishbone told him.

"Indeed!" said Catman. "You're good with that slingshot, too."

Ghoulina stood beside Nikki and held her right hand. "You've seen me do this many times," said the Healing Witch. "I will guide you and instruct you, and once you do it, you'll never need my help using this kind of magic again. Ready?"

Nikki nodded. "Ready," she said.

"First, close your eyes and think only about what you want to use your magic for, which in this case is removing the barrier," said Ghoulina. "Now raise your left arm into the air, and I'll raise my right. Concentrate on what you want to do. Then open your eyes and say whatever words pop into your head. You'll see that they will come out as a Spell. Go for it!"

When they raised their arms into the air, Nikki thought about making the barrier melt away and disappear. Then she opened her eyes and said:

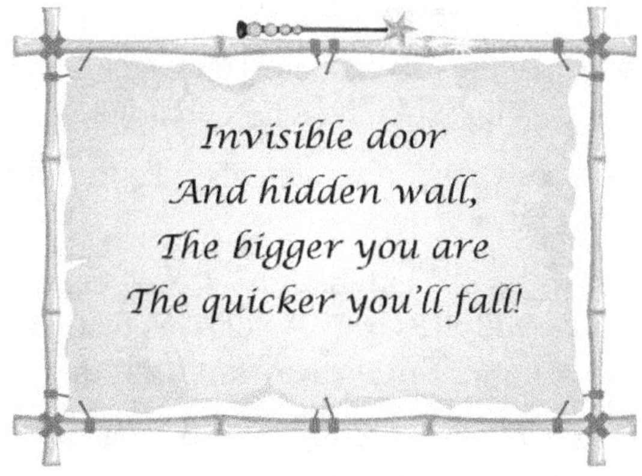

With the sound of water gurgling down the drain, the invisible barrier vanished. Now everyone could see clearly beyond the entrance and into the valley.

"Most excellent!" Ghoulina told Nikki.

Wishbone smiled and bowed to Nikki. "Well done," he said.

"You did it, Nikki!" Jack shouted, being very proud of his cousin.

"Yes, very good, and it's surely going to bring old Gnarly running to see what's going on," said Catman.

"Thank you," Nikki told Jack and her friends, blushing and basking in their praise.

Quicker than a bird snatches a worm out of the ground, there was a great commotion in the valley among all the creatures living there.

"See? I told you," said Catman.

From a shabby-looking castle made of mud, stone, twigs, and branches a big fat rat-like creature, as tall as a man, marched towards them. Behind him followed a procession of field mice, normal-sized rats, squirrels, skunks, foxes, and other animals. A large brown bear and two gray wolves brought up the rear.

"Mice and rats. Yummy food!" said Sparky.

He swooped down from Jack's shoulder and grabbed a small mouse that couldn't scurry away with the others fast enough.

"I'm Gnarly, the Rat King" the fat rat roared. "You are intruders in my kingdom. How dare you enter and how did you get in?"

"We broke through your magical barrier," Catman replied.

Gnarly hissed at Catman. "What do you want and what are you, pointy ears? You don't look like Nature's creature."

"I'm part man and part cat," Catman hissed. "Look who's talking? What are you? A fat rat or a dog?"

"I'm a rat!" Gnarly shouted indignantly. "You see, there was a glitch when... Poo sneezed and the Grim Witch was distracted and my face changed and...never mind. I'm the Rat King and that's that!"

"King you are, you say. Not!" Catman told Gnarly. "You're nothing but a fat cross between a dog and a rat."

Gnarly roared with anger and in his blind rage threw a punch at Catman. But Catman moved fast. Blocking the punch, he grabbed Gnarly's fist and threw him over his shoulder. The Rat King hit the ground with a loud thud and didn't move for a few seconds.

All the animals squawked and squealed, and yapped and yowled. The brown bear and the two wolves crept closer, with menace and hunger in their eyes.

Wishbone stepped forward and raised the blue, enchanted Sword of Moriah. "I wouldn't come any closer, if I were you," he warned them.

The bear took another step forward.

"Too close," Sparky said, sneezing fire at the bear's foot. "I'm eating here." He laughed between two bites when the bear yelled, jumped and tried to smother the fire on his leg that burned a patch of his fur.

"Watch it!" the bear mumbled but retreated.

The wolves exchanged frightened glances with the bear, and then they all backed away. Many of the smaller animals turned and ran off into the forest.

Slowly, Gnarly rose to his hind legs. "I'm the Rat King. You can't defeat me!" he snarled. Gnarly then gave Catman a head-butt to the stomach, knocking him backwards onto the ground. For a moment, Catman laid there, stunned.

Nikki wanted to cast spell. Jack picked up a stone and loaded his slingshot. Wishbone flashed his sword over his head, letting the other animals know that he wasn't one to mess with.

Ghoulina clenched her fists. "Do nothing, yet," she told the kids. "Wait."

Gnarly was ready to pounce again when Catman sprang to his feet and hit the Rat King with two quick punches to the jaw. Stumbling backwards, Gnarly rubbed his jaw and then tried to kick Catman in the knee. Catman moved as quickly as a cat, leaping into the air, avoiding Gnarly's kick, and then kicking the big rat in the belly. When the Rat King doubled over, holding his fat belly, Catman threw an upper-cut punch and socked him right underneath his jaw. The blow caused Gnarly to stand upright, and when he did, Catman aimed another punch straight for his nose. The Rat King ducked and hit back with a jab to Catman's chest that knocked him to his knees, gasping for air. The Rat King raised his front paws into the air and started hopping up and down and whirling around in circles. But his victory dance didn't last long.

Catching his breath, Catman hopped to his feet and grabbed Gnarly's long tail. He held onto the tail and began twirling the Rat King around and around in circles until the big rat started moaning and went limp. Then Catman let go of Gnarly's tail. The Rat King flew through the air and crash-landed against a pile of rocks and boulders. He groaned in pain, lying there on the ground, defeated.

Nikki and Jack applauded. The forest creatures that had not fled yet, including the bear and the two wolves, all bowed to Catman.

Turning to Wishbone, Catman said, "Let's find the Crystal Heart and get out of here."

As they started to go forward, Gnarly picked up a large rock and was ready to stand up and throw it at the back of Catman's head. But Jack saw what the Rat King intended, took aim with his slingshot, and let the stone fly. Faster than an arrow whooshing through the air, the stone whacked the Rat King right on his nose.

"Ouch!" he yelled.

"Take that, you dirty rat!" Jack told him.

"You punk, I'll turn you into a skunk!" said Gnarly, rising from the ground.

Wishbone and Catman turned around.

"You leave my cousin alone!" Nikki shouted, pointing at the Rat King. Raising her arms into the air, she chanted:

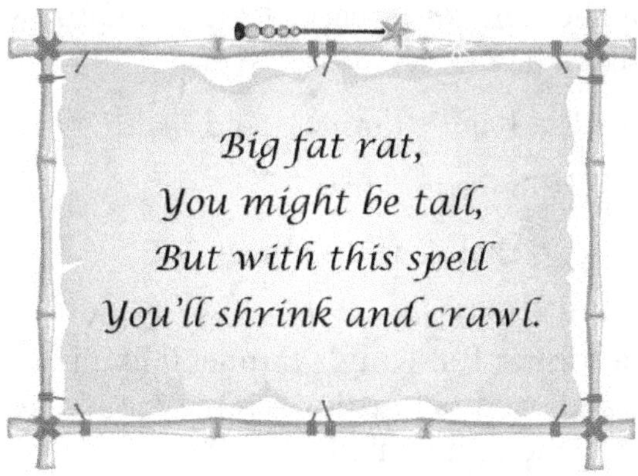

A sharp, popping sound echoed in the valley. This was followed by a flash of blue light, and a split-second later the Rat King had shrunk to the size of a normal rat again.

"Help!" he squealed as he started to run away. "Help!"

Nudging Catman in the ribs, Wishbone grinned and said, "You're a cat. Go eat that rat."

Catman laughed. "I'm not in a mood to eat junk food," he replied with a wink.

Sparky, still hungry, saw little Gnarly running away. "A juicy rat!" cried the dragon. He took off in a flash, flying after the former Rat King and snatching him up in his jaws.

At that moment Champ raced into the valley. "Sparky eat rat! Sparky eat rat!" said the young foal, snuggling up to Jack.

"Bravo!" said Ghoulina. "Well done!"

Nikki blushed. "Thank you, Ghoulina. But I didn't intend for *that* to happen."

"But it was *so* cool!" said Jack.

The other forest creatures returned to their homes, and soon the valley was empty and quiet. Domino, Fiona, and the three white mares galloped into the valley to rejoin their friends.

"Come on," said Wishbone. "The Crystal heart is here somewhere."

Everyone followed the Silver Knight. They searched the filthy castle of the Rat King high and low. Finally, they entered a room where they saw a large stone chair set upon a high dais, with five steps leading up to it. On top of the chair in a carved niche they saw a small, clear crystal shaped like a heart.

"That must be the Rat King's throne," said Jack.

"Not anymore," Wishbone told him.

"Now it's just a stone chair," said Catman.

Ghoulina climbed the five steps to the dais, followed by Nikki. When they reached the former Rat King's throne, Ghoulina took the Crystal Heart into her hands and held it for a few seconds, feeling its power and energy. She handed it to Nikki.

"Can you feel the crystal's magical power?" Ghoulina asked her.

Nikki nodded as she sensed and felt the power of the Crystal Heart. "It feels weird," she said. "It's vibrating and moving rhythmically like a real beating heart."

"That's because it *is* alive," Ghoulina told her."

"How did it get here?" Nikki asked, handing the crystal to Ghoulina.

The Healing Witch put the Crystal Heart into one of her pockets. "Evila stole it from your grandmother and hid it here, where she thought no one would find it."

"Look!" cried Jack, pointing at the sky. "We've got company!"

Down from the sky floated the ghosts of twelve warriors, each one wrapped in a silvery light. They descended slowly and landed at the foot of the dais. To Nikki's surprise, they bowed to her.

"Welcome home, Princess Nicolette," said the leader of the twelve spirits. "We have been expecting you and your friends."

"You—you know who I am?" asked Nikki, totally amazed. *That's right! I'm a princess! Just like my Mom. And Grandma is the Queen of Willow Haven!*

"Awesome!" said Jack, smiling proudly at Nikki. "My name is Jack. What's yours?"

"I am the Captain of the Ghost Warriors," said the leader.

"Each of you died in the battle against Evila," Wishbone said to the ghosts. "You once belonged to the Order of the Silver Knights."

"We still do," said the ghostly leader. "We were told to await your arrival."

"Who told you?" asked Catman.

"The messenger bird," answered the Captain. "We have been in contact with the Wishmothers ever since you left Celestria."

"And now you are free," said Ghoulina. "Nikki—the Princess—broke the barrier that held you prisoner here. You're no longer lost and can finally find your way to Celestria."

"That's correct, and we thank the Princess with all our hearts," said the Captain of the Ghost Warriors. He bowed to Nikki again. Uncertain how to respond, she curtsied to him. "We shall soon return to Celestria, to confer with the Wishmothers."

"What, may I ask, are you going to confer with the Wishmothers about, Captain?" Wishbone asked.

The ghostly knight smiled. "We know of your quest and we have vowed to help you," he replied. "We have a plan."

"What sort of plan?" asked Wishbone.

"A plan to sneak into Dreadful Hall and free not only your daughter, but the parents of Princess Nicolette, as well," the Captain told him.

Wishbone and Ghoulina turned and embraced each other, both of them weeping with joy and renewed hope. Catman wiped tears from his eyes. Jack sniffled and fought to hold back his tears. Nikki let her tears roll down her cheeks like gentle drops of rain.

"What is your plan?" Nikki asked, her heart pounding and racing in her chest. "How can you sneak into Dreadful Hall, with all of Evila's soldiers and guards?"

The Captain of the Ghost Warriors smiled and bowed again. "My Princess, we are ghosts, and ghosts can go places no living person can go."

Chapter 15

Nikki, Jack, Ghoulina, Wishbone, and Catman stood hidden by dead trees and bushes on a hilltop overlooking the barren lowland spread out below them. They watched as Evila's army marched to war. Above the five friends hovered the spirits of the twelve Ghost Warriors, and behind them were Domino, Champ, Fiona, and the three mares. Sparky sat on Jack's shoulder like a large bird sitting on its wooden perch.

Dreadful Hall was a huge, sprawling manor house that looked like a castle. It had two floors and a basement, and a watchtower standing at each of its four corners. Its walls were tall and strong, with battlements and a wide drawbridge spanning a deep moat surrounding the castle. Four black, triangular banners decorated with a red ball of fire and a pair of crossed Wands flapped in a mild breeze, one atop each of the watchtowers. High atop Dreadful Hall stood a tall, iron pole flying the flag of the Grim Witch. The flag was pitch-black, with the insignia of a crimson claw. A crimson skull graced the very top of the flagpole.

The sky was cloudy and gray, with sunlight struggling to break through. The air had a moldy smell to it, mixed with the odor of rotten eggs. Dreadful Hall itself was built of black stones and blood-red mortar, and its four chimneys belched foul, gray smoke into the air. Spreading out from the foot of the lowered drawbridge for miles in all directions was a desolate plain of sand and rock, where nothing grew except for a few withered plants, shrubs, and weeds. The castle was a beehive of activity as the army of the Grim Witch prepared for war. Short Gnomes with large, ugly heads guarded the battlements, each one armed with a bow and quiver of arrows. Ranks of floppy-eared and long-nosed Goblins carrying battle axes and war hammers marched across the drawbridge to join up with a platoon of Wolfmen and a battalion of Gnomes armed with swords and spears. Behind them shambled forty, monkey-faced Ogres holding wooden clubs.

"So this is it," Wishbone sighed. "If we don't defeat Evila and her army today, she will destroy everything that is good and beautiful in Creepy Hollow."

Catman's sharp eyes studied the enemy forces emerging from inside the Hall of the Grim Witch. "We will win this fight if everyone who can help us gets here on time!" he said.

"I don't see those Wolfmen who attacked us at Grandma's house," said Jack.

Nikki looked around. "I don't see that guy who looked like Frankenstein's monster, either," she said.

"They'll show their faces when the time is right," Wishbone told her.

"And so will Evila and the witches of her coven, the Silent Sisters," said Ghoulina.

Everyone turned around at the sound of marching feet coming up the hill behind them. Then seven Silver Knights, the last of their Order, appeared, along with a great host of the armed people of Willow Haven.

Wishbone and the Sergeant of the Silver Knights bowed to one another. "You have come with my brothers and sisters!" Wishbone said with relief and joy as he bowed to the Silver Nights one by one.

The Sergeant nodded. "All who can fight and remain loyal to Queen Leandra have come to defend Willow Haven as well as the entire land." He nodded to the twelve Ghost Warriors and saluted their Captain. "Greetings, my long-lost brothers. At last, you have returned. But you are spirits, my brothers. How can you help us in battle?"

"We have a plan, sir," spoke the Captain of the Ghost Warriors. "And soon we shall put our plan into action."

A moment later the sound of thundering hooves brought all further conversation to a halt. The ground trembled and the hill shook as a herd of one hundred Wild Horses galloped up the hill. These were tall, strong stallions and mares of all breeds and colors, and when they slowed to a stop, they bowed their heads to Domino. Young Champ neighed and pranced around, proud and happy.

"The horses are here!" he shouted, but only Jack, Catman, and the other horses could understand what he said.

Domino turned to Jack and Catman. "They have answered my call," he told them. "The horses of Scarlet Canyon have come to help—not to bear riders into battle, but to fight alongside you as equals and allies."

"Thank you, Domino! Thank you all!" Jack spoke to the horses while Catman told his other companions what was happening.

"We are all most grateful to you," Catman said to the herd of Wild Horses.

"Excuse me, sir," Nikki said to the Sergeant of the Silver Knights. "Where is my Grandmother? I mean, where is Queen Leandra?"

The Sergeant's eyes opened wide. Then he and his soldiers kneeled and bowed their heads. "The Queen and the Nine Guardians of Willow Haven will be here once she has rung the great bell, Princess."

Nikki blushed. She wasn't used to all this stuff about being a Princess of the Royal Family. But she had seen a lot of movies and had read many books, so she knew what to say. "Thank you, Sergeant. Please rise. Today is not the day for traditions and ceremonies. Today we fight for the survival of the land."

The Sergeant looked at her with awe, and then a slow smile crept across his face. "Truly you are you the granddaughter of our Queen." Rising to his feet, his troop followed his example. "Now it is time to march," he said.

"The time for us to put our plan into action," said the Captain of the Ghost Warriors. As he rose higher and higher into the air, followed by the other eleven spirits, he bowed to Wishbone, Ghoulina, and Nikki. "With great luck, we shall soon save your daughter—and the parents of our young Princess!"

The twelve magnificent Ghost Warriors headed straight for Dreadful Hall and were soon hidden by the gray clouds hanging in the sky.

Tears rolled down Ghoulina's cheeks. Nikki took hold of her hand, fighting to hold her own tears at bay as Catman wiped his eyes.

"Time for us to move out, too," said Wishbone, blinking rapidly.

Catman turned to Jack. "You stick close to me, lad," he said. "Don't you go running off on your own, trying to be a hero. An army is strong only when the soldiers fight together."

Jack grinned, reached into his pouch, pulled out a Dragon Rock—one of Sparky's silver poop balls—and loaded it into his sling. "Got you, Catman," he said.

"And you stay at my side, Princess Nikki," said Ghoulina. "Together we will use our magic powers to help each other."

"Of course," Nikki told her. "But please...just call me Nikki, okay?"

Ghoulina smiled, leaned down, and kissed Nikki on each cheek.

"I come, too!" said Champ.

"No, you eager little colt," Fiona said sternly. "You stay with us."

"Your job is to guard your Mother and her three sisters, son," said Domino. "They are the last of their royal bloodline and will not fight unless they have to."

"But Mom, Dad," Champ said.

"He finally called us Mom and Dad!" said Fiona.

"I'm very happy that Jack is helping you to speak so quickly, Champ," said Domino. "But there will be no *buts* about this. Understand?"

Champ lowered his head and shook it sadly a few times.

Jack walked over to Champ. "You're brave and strong and courageous, my friend," he told the foal. "You have a job to do, just like I have. Now listen to your parents and make them proud. I'll be back soon and then we can go play."

Champ neighed and raised his head. "Play! Yes, yes!"

Jack wrapped one arm around the foal's neck, hugged him fiercely, and kissed him on the nose. "Just do as you're told," he told Champ. "We must all obey orders."

"Well, *I'm* coming—and you can't stop me!" said Sparky.

Flapping his wings, the young dragon took off from Jack's shoulder and hovered in the sky above everyone's heads, waiting for them to get moving. Jack shook his head, knowing full well there was no way he could stop the dragon.

With that, Jack joined Nikki and their friends, and everyone marched down the hill, heading straight for the barren plain that would soon become the field of battle.

Evila the Grim Witch stood at the foot of the lowered drawbridge, watching her army of Goblins, Gnomes and Ogres march off to war. Armed once again with his huge mace—the war club with the hammer head and sharp metal spikes, Mutanto stood beside her. Howler and his Wolfmen stood on the other side of the Grim Witch, their fangs sharpened and bared, and their knife-like claws extended.

Lined up in front of Evila were the Silent Sisters, the twelve witches of Bleakvale Coven. Although Evila had taken their Wands from them, to blend their power with her own, the Silent Sisters could still work small, basic magic. But Evila didn't need them to use their magic; they were merely pawns, witchy shields to protect her. Evila planned to make sure they would not survive the coming battle, for the Grim Witch no longer wanted to share power with anyone and had decided to rid herself of the Seven Sisters.

"Look at those fools coming down the hill towards us, thinking they can stop us from marching on Dwarf Hill and the other towns along the coast," Evila said.

"Let them destroy as many of our foes as they can before we join in, Your Majesty," said Mutanto. "Then I'll deal with Wishbone and his Silver Knights."

Howler's fangs dripped and drooled with saliva. "And I'll show that Catman a thing or two, Your Majesty, both him *and* that little brat who acts like his sidekick," he growled.

"And I and my Silent Sisters will show Ghoulina and her young apprentice what it really means to come face to face with the powers I command!" Evila said.

"Yes, Your Majesty!" said Howler. He licked his fangs in hungry anticipation as they watched their forces march to war.

Domino bowed to the Silver Nights and said to Catman, "Tell them that we will lead the battle. My herd will scatter many of the enemies, and then they can follow us."

Catman told everyone what the majestic horse said as they watched him lead the Wild Horses of Scarlet Canyon galloping down the hill. The snowy crescent marking on his forehead blazed with light as he urged the mighty herd of horse warriors towards the field of battle.

"Attack!" he shouted.

Raising their great heads, the Wild Horses joined their voices together in a chorus of neighs and whickers that thundered across the sky. The pounding of their hooves made the ground tremble and shake as they charged straight into the line of Ogres advancing towards them. The mares and stallions slammed into the Ogres with the force of a speeding train, crashing through their ranks, riding over them and trampling them beneath a stampede of hooves. The Ogres growled and hollered as they tried to fight back, swinging their wooden clubs, and doing their best to clobber the heads of the mighty horses. But the Ogres were clumsy and moved too slowly, and many of those monkey-faced giants were knocked to the ground by a mare or stallion. Many Ogres were sent flying through the air or tumbling over onto their backs. The Wild Horses bucked and kicked out with their hind legs, their hooves whacking and smacking their foes. Mares and stallions rose on their hind legs, using the hooves of their front legs as if they were fists, stomping and kicking the Ogres without mercy. Within moments the ranks of the Ogres buckled and broke. Many turned to flee back to Dreadful Hall, only to be squashed into the ground by the hooves of the Wild Horses. A few escaped and fled north and west, back to Ogre Mountain where they had been born.

"Onward, my kin!" Domino cried out. "For the victory of Queen Leandra!"

But then the bravest of the Ogres rallied and closed ranks, standing bold and firm as they fought on, hoping to destroy the herd of great horses.

Wielding the Sapphire Sword of Moriah, Wishbone led the Seven Silver Knights and the large militia of brave, strong people and magical creatures who had volunteered to fight against Evila's wicked warriors.

"For Queen Leandra!" Wishbone's cry of battle rang out. "For the Royal Family and for my daughter! Let's show these evil creatures how to fight…and then send them to where they belong!"

Wishbone's brigade clashed with the army of Goblins, driving straight through to the center of their forces. The Goblins fought back with a ferocity that startled Wishbone and his company of Knights and volunteers. Startled, yes, but they were not to be deterred and they were unafraid as their swords and spears clashed with the battle axes and war hammers of their foes. Both man and Goblin fell, wounded or killed as they fought one another. Cries of war from both sides nearly drowned out the roar of battle as the crash of steel against steel rang out loudly in the afternoon. The field of battle became an arena of growling, shouting, and howling voices.

In Wishbone's hands, the Sapphire Sword swept aside rank after rank of Goblins, and it became like a banner of a war, a flag of victory around which the Knights and the other fighting warriors rallied. The Sword of Moriah was unstoppable and unbreakable, and Wishbone sent Goblins by the score down to the place from which there was no return.

"Fear not, my brothers and sisters!" Wishbone yelled above the roar of battle. "We will win this day and teach these Goblins a lesson they'll never forget!"

The battle raged on for what seemed forever as the two armies hammered and battered each other, slammed and rammed into each other under gray clouds that hid the face of the sun.

The Gnomes charged into battle, waving their swords and spears in the air. Short and stout, their skinny little legs couldn't carry them as fast as those of the Goblins. But what they lacked in speed they made up for in strength, for their ranks moved forwards like army tanks made of flesh and blood. They fought well and bravely, too.

As the Gnomes broke rank and divided their forces in two, one half joined with the Goblins to fight against Wishbone and his warriors. The other half marched at a quick pace towards the hill upon which stood Nikki, Ghoulina, Jack, and Catman, who were waiting for the moment when they must join the fight. Behind them huddled Champ, Fiona, and the three white mares. They, too, were well aware that if it came to it, they would also have to join the fight.

"Looks like we might have to change our tactics," said Catman.

"Yes," said Ghoulina, worried about Wishbone and his men. "Mutanto and the Wolfmen have not yet joined the battle, and neither have Evila and her twelve Silent Sisters. I wonder what they're waiting for."

"The Gnomes split their forces and will soon be upon us," Catman said to her.

"Then we'll just have to deal with them before we tackle the evil power that commands this army," said Ghoulina.

Jack was frightened, but tried not to show it. "I have my slingshot, and there are plenty of stones lying all around us, if I need them. I'm ready," he said.

"Look!" cried Nikki, her fear overcome by her excitement. "Dwarfs!"

Sure enough, from the south marched a battalion of short, stout, and bearded Dwarfs, each one armed and ready for war. As they drew closer to the base of the hill, the Dwarf with the longest beard and carrying a large axe over one shoulder turned and waved to Nikki, Jack, Catman, and Ghoulina.

"The Wishmothers sent for us," he called out. "Their messenger bird told us that the Grim Witch plans to march on Dwarf Hill next, and that you could use a little help here."

"The Wishmothers told us we'd find help along the way!" said Nikki.

"And so we have," Ghoulina told her.

"Your arrival is spot on," Catman yelled down to the Dwarf. "We thank you with all our hearts! We'll soon be joining the battle, because there are foes of a special nature we must deal with."

The long-bearded Dwarf waved back and then he and his warriors charged forward to fight in the Bleakvale War.

When the Gnomes saw the Dwarfs charging towards them, they drew to a halt, many of them bumping into one another. The Gnomes hadn't expected to be fighting the Dwarfs in this battle. All of that was to come later, when they attacked Dwarf Hill. Now they had three choices: to turn around and rejoin the main body of their army, to meet the Dwarfs in battle, or to flee. Many chose to flee into the west and return home to Gnome Town. Some ran back to rejoin the other Gnomes and Goblins. Most, realizing that one fight was pretty much the same as any other fight, turned to face the Dwarfs. But they underestimated the strength and ferocity of the Dwarfs, who tore into them like a battering ram breaking through the gates of a city under siege. The battle was fierce and riotous, loud and deadly, for the Gnomes were no match for the slightly larger Dwarfs, who battered them and shattered their weapons. Gnomes began to flee by the score, but the Dwarfs refused to let them escape, and chased after them until they had no choice other than to fight or surrender.

<hr>

Back at the foot of the lowered drawbridge leading across the moat and into Dreadful Hall, Evila watched her forces clash with her foes. The battle was as yet undecided, although the timely arrival of the Dwarfs was something she had not expected.

No matter, she thought. *There is no way under the sun and stars of Creepy Hollow that we can lose this battle.* But she realized she had no more time to wait, no more time to lose.

"Mutanto, you know what to do. Howler, lead your wolf pack into battle, *now!*" the Grim Witch told them.

"Yes, Your Majesty," said the towering Mutanto, rushing forward and swinging his wicked-looking war club high above his head.

Howler drooled and howled, and then took off at a quick pace. Behind him, his Wolfmen snarled and followed closely on his heels."

Evila turned to her twelve silent witches. "March to war, my sisters," she said. "Our time has come. Victory is ours!"

In utter silence, the Silent Sisters went forward, their hooded heads and veiled faces now raised to face their enemies in battle.

Evila marched forth as if she was Queen of the Universe—arrogant, self-assured, and totally confident that victory would soon fall into her hands.

Chapter 16

Sweet Freedom

As the battle raged on, Wishbone, the Silver Knights, and the people from Willow Haven continued to battle the army of the Grim Witch. Many fell on both sides, wounded or slain. Those fighting for Queen Leandra proved their worth and their bravery. They were unstoppable, relentless in the pursuit and destruction of their foes, and yet merciful and kind to all those who surrendered. But a regiment of Goblins and a platoon of Ogres put up a good fight, while the Gnomes were still trying to stand against the Dwarfs.

Howler and his great pack of Wolfmen joined the battle, fighting against the Silver Knights and the other warriors of Willow Haven.

Atop the hill overlooking the field of battle, Nikki, Ghoulina, Catman, and Jack watched and waited, while Fiona, her sisters, and little Champ stood behind them.

"It's our turn," Catman said to Jack. "We must join our allies and do what we can. Are you ready?"

Jack swallowed the lump of fear in his throat, summoned his courage, and nodded. "I'm ready," he said with a determined look on his face.

Champ raced forward and nuzzled Jack affectionately. "Champ love," the foal told him.

"I love you, too, Champ," said Jack, giving the cinnamon-colored foal a big hug.

"Jack, take care and listen to Catman," said Nikki. "I hope you know what you're doing."

Reaching into his pouch, Jack pulled out a Dragon Rock—one of Sparky's silver poop balls. He winked and said, "Those Wolfmen won't know what hit them!" Loading his slingshot, he nodded to Catman.

"Let's go!" said Sparky, flapping his wings.

"May the sun and stars of Creepy Hollow protect each and every one of you!" Ghoulina yelled to them.

Jack turned, gave her a smile and a thumbs-up, and then raced down the hill.

As soon as they got close enough to face the Wolfmen, Sparky flapped his wings and took off like a rocket ahead of the group, reaching the Wolfmen first. He swooped down quickly, scratching their eyes and noses and biting their ears. The Wolfmen swatted at him but the little dragon moved as fast as lightning to get out of their reach. He sneezed sparks into their faces, scorching their eyes and snouts. He even discovered by accident that when he coughed, a small ball of fire flew from his mouth. It struck a Wolfman's back and burned the fur from most of his body, sending the beast rolling on the ground in pain.

When Jack and Catman got closer, he watched the little dragon with pride as he flew circles around the werewolves, swooping in and out among them like a jet. Sparky did his best to disrupt the ranks of the Wolfmen, to cause confusion among them so their platoon would be in complete disarray when Jack and Catman charged in to attack.

"Sparky is a smart little dragon," Jack said to Catman as they were running side by side. "He's disrupting the ranks of the werewolves and causing confusion."

"He's doing great! Look at them scrambling around," Catman replied. "We're close enough to attack. Remember: don't get too close because your slingshot will be useless. Circle around the werewolves and fire at them from a distance. Silver is poison to werewolves, so it doesn't matter which part of their bodies you hit. I hope you have enough ammunition."

"Don't worry, Catman," Jack assured him. "Thanks to Sparky, I do."

Catman roared like an enraged tiger and then together he and Jack charged forward.

Catman was a black, furry whirlwind of booted feet and clenched paws as he moved with a speed and agility that surprised Jack. He leaped into the air, punching, kicking, and clawing the werewolves.

Jack quickly loaded his slingshot with Dragon Rocks and sent the silver balls flying rapidly, hitting the werewolves.

Every time Catman punched, kicked, or clawed a Wolfman, Jack's slingshot twanged like a bowstring and a Dragon Rock *whooshed* through the air to strike the hairy monsters. Jack rarely missed and each time he scored a direct hit, a Wolfman howled in pain and fell to the ground, mortally wounded.

While Jack was reaching into his belt pouch for another Dragon Rock, he saw a Goblin armed with a war club charging towards him. Remembering how he used his shield against the Creeps, he quickly removed it from his back and threw it at the Goblin. But the Goblin batted the shield aside with his club, picked it up, and threw it back at Jack. Ducking so the shield wouldn't hit him, Jack picked up a large rock, loaded his slingshot, took aim, and fired. The rock struck the Goblin right between his eyes and knocked him out cold.

Catman and Jack fought together like a well-trained combat team. Catman's boots kicked Wolfmen in the stomach, knocked them down with one or two punches, and then Jack would destroy them with a Dragon Rock fired from his slingshot like a silver bullet. But there were just too many werewolves.

"We need help!" Jack cried out.

Catman seized a Wolfman, picked him up, and threw him at three others, knocking them down as if they were bowling pins. "Look, Jack!" he shouted. "Reinforcements have arrived!"

Then Jack saw the herd of Wild Horses stampeding through the ranks of the Wolfmen, trampling the werewolves under their thundering hooves.

While Catman continued the fight with the help of the Wild Horses, Jack saw two Ogres sneaking up behind his friend. Picking up his shield, Jack threw it at the Ogres, not wanting to waste any Dragon Rocks on them. This time, he didn't miss. Not only did his shield hit one Ogre on the head, it bounced off and smacked the other one on the forehead. Both Ogres fell flat on their faces and didn't get up.

"All right! Two with one shot!" Jack shouted.

And then, from out of the cloudy sky the Nine Guardians of Willow Haven magically appeared, flying through the air towards them.

"Grandma sent us more reinforcements!" Jack cried.

The good witches of the Weeping Willow Coven landed and immediately attacked the Wolfmen from the rear, blasting them with fiery beams from their Wands until the monsters dissolved into wisps of smoke. The remaining Wolfmen now turned to attack the Nine Guardians, only to find that they were no match for the good witches of Willow Haven.

Howler, the leader of the wolf pack, knowing that his army was losing the fight, pushed his way towards Catman. He wanted to defeat him and show him who was stronger. "It's just you and me now, hairball," he growled.

Catman snarled. "Then it's time to send you back to the kennel, you mutt," he said.

Howler growled and leaped towards Catman, who caught him in his paws and threw him to the ground. Lurching quickly to his feet, Howler attacked Catman again. They punched, kicked, clawed, and scratched one another, tearing and ripping clumps of fur from each other's body. Jack stood there, unsure what to do, unable to take a clear shot at the Wolfman. Catman and Howler grappled and fought, tumbling to the ground and wrestling with a ferocity Jack had never before seen. Over and over they rolled on the dirt of the barren field, slapping and snapping at one another. Then Howler gained the upper paw when he ended up on top of Catman, held him down, and bit down hard on his shoulder. Catman yowled in agony. Howler cried out in victory.

"Catman!" Jack shouted.

Howler glanced up from the mortally wounded Catman, looked at Jack, and said, "Now it's your turn!" he said.

Rising to his feet, Howler moved slowly towards Jack.

Jack backed away, afraid and worried about Catman. Tears flooded his eyes as he stuck his hand in his pouch to grab the last of his Dragon Rocks.

"Hang on, Jack! I'm coming!" yelled Sparky. He swooped down and sank his talons into Howler's eyelids. The Wolfman wailed in pain as the dragon flapped his wings and tugged hard, causing him even more pain. "Now, Jack! *Now!*"

Heart pounding, Jack knew he had to make his last Dragon Rock count.

With his hands shaking, Jack loaded the silver Rock into the pocket of his slingshot. Then he steadied his nerves and his hands, and took careful aim.

Just as Howler finally managed to get free from Sparky's claws, Jack pulled back on the thick, rubber strap of his slingshot.

"Nobody hurts my friends, you dirty dog. *Nobody!*" Jack yelled.

As Howler charged towards him, Jack released his grip on the pocket of the slingshot and let the Dragon Rock fly. The silver Rock struck the Wolfman between the eyes. With a ghastly howl filled with animalistic rage and terrible agony, Howler fell to the ground like a ragdoll and did not get up again.

Jack dropped his slingshot and ran over to kneel beside the fallen Catman. His shoulder had a deep, torn wound that oozed blood.

"Good shot, Jack," said Catman, gritting his teeth in pain. "I'm proud of you."

Sparky landed on Jack's shoulder and nuzzled his cheek. "Sparky, go get help!" Jack told him, choking back on his tears.

The little dragon nodded and flew off to find help. Jack didn't know what to do, didn't know how to stop the bleeding. He lifted Catman's head, laid it in his lap, and held one of his friend's paws.

"Catman!" Jack cried. But Catman's eyes had already closed and he didn't say another word. "Somebody help! Catman's hurt! Somebody! *Help!*"

Meanwhile, Ghoulina watched as the twelve Silent Sisters of Bleakvale Coven marched forth into battle. Her eyes narrowed in anger when she saw that Evila stood safely behind her Coven, watching and waiting.

"Now it's our turn, Nikki," Ghoulina said. "Stick closely to my side and don't be afraid. We are under the protection of the Wishmothers, and I have a few defensive tricks up my sleeve. Are you ready?"

"I'm ready!" Nikki said, ignoring the cold ball of fear in her belly.

Ghoulina smiled at her and unclasped her Key Stone from her necklace. "Nikki, take yours off, too. When we hold hands with our Key Stones, they will unite and strengthen our combined powers.

As they walked down the hill holding hands, Ghoulina whispered a spell and slowly, a colorful vapor enveloped them, forming a domelike barrier around them.

"The love and protection of the Sacred Herd follows you!" Fiona called to them.

Nikki's legs were a little shaky and her stomach was in a knot, but she kept on walking. As they reached the bottom of the hill her fear lifted, and with every step she felt the combined power of the sacred stones growing stronger and stronger.

The twelve witches of Evila's coven marched with bowed heads towards Ghoulina and Nikki. When they were just a stone's throw away, the Silent Sisters removed their hoods and veils, and revealed their faces.

When Nikki saw that the witches were very young children, less than half her age, she was stunned. She stumbled but didn't fall because Ghoulina had a tight hold on her hand.

"The Grim Witch is crueler than I imagined," Nikki whispered. "She uses children to fight her battles."

"They're grown witches, but because Evila has been draining their powers and strength for so long, she stunted their growth," Ghoulina explained. "They may look like children, but don't be fooled by their looks. They still have some powers left and they're loyal to their mistress."

They raised their arms together just as the Silent Sisters attacked. Crimson-colored, crackling bolts of energy went hurling towards Ghoulina and Nikki. But these exploded harmlessly against Ghoulina's magical shield.

Ghoulina waved her arm, conjuring a shimmering, purple wave of heat that slammed into the twelve witches, causing them to stumble and fall back a few steps.

They gathered themselves together and launched another assault, throwing balls of black fire and streaks of red lightning towards Ghoulina's shield. These, too, slammed into the protective barrier and died out. The explosions shook the ground and rocked Nikki and Ghoulina, making them wobble, but they remained standing. Again, Ghoulina waved her arm and conjured a ring of blue and purple fire that wrapped itself around the witches.

As a counterattack, they summoned up a dark wind to blow and extinguish the flames. Then the sisters gathered the last sparks of their dark magic and wove a black and crimson energy bundle that burst against Ghoulina's protective dome with enough power to crack the shield.

The ground trembled beneath her and Nikki's feet, and the force of the attack nearly knocked them down.

The twelve Silent Sisters moved towards them.

"They're breaking your shield, Ghoulina!" Nikki said. "Are they too powerful for us?"

"No way!" Ghoulina shouted. "Hold onto my hand with all the strength you can muster, and make sure our Key Stones are in constant touch. Stand tall and strong, and cast aside your fear. I'm going to lower my shield so I can send these pitiful creatures back where they belong!"

Ghoulina whispered a spell, clenched her upraised hand into a fist, and then unclenched it. Their shield melted away and Ghoulina's entire body started to glow. Nikki looked down and her heart skipped a beat when she saw the white glow emanating from her body, as well.

"Point your fingers at them. *Now!*" Ghoulina said, her voice sounding eerie.

Nikki complied and a glowing white energy beam shot out from their hands, hitting the ground at the sisters' feet. The ground shook and lush green vines sprouted from the earth to wrap themselves around the Silent Sisters. The witches hissed in anger, trapped and unable to move. Struggling with all their might, they could not break free from the vines that were twisting and tying their arms and legs.

"I think it's time we can finally end this, once and for all," said Ghoulina. She chanted:

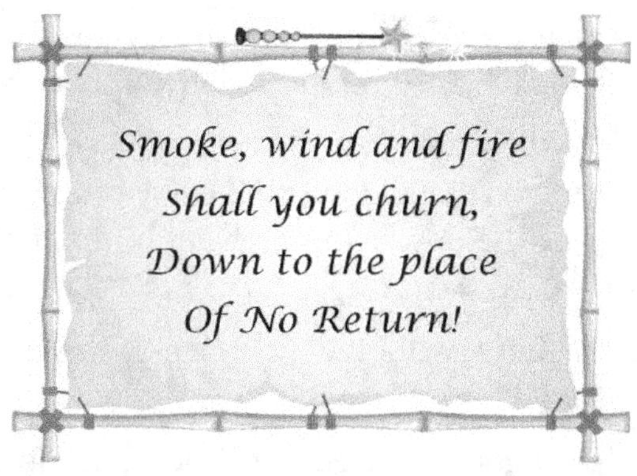

Dark whirlwinds appeared in the air, one above the head of each Silent Sister. They looked up and cried out in fear and horror as the whirlwinds descended and wrapped around them until all that could be seen were twelve spinning and whirling figures that drilled themselves into the ground like giant screws. A few seconds later there was nothing left but wisps of dust and dark smoke.

"Where did they go?" Nikki asked, feeling dazed and a little confused.

"They were sent down to where all their kind ends up: in the Realm of No Return," Ghoulina replied. She let go of Nikki's hand and clasped her Key Stone back on her necklace.

Goosebumps crawling up and down her arms, Nikki stood there stunned, staring at the ground.

Ghoulina, sensing Nikki's distress, wrapped her arms around her and whispered, "It's over. We're okay, but we still have things to do."

Nikki shook her head and felt calmness flowing through her body from Ghoulina's touch. "Thank you, Ghoulina, I feel much better," she said and worry made her cringe with fear. "I hope grandma is okay; and now we have to help the others, too."

While the fierce battle took place outside, down in the basement of Dreadful Hall, the three hapless Wolfmen sat at their card table, listening to the sounds of the battle raging outside. But they were too afraid to play cards or do anything else while on guard duty. Instead, they talked quietly and made their secret plans.

Poo grinned. "Maybe if we rescue the baby, Angelina, and Mike, the Wishmothers will look kindly on us, break Evila's spell, and turn us back into men," he said hopefully.

"Lower your voice, you knucklehead!" Boo told him. "That Tattler fellow is right outside the door. Do you want him to hear us?"

"We have the key to the glass cage," said Goo. "But how are we going to slip outta here with the prisoners? Have you thought of that?"

The three cursed but good-hearted Wolfmen had no answer to that, and they looked at the cage made of Wizard's Glass, where Angelina still lay in the bed, rocking the sleeping baby Ava in her arms. Mike kneeled beside the bed, talking softly, comforting them.

Boo was about to make a suggestion when the spirits of the twelve Silver Knights suddenly floated through the ceiling and down to the floor.

"Ghosts!" cried Poo, backing up and falling over a chair.

Goo and Boo stood there, shaking and unable to move.

Inside the glass cage, Mike stood and walked over to stand by the wall, watching and trying to hear what was going on.

"Don't be afraid, for we mean you no harm," spoke the Captain of the Ghost Warriors. "The Wishmothers sent us here to free these prisoners. We've been spying on you three and know you want to help them. If you help us, I'm certain Queen Leandra will break Evila's spell and turn you back into men again."

The three werewolf brothers stared at each other.

"The Queen of Willow Haven is alive?" Boo asked. "She's returned to Creepy Hollow?"

"Will she really help us?" asked Poo, rising to his feet.

"If you help us, we'll put in a good word for you," said the Ghost Captain. "Otherwise, without the key, we'll have to push the glass cage out of here, which will cause us a little difficulty and slow us down a bit. Furthermore, Angelina is Queen Leandra's daughter, Opal, and rightful heir to the throne of Willow Haven. Serve the Royal Family and all your sins and crimes will be forgiven."

Goo stared at the ghosts in disbelief. "*Princess Opal?* Angelina is Princess Opal?"

"Yes!" said the Captain. "Now, do you have the key to that cage? Will you help us?"

"Yes, and yes!" said Boo. He grabbed the keys hanging on the wall near the outer door and quickly unlocked the glass cage. Almost immediately the front wall of the cage slid down into the floor.

The Silver Knights entered the cell and bowed. "Princess Opal," said the Captain. "We have come to save you."

Angelina rose to a sitting position, trying not to wake Ava. Confusion darkened her face. "I don't understand," she said.

"What's going on?" Mike asked in a weak voice.

"A great battle," said Boo, stepping forward with his two brothers.

"Your mother, the queen, thought you long dead, Princess," said the Captain. "But when the truth was discovered, she returned to Creepy Hollow, and your daughter Nikki is with her."

"My…my mother? My…oh, Nikki!" said Angelina, and she started to cry.

Mike wiped tears from his eyes. "But we're too weak to travel far," he said.

"I can carry you and baby Ava, if Your Highness will allow me the honor," said Boo.

Goo nodded. "I can carry you, Sir," he said to Mike. "Trust us, please, for you know we have never hurt anyone, never caused you harm, and did not take part in your abduction, although we were there. Forgive us, for we were too cowardly to stand up against Mutanto, Howler, and the others. Now is our chance to regain our honor and redeem ourselves."

"I'll lead the way out of here," said Poo. "I know a few secret tunnels and passageways."

At that moment the outer door flew open and Tattler, the shape-shifting gossip, stormed into the chamber, demanding, "What's with all this noise? What's going on in here?"

Then he saw the twelve ghosts, cried out in fear, and fled from the chamber.

The Captain of the Ghost Warriors turned to three of his brother spirits. "Float towards the roof and hover in the sky above it so Queen Leandra and our friends can see you. That is the signal to let them know we have the prisoners safely in our care."

The three Ghost Warriors floated up to the ceiling and vanished.

"So what do we do now?" Mike asked.

"Cover your ears and wake little Ava," said the Captain.

But no one needed to wake Ava, for her eyes popped wide open at that very moment, and when she saw the ghosts and the three Wolfmen, she began to scream. She cried louder and with more shrill and greater power than she had ever cried before.

Just as Tattler climbed the stairs from the basement to the first floor of Dreadful Hall, he heard baby Ava's ear-splitting cry. Not a moment later the building shook and trembled, the walls began to crack, and stones and plaster rained down from the ceiling behind him. Dreadful Hall was beginning to fall apart and crumble into ruin.

"I didn't sign up for this. I'm out of here!" Tattler shouted as he raced down a corridor in a frantic attempt to escape. He screamed with fright when the ceiling up ahead collapsed, and stones and bricks fell and filled the corridor, blocking his path.

He was trapped.

The splitting pain in his ears caused by Ava's cry was driving him mad and his eardrums were about to pop from the pressure, but Tattler was not going to give up. He turned around, frantically looking for an escape route. Then he saw a tiny gap in the wreckage blocking his way. He could see light and feel the stirring of fresh air passing through the gap.

That hole's just big enough for me to crawl through, he thought, quickly turning himself into the snake. Having no external ears, the pain he felt as a human was gone and he could only hear the muffled sounds in his inner ears and feel the vibration of Ava's powerful voice. *I always knew it's better to be a snake than a human*, he thought, crawling through that tiny gap.

Chapter 17

At the same time his wife and friends were fighting for their lives, and well before the Ghost Warriors slipped into Dreadful Hall to complete their rescue operation, Wishbone strode into the other part of the battle. The Sapphire Sword of Moriah flashed left and right, sweeping his foes aside and defeating them as fast as he could.

The Silver Knight fought his way to reach the scarred giant, Mutanto.

Mutanto waved his heavy mace high above his head, and then he bowed. "So we meet again, Wishbone Jones," he said in his low, gruff voice.

Wishbone started circling around Mutanto, watching and looking for a chance to attack. "Such a shame we couldn't meet under better circumstances," he said with a mocking laugh.

"I would think the circumstances are just right, wouldn't you agree?" Mutanto asked, turning clumsily to face the Silver Knight.

"Most definitely," Wishbone replied, gently swinging his sword of sapphire-blue steel back and forth like the pendulum of a clock. "So, let's make the most of it, shall we?"

With a war cry that rang out across the field of battle, Mutanto attacked.

Wishbone met his foe's charge with a speed almost too quick for the eye to follow, beating aside Mutanto's mace with a savage ferocity. The giant tightened his grip on the handle of his weapon, swinging it up, around, and down again to crash into Wishbone's blade. The Silver Knight blocked the monster's weapon with a mighty blow from his sword, knocking Mutanto's war club aside. Mutanto brought his mace up and around again, aiming a blow for Wishbone's head. The Sword of Moriah was like a winged serpent of blue steel as it crashed with a sharp clamor against the weapon of Wishbone's monstrous foe. Sword and mace grated against each other. Gray and blue sparks flew through the air like dozens of lightning bugs on a warm summer's night.

Mutanto took one step backwards to catch his breath. "Not bad, not bad at all," he said.

Raising his sword, Wishbone said, "I think it's time to get down to business and end this, don't you?"

"Most assuredly," Mutanto agreed.

The two warriors went at it again, hammering and battering each other's weapons. Back and forth they fought, with the the sound of metal ringing out as they clashed. The sweat of exertion stung Wishbone's eyes as he fought against Mutanto, using all his skill and every trick he knew to stand up against the great strength of the giant. Mutanto may have been bigger and stronger than Wishbone, but the Silver Knight was a great warrior and swordsman. Still, he had to muster all his strength in order to avoid being overcome by the scar-faced giant.

Sword kissed mace as Wishbone and Mutanto tried to beat down and break each other's weapons. Wishbone's sword was a blur of blue steel—dipping, slicing, sliding in and out of the silvery web spun by the metal spikes and hammer-head of Mutanto's war club, and then striking fast and hard. But Mutanto's powerful arm and the great fist clutching the shaft of his mace was almost too much for Wishbone to stand against. His sword arm was tired and sore, and against his will he lowered his guard. That's when Mutanto struck, swinging his mace sideways, aiming for Wishbone's neck. The Silver Knight moved quickly, dancing backwards out of the way, and the sharp spikes of Mutanto's weapon grazed his shoulder, causing a long but shallow cut.

Wishbone fell back as Mutanto pressed his advantage. But the Silver Knight was not one to retreat from a fight. He spun around on the heels of his boots and bashed his sword against his foe's huge weapon with every ounce of strength in his body. Chips of grey steel from the giant's war club buzzed through the air as Mutanto fought back with everything he had. Blue sword and heavy mace clashed and clanged with a deafening sound. When Mutanto raised his wicked weapon high above his head and brought it straight down towards Wishbone's head, the Silver Knight turned sideways, and the steel spikes of the giant's weapon struck the ground and stuck there.

Wishbone planted one boot on the mace and stared into the mismatched eyes of Mutanto. They glared at each other, taking a moment to catch their breaths before resuming their duel.

And then, high above Dreadful Hall behind them, Wishbone saw the three spirits of the Ghost Warriors soaring into the sky.

The signal! The Ghost Warriors have succeeded, he thought and rejoiced.

A second later, Wishbone and Mutanto heard a cry unlike any cry either of them had ever heard before. But Wishbone recognized the frightened voice of his daughter.

"Ava!" he cried out, his heart thumping in his chest.

The ground then rumbled and shook, and Dreadful Hall began to crumble, its walls and towers and buildings cracking and falling into ruin. A massive earth tremor nearly knocked Wishbone off his feet, and his boot slid off of Mutanto's heavy war club.

"What is the meaning of this?" Mutanto demanded.

"It means we've won," the Silver Knight told him.

Mutanto pulled his war club free and was ready to bash Wishbone's head when the dark clouds lifted and the sun shined on the barren land. Wishbone raised the Sapphire Sword, and a shaft of sunlight shined on his blade, which began to glow with a blinding blue light. The light struck Mutanto in the eyes and he cried out in pain. The blue radiance began to cover him. He screamed as he and his huge mace started to dissolve, melting away like an ice sculpture under the light and heat of the blazing sun. It took only a few seconds, and then he was gone.

"Thank you, bright sun of Creepy Hollow!" Wishbone shouted with joy.

He turned and raced back to rejoin the battle, and to see it finished. That's when he heard Jack's voice, crying out above the noise of battle.

"Jack! Hang on, I'm coming!" yelled Wishbone, running as fast as he could.

Teleporting herself directly to the field of battle, Queen Leandra landed right in front of Evila, near the foot of the lowered drawbridge of Dreadful Hall. The eyes of the Grim Witch went wide with surprise. The battle raged on all around them, but they were well out of harm's way.

"Queen Leandra—you're alive!" cried Evila.

"Yes, I am," said the Queen of Willow Haven. "And surely you must know the reason why I have returned to Creepy Hollow."

The face of the Grim Witch wrinkled as she frowned and gave thought to the queen's words. Then her eyes went wide again when she guessed the truth. "Angelina. She was born in Creepy Hollow. She's Opal, your daughter!"

"Indeed she is," Queen Leandra replied.

"All these years," said Evila. "All these years she has been my prisoner and not once did I ever suspect the truth of who she really is."

"Your arrogance and wickedness have blinded you, Evila," said Queen Leandra. "All you can see is your own greed and ambition."

"But I never sensed that her magic was of the Royal Blood!" Evila said.

"That's because you're ignorant!" Leandra told her. "Only a fool would fail to recognize the magic of the Royal Blood when it was right under their very nose all these years."

The Grim Witch laughed. "If your powers are as weak as your insults, then this is going to be short and sweet," she said.

"Then let us begin, shall we?" Queen Leandra asked.

Evila raised her gnarled and twisted, moss-covered Wand and waved it over her head. Without the need for a Spell, she conjured a hailstorm that fell upon the Queen of Willow Haven.

Queen Leandra, waving her Sapphire Wand, summoned a shimmering, silver heat wave to melt the rain of hailstones.

Evila shrieked with anger and from the tip of her Wand flew three large, black bats with fiery eyes. Straight towards Leandra they flew, and in the blink of an eye the Queen conjured three ropes made of blue light. She flung the ropes at the bats, lassoed the first pair and tossed them into the sky, where they vanished with a *pop!* But Queen Leandra's rope missed the third bat, and the creature slammed into her belly, knocking the wind out of her and causing her to fall upon her knees. When the bat crawled over Leandra, seeking to bite her throat, she touched it with her Wand and the bat turned to dust. She smiled and slowly rose to her feet.

"Really, is that the best you can do?" she asked Evila.

With a cry of rage, Evila summoned sharp-edged disks and iron balls with spikes, and hurled them at Leandra. The Queen of Willow Haven batted them aside with her Wand. Evila next conjured up snakes that flew through the air towards her opponent. Nikki's and Jack's royal grandmother waved her Sapphire Wand and trapped the snakes in a huge net. Two seconds later both net and snakes vanished. Evila's Wand then hurled sharp daggers at Leandra, whose own Wand conjured up a wall of blue steel that shielded her. Both the knives and the shield then exploded into puffs of black and white smoke.

Evila waved her gnarly Wand twice in the air, causing Leandra's head to snap to the left and then to the right, as if she had been hit in the face by two invisible fists. Leandra staggered backwards, almost fell over onto her back, but quickly regained her balance and used the power of her Sapphire Wand to hurl invisible punches at Evila. The first hit Evila square on the nose, causing it to bleed. The second slammed into her belly, and when she doubled over the third punch struck her with an upper-cut blow to the jaw that knocked her flat on her back.

"Ready to give up, Evila?" Queen Leandra asked.

"Never!" cried the Grim Witch, hopping to her feet.

The two witches went at it again.

Fireballs and lightning bolts flew back and forth between the two witches. Ropes of crackling electricity and rays of white-hot energy sizzled in the air. Swords battered each other in the middle of the air, with no visible hands wielding them. Lengths of fiery rope shot back and forth between them. Coils of hot wire wrapped themselves around the witches, only to be vanquished by streams of cold water. Back and forth Evila and Leandra hurled laser-like beams and weapons of all kinds at each other. Leandra was forced to duck as flaming torches flew towards her and passed harmlessly over her head. Blazing darts and scorching needles *whooshed* through the air and burned both witches. The Grim Witch screamed in agony and stumbled backwards. Queen Leandra cried out in pain, but then waved her Wand in the air. Evila screamed again, tripped and nearly fell when burning red charcoal flew straight for her, barely missing her. Then Leandra flung her Wand at the Grim Witch, who fell to her knees when it struck her on the head. Once the Sapphire Wand flew back into Leandra's hand, she walked right up to Evila and slapped her on each cheek, once with the palm of her left hand, and then with the back of her right hand.

Evila didn't move. She was burned and bruised, and trying to catch her breath. Queen Leandra smiled and shook her head at the Grim Witch.

"You know, Evila, you always enjoyed breaking and destroying things that belonged to other people, like you broke and destroyed my kingdom and my husband," Leandra told her.

At that moment the loudest and most shrill, ear-shattering scream sounded from the direction of Dreadful Hall. Then the ground trembled as if from an earthquake, and the noise of buildings cracking and falling apart soon followed.

"Is—is that what I think it is?" Evila asked.

"Yes," Queen Leandra told her. "It's the sound of all your hopes and dreams being destroyed. Let's see how *you* like it when someone breaks *your* things."

When Evila turned her head and saw Dreadful Hall breaking and falling apart, she screamed, "No!"

That's when Leandra seized Evila's twisted and moss-covered Wand, broke it in half, and tossed it on the ground.

When she heard the snapping of her Wand, Evila swung around to face the Queen. "What have you done?" she cried out.

"Your power is broken, Evila," said Leandra. "Now you must go where you belong, to the place below where all your kind eventually go...to the Realm of No Return."

"No! Not that!" Evila screamed. *"Not that!"*

Queen Leandra then stabbed the ground with her Sapphire Wand.

There was a flash of blue light as the earth suddenly quaked, cracked, and split wide open, right where Evila kneeled, leaving a great chasm between her and Queen Leandra. The Grim Witch kneeled on the very edge of it, paralyzed with fear. When another tremor hit, she lost her balance and tumbled head-first into the chasm. Down and down and down she fell, screaming all the way until the great hole in the ground closed again and the earth swallowed her up.

Rising to her feet, Queen Leandra pointed her Sapphire Wand at the two halves of Evila's Wand lying on the ground. They burst into flames at once and turned into ashes.

The Queen of Willow Haven did not celebrate her victory over the Grim Witch, for her destruction was not something she wanted to do, but *had* to do, having no other choice. But there was still fighting going on, and a moment before she teleported herself out of there she heard Jack's cry for help. Heart pounding with fear, she silently begged the sun and stars of Creepy Hollow, *Please, help my grandchildren! Do not let any harm come to him or Nikki!*

Jack wept heavily, his face dirty and streaked with tears. He sat on the ground, still holding the unconscious Catman's head in his lap.

Queen Leandra appeared out of thin air at Jack's side. She kneeled beside him and wrapped an arm around his shoulders. "Are you hurt?" she asked him.

"Oh, Grandma, I'm okay," he said, not bothering to wipe away his tears. "But Catman was bitten by a werewolf and it's bad. Real bad. I can't wake him up!"

"I'm very sorry, Jack," Leandra said to him in a kind and loving voice.

Jack's tears fell like rain and his grandmother hugged him more tightly.

Sparky flew down and landed on Jack's shoulder, dragon tears dripping from his eyes. Champ trotted over and lay down beside him. Leandra looked at them with great curiosity, but said nothing. She understood. She knew then that her grandson had the Gift to talk to animals.

Having heard Jack's cry for help, Nikki, Ghoulina, Wishbone, Domino, and Fiona joined them. When Nikki saw Catman lying there, eyes closed and hardly breathing, she broke down in tears and kneeled beside her grandmother, who put her other arm around her.

"Isn't there anything we can do, Grandma?" Nikki asked, her voice choking back her tears. "There must be something we can do. Ghoulina and I both have the Healing Gift. I healed you when that werewolf clawed you."

Leandra shook her head sadly. "But remember what I told you," she said. "There's no cure for a werewolf's bite."

"You mean Catman's going to die and come back as a Wolfman?" Nikki asked, horrified and frightened.

"No!" Jack wailed. "Not Catman—*no!*"

Wishbone looked at his friend sadly and wrapped his arms around Ghoulina. He said nothing, just lowered his head and held his wife.

"Grandma! Catman is going to turn into a Wolfman!" Jack yelled. "Help him, please!"

"There is no power in Creepy Hollow that can save him, Jack, not even the power of my Sapphire Wand," said Leandra, feeling helpless and powerless.

The unconscious Catman started having convulsions. His body writhed and squirmed on the ground.

"Ghoulina, please, save him!" Jack pleaded. "You healed me when I was bitten by the Tasmanian Devil."

Ghoulina shook her head sadly. "I'm so sorry, Jack," she said with tears rolling down her cheeks. "This is not the same thing. There is nothing we can do."

"No, no! We can't let Catman die! There *has* to be a way to help him!" Jack said, weeping as his heart began to break. "Oh, I wish there was something we could do to save him!"

Ding!

Everyone heard the bell-like sound and looked at Jack.

Jack's second wish was granted in the form of an idea that suddenly popped into his head like a lightbulb being switched on. "Ghoulina," he said. "You have a Dragon Rock in your pocket, remember?"

Ghoulina wiped her tears and nodded. She reached into her pocket and pulled out the silver ball. "What do you have in mind, Jack?" she asked

"Maybe the Dragon Rock can save Catman," he said.

"But Jack," said Nikki, "that's dragon poop!"

"It's *silver* dragon poop, Nikki," Jack told her. "Don't you get it? My wish was granted. If silver can destroy a werewolf, it can also heal Catman's wound!"

Ghoulina looked at Nikki. "We have to hurry," she said. "Nikki, you healed your grandmother's wound, so you can do this. I'll help you."

Placing the Dragon Rock on Catman's wound, Ghoulina said, "Nikki, hold onto your Key Stone and place your hand on the silver Rock."

"Hurry!" said Jack. "Please hurry!"

Without question, Nikki did as Ghoulina instructed her to do.

"Now, Nikki," she said. "Just remember everything you've learned."

In spite of her uncertainty, there was a confidence and determination in Nikki's heart that felt like fire when she clutched her Key Stone. Closing her eyes for but a second, she opened them and spoke the Spell that formed in her mind:

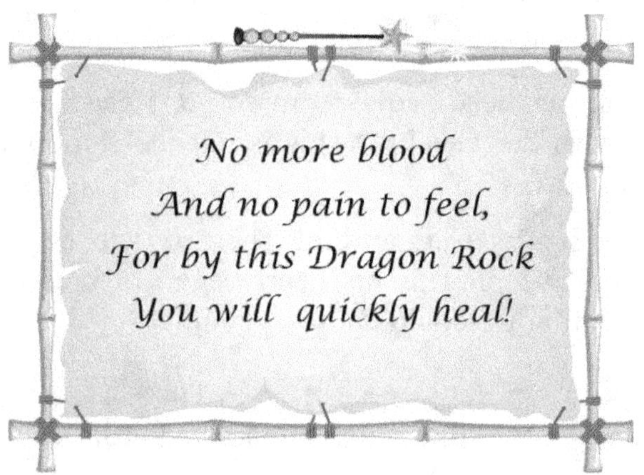

"Something's happening," said Nikki. "My hand feels warm, like when I healed that robin. But this is much more intense."

"Nikki, please remove your hand," said Ghoulina, hoping that Jack's idea would work. But then she realized, this *had* to work: the Wishmothers had granted Jack's second wish.

Nicki slowly removed her hand and watched as the silver Dragon Rock began to melt into Catman's wound. His convulsions stopped and then slowly his wound began to close as it healed itself. Within a matter of seconds the gashing wound vanished, as if it had never been there at all.

"It worked!" Jack shouted happily.

Queen Leandra smiled, giving him a big hug. "The Wishmothers granted your wish and the wish told you how to do it!"

Catman's eyes fluttered open and he saw everyone standing around him. "Oh," he said. "What happened?"

"We won," Wishbone said, helping Catman to his feet.

"Howler bit you and you almost died," said Jack.

"You almost turned into a werewolf, too," said Nikki.

"But Jack made a wish and got the idea to use one of his Dragon Rocks to save you, and it worked," said Ghoulina.

Catman looked around, totally confused. Then his eyes went wide and he asked, "Wait, you mean Sparky's poop helped to save my life?"

"Indeed, it did!" Sparky said proudly.

Jack threw himself at Catman, hugging him tightly while the others explained how the battle ended, leaving them victorious.

"Wow!" Catman said when Ghoulina was finished. He bowed to Nikki and Jack, and said, "My dear friends, I thank you both for saving my life," he said. "I'm forever in your debt and at your service." Then he saw something in the distance and pointed. "Look! Someone's coming!"

Everyone turned as three Wolfmen walked towards them. Floating in the sky above them were the twelve Ghost Warriors. One of the Wolfmen carried a woman, and in her arms a baby nestled quietly. The second werewolf carried a man.

"My baby!" Ghoulina shouted with joy.

"Ava!" cried Wishbone, squeezing Ghoulina's hand.

"Angelina! Mike!" Leandra cried out with joy.

Boo put Angelina down and she handed Ava to Ghoulina. "She's a really good baby," the Wolfman said. "She stopped crying once she got used to us and knew we weren't going to hurt her."

"Thank you, thank you so very much for saving my baby," Ghoulina said.

"We are deeply grateful for your help," Wishbone told the three Wolfmen.

Leandra's heart was bursting with happiness. But there was sadness in her heart, too, because Angelina and her husband Mike looked so frail and pale, so much older than their real age.

"Mom!" said Angelina, trying to stand. Mike rose and helped his wife to her feet as the Queen hugged and kissed her, then hugged and kissed Mike.

"All these years, all these many long years you two were lost to me," said Leandra, crying tears of joy. "We all thought you drowned and were gone forever when your car was found. I never knew. I never even suspected."

"Oh, Mom, it's gonna be okay," said Angelina. "We're safe and we're home again."

With a broad and loving smile, Queen Leandra caressed Angelina's pale cheek. "Your daughter has the Healing Gift, too, and just helped save Catman's life," she said, nodding in Catman's direction. She turned to her granddaughter. "Come and meet your parents, Nikki."

Nikki, speechless, burst into tears and ran straight into the arms of her parents. Nikki was at long last reunited with the mother and father she had never known.

"Nikki!" said Angelia, tears filling her eyes. "It's been so long and we have so much time to make up for."

"Mom! Dad!" Nikki managed to say. Not once had she ever imagined that her parents were alive and she'd meet them one day.

"And look at *you*, all grown up," said Mike sniffling.

"Well, *almost* grown up," said Jack, grinning.

"And who's this handsome young man?" Angelina asked.

"This is Jack Brady, Frank's and Mary's son," Leandra replied.

"Come here, son," said Mike, holding out his arms.

Jack rushed without hesitation into Mike's arms, and then they, Nikki, and Angelina embraced and held onto each other for what seemed like forever.

"Oh, Mom and Dad! I have *so* much to tell you!" said Nikki.

"Jack and Nikki happy!" said Champ, prancing around. Of course, only Jack and Catman knew what he said.

"Yes, *everyone* is happy now," said Sparky.

Jack glared at the three werewolves. "Who are these three guys?" he asked.

"These are the three Wolfmen my friends captured and questioned, and then had their memory of it erased by the Wishmothers," Catman told him.

"So *that's* what happened to us!" said Poo.

"We were there the night the princess and her husband were abducted," Boo explained. "But we took no part in that and we never hurt anyone."

"We've guarded their prison cage ever since the night they were abducted," said Goo. "We were under orders to do so. Evila's orders."

Poo started crying. "We don't want to be werewolves anymore," he said. "But Evila put a spell on us and made us her slaves. We had no choice!"

"That's true," Mike said. "I overheard them talking many times. All they wanted was to get away from Evila and try to set us free, too."

"We just want to go back home to Stone Mill," said Boo.

Goo nodded. "We're not really bad people, you know," he said.

"We never even wanted to be werewolves," Poo explained.

"It's all true. In return for helping us escape, we promised them that you would break Evila's spell and turn them back into men again, Mama Rose," Mike said, calling Queen Leandra by the name he called her since the day he first met her.

Queen Leandra stepped towards the three Wolfmen. "Sounds like you're just innocent victims of circumstance," she said. Then, raising her Sapphire Wand, she touched each of them with a burst of blue light from the tip of her Wand. Moments later the Wolfmen were turned back into men, each dressed in a black tuxedo.

"Hey, Boo! We look just like real gentlemen!" Poo said.

"Now it's time for us to act like gentlemen, too," said Boo.

Goo nodded eagerly and said, "Yep! No more following evil witches, either. From now on, we will help people."

"My name is Brian, Your Majesty," said the man formerly known as the werewolf Boo. "I'm a mason, by trade, and my brothers and I thank you. We hereby swear allegiance to you."

"For the rest of our lives, Your Majesty," said the man once known as Goo. "My name is George, and I'm a carpenter."

The brother who was once called Poo bowed to the Queen. "My name is Peter, and I help them," he said. "I taught them everything I know, Your Majesty."

"Our last name is Wolfe, by the way," said Brian. He and his brothers laughed.

"Well, then," said Leandra, "if you'd like to live in Willow Haven for a while, you will find good jobs. We can use masons, carpenters, and even their helpers."

The Wolfe brothers then kneeled and gave the queen their oaths of loyalty.

The Nine Guardians of Willow Haven approached, now that the battle was truly over and won. They bowed to Queen Leandra.

Leandra turned to Ghoulina. "My dear, please show me the Crystal Heart you recovered from the Valley of Lost Souls," she said.

When Ghoulina removed the heart-shaped crystal from her pocket, Jack laughed and said, "That dress sure has a lot of pockets!"

Queen Leandra told Ghoulina to take the Crystal Heart in both hands and hold it high above her head. Then Leandra nodded to the Nine Guardians, and together they raised their Wands and pointed them at the battlefield.

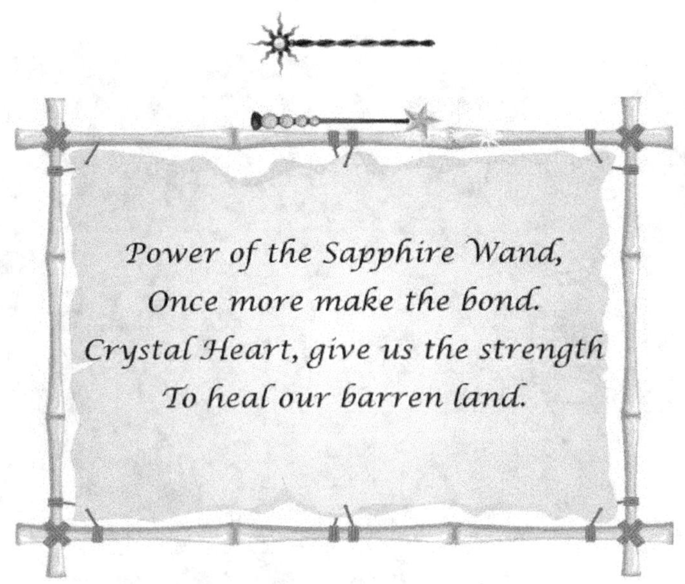

Suddenly time sped up and grass and flowers began to grow all around them with lightning speed. Trees and bushes sprang up from the earth. A narrow stream and a small lake materialized, too, right there on the former field of battle. Birds, squirrels, beavers, foxes, and all sorts of forest creatures soon appeared and took their places in the beautifully restored land. Farmlands grew lush and whole again, with corn and wheat, fruit trees and vegetable patches, all sorts of growing things sprouting from the ground. The once barren land of Bleakvale turned into a lovely realm where everyone could once again live in peace and harmony with nature. Even the color of the sky turned a deeper blue, and the sun blazed all the brighter.

"From this day forward this land shall be called Sweetvale," Queen Leandra announced.

Sparky flapped his wings. "I'm hungry, Jack," he said, and flew off.

"The poor creature must be starving. Now that the small animals returned, Sparky has plenty to eat," Wishbone told Jack.

Nikki and her parents laughed and watched the dragon flying off in the direction of the brand-new forest by the foot of the hill.

"Champ hungry," said the little foal.

"I'll pick some apples for you, in a little while," Jack promised.

"Now the time has come to bring a lasting peace to this realm," said Leandra. Raising her Sapphire Wand, she pointed it at the ruins of Dreadful Hall.

A ball of blue light appeared in the sky, followed by the sound of grinding stones, crumbling rock, and shifting stones. And then a magnificent, towering pillar of white stone and gray marble emerged from the ruins, rising higher and higher until it seemed to scratch the sky.

"Ghoulina, please open your hands and release the Crystal Heart," said Queen Leandra.

The Healing Witch did as she was told, and the Crystal Heart rose into the air and floated in the direction of the great pillar. The Crystal Heart then came to rest on the pinnacle of the tower, where the sun's light turned it as red as a ruby.

"Let the light of this Tower of Sweet Freedom stand as a beacon to all who would live in peace and harmony," Leandra proclaimed.

Everyone cheered and applauded the rebirth of the land and the beginning of a new realm in the world of Creepy Hollow.

Flying around looking for something to eat, Sparky caught sight of something crawling on the ground, through the brand-new forest.

"A snake!" he shouted.

Flapping his wings, he veered to the left, nose-dived, swooped down, and snatched the snake with his sharp teeth.

"I'm not a snake!" cried Slither, his serpent body coiling and twisting as he tried to get free. But all Sparky heard was the angry hissing of his food.

Tattler, the evil-minded, shape-changing town gossip and one of Evila's most sneaky spies, never had a chance to say another word as Sparky bit his head off, spit it out, and gobbled up the rest of him.

Epilogue

The people, creatures, and ghosts of Creepy Hollow celebrated the victory. A bright and beautiful crescent moon hung high in the sky overlooking the realm of Celestria and the mausoleum of the Wishmothers.

Ghosts floated happily across the night sky, for flying was something they greatly enjoyed. Candles burned everywhere with flames of every color imaginable. Numerous Jack O'Lanterns were hung with loving care from the trees and bushes. Pumpkins of all shapes and sizes lined pathways and decorated the tombstones and mausoleums in the cemetery of Wormbelow.

It was Saturday night, the night before Halloween, but Nikki and Jack didn't care if they returned to Earth in time to celebrate. They had more reason to stay in Creepy Hollow to celebrate.

After the battle, the Dwarfs pledged their everlasting loyalty to Queen Leandra and the Royal Family, for without them Evila would have conquered and destroyed their realm. They spread the word to Elf Harbor and Mermaid Landing on the southern coast that the wicked old Grim Witch was dead. When the Dwarfs returned to Dwarf Hill, the great herd of Wild Horses bowed to Queen Leandra and then set out for their home in Scarlet Canyon. The Silver Knights and the men and women who had helped win the war with the Grim Witch returned to Willow Haven, accompanied by the Nine Guardians of Weeping Willow Coven. The three former Wolfmen known as Boo, Goo, and Poo, went with them to Willow Haven, to help with the rebuilding of Starvale. Last but not least, the twelve Ghost Warriors had finally found their way to Celestria.

When everyone reached the mausoleum where the Trinity of Wishmothers dwelled, they found the three ghosts standing there, waiting for them. The Wishmothers bowed to Leandra, the Queen Mother, and to Angelina, the Princess of Willow Haven.

"Welcome home, Your Majesty and Your Royal Highness!" said Minerva Terrapin, holding her black onyx Wand in one hand.

"Finally," said Prunella Pickles, tapping the palm of her hand with the tip of her jade Wand.

Gladiola Scales twirled her amethyst Wand in one hand. "I do declare, this is such a joyous reunion on such a glorious evening," she said in her Southern Belle voice.

Minerva bowed to Angelina. "Please, come closer towards us, Princess Opal. You and your husband need rest and recuperation, and you will receive it while in our care," she said.

"Thank you, Wishmother. It will take some time before I get used to being called by my rightful name and title," Angelina replied.

Nikki watched her parents, but it all felt like a dream. She stayed close to them and wouldn't let their hands go. She was afraid they would disappear.

"Let us rejoice in the return of Queen Leandra!" said Catman.

Everyone shouted at once, *"Hail, Queen Leandra!"*

"Grandma, where's your crown?" Nikki asked.

Leandra smiled at her beloved granddaughter. "I retired my crown. It's time for a new crown for the new Queen and King."

"You can't retire, Grandma," said Jack. "You're the queen!"

"I'm the *Queen Mother*, Jack, which is exactly why I *can* retire," Leandra told him.

Holding out her Sapphire Wand, Leandra pointed it at Angelina and Mike, and in a flash of blue light, gold and diamond crowns appeared on each of their heads.

"Long live the Queen Mother, Queen Opal, and King Michael!" Wishbone cheered.

Once again, everyone joined in on the cheer.

Ghoulina turned to Nikki. "This officially makes you Princess Nicolette," she said.

"Hail to my cousin, Princess Nicolette, but for me, she will always be Nikki, the best cousin in the whole world!" Jack shouted.

Everyone cheered and applauded.

Nikki blushed. "Thank you, Jack, and thank you, my friends," she said.

"Now, there are two final matters that must be addressed," said Wishmother Minerva.

"Moriah has begged for forgiveness, freely given up her weapon to aid our cause, and has thus redeemed herself," said Wishmother Prunella.

"Since it was you, Queen Mother, whom Moriah betrayed, it is now up to you to decide her fate," said Wishmother Gladiola.

"And so I shall," said Leandra. Raising her Wand high above her head, she sent a shower of blue sparks flying south with the speed of light, in the direction of Moriah's lair.

Seconds later, the sparks returned, and wrapped inside them, as if in a cocoon, was Moriah the Scorpion Woman. No longer a scorpion, she was now a beautiful woman with long black hair, sparkling blue eyes, and pale skin. Dressed in a simple blue dress, she kneeled before the Queen Mother, humble, respectful, and repentant in her manner.

"Your Majesty," she said. "Although I strayed and lost my way, I am saved and redeemed, and most grateful. I would make amends for my crimes."

"We all thank you, Moriah, for finding your way out of the darkness of Evila's curse," Leandra told her. "But I am no longer your queen or anyone's queen. My daughter, Opal, is now Queen of Willow Haven, and Michael is her king."

Still on her knees, Moriah turned to the new Queen and King. "I hereby renew my vow of service and pledge my allegiance and everlasting loyalty to you both, if you will honor me with your acceptance, Your Majesties," she said.

"Gladly," Angelina said in a weak voice. "Please, stand up and be welcomed back into the good graces of the Royal Family."

Leandra pointed her Wand at Moriah, and in a flash of blue light the woman rose to her feet, once again a warrior wearing armor forged of sapphire-blue steel. Tears came to Moriah's eyes and her shoulders shook as she wept with joy.

Wishbone walked over to Moriah, removed the Sapphire Sword and its scabbard from his belt, and presented it to her. "This is your sword and I happily return it to you, Moriah. Without your sword, I could not have defeated the giant Mutanto," he said. "You are once again a Sapphire Knight, Warrior and Guardian of the Royal Family."

Everyone cheered and applauded.

"Thank you, thank you, everyone!" said Moriah. She hung her Sapphire Sword from her belt and walked over to stand behind Angelina and Mike.

Minerva Terrapin turned to Jack. "Master Jack," she said. "You have earned the right to become a Warrior and Guardian of the Royal Family."

Jack blushed and hardly knew what to say. "Thank you, Wishmother!" When he glanced at Wishbone, the Silver Knight grinned and secretly gave him a thumbs-up sign.

"Furthermore, Jack," said Prunella Pickles, "you still have one wish remaining to you. Is there anything you would wish for right now?"

Frowning thoughtfully, Jack rubbed his chin for a few minutes and then said, "I have everything I want. But can I save that wish for later? For something *really* important?"

Gladiola Scales smiled at him. "Why of course you can," she said.

"Ghoulina and Princess Nicolette, please come closer," said Minerva.

Glancing at each other, Nikki and Ghoulina approached the Trinity of Wishmothers.

"You have both earned your Wands," Prunella told them.

Gladiola gestured with one of her hands. "Please, hold out your Key Stones," she said.

When Nikki and Ghoulina presented their Key Stones to the Trinity, each Wishmother touched the Stones with her Wand. In a flash of silvery light, Nikki's Key Stone turned into a blue topaz Wand, while Ghoulina's Key Stone was transformed into a turquoise Wand. After Nikki and Ghoulina bowed and thanked the Wishmothers, Jack and Catman were told to come forward. Hesitantly, they approached the Wishmothers, neither of them having any idea what to expect.

"Hold out your hands," Minerva told them.

"Palms facing upwards," Prunella said.

Without question, Jack and Catman did as they were told.

"Jack, by your courage and unselfishness when you wished to save Catman's life, and you, Catman, for your own acts of bravery, you are both awarded your very own Key Stones," said Gladiola.

Jack blinked, and as quick as that, he and Catman found clear crystal Key Stones sitting in the palms of their hands.

"Oh, thank you!" Jack said.

Catman bowed. "I am honored," he said.

Leandra then stepped forward. "This is my gift to you, Angelina, who will be known far and wide as Queen Opal of Willow Haven," she said. Then, with a wave of her Sapphire Wand, a beautiful Wand cut from a single, large diamond appeared in Angelina's hand. "A Diamond Wand for a Diamond Crown!" said Leandra, the Queen Mother of Willow Haven.

"Mom...Mom, this is truly wonderful!" said Angelina.

"What about Grandpa's Key Stone?" Nikki asked her grandmother. "Shouldn't that be passed on to my Dad?"

"I'm afraid, not," said Leandra. "Evila always kept the Stone on her and I'm afraid it was lost when she fell into the Realm of No Return. But fear not!" She turned to her son-in-law. "Hold out your hand, King Michael," she told him.

No sooner did Mike hold out his hand when a purple and orange Key Stone appeared there. His eyes opened wide. "Thank you, Mama—I mean, Your Majesty," he said. He looked at his wife. "How do I use this?" he asked.

"Don't worry, Mike. I'll teach you," Angelina replied.

Now at last they were finished, and Angelina and Mike, who had no other family back on Earth, decided that, as Queen and King of Willow Haven, they must remain in Creepy Hollow, to reign in peace and prosperity. Staying there also meant that they would heal, grow stronger, and recuperate more quickly. But they decided that Nikki and Jack should return to Earth and finish their schooling, and Jack's parents must finally be told the history and heritage of the Royal Family. Nikki's face then scrunched up as tears filled her eyes.

"But if we leave, we won't be able to return to Creepy Hollow until next year!" she said.

"Nikki, dear," said Grandma Leandra. "You forget: the Key Stones of the Royal family allow us to travel to Creepy Hollow any time we wish. You can go to school during the week and spend weekends and holidays and summer vacations here with your parents."

Nikki threw her arms around her grandmother. "I love you, Grandma," she said.

It was now time for everyone to say farewell until the following weekend, when Grandma Leandra, Nikki, and Jack would return to spend the weekend in Creepy Hollow. Domino told Catman that he and his family of Wild Horses would like to live in Sweetvale.

Little Champ pranced around happily. "Sweetvale! Live in Sweetvale!" he told Jack.

"Now be a good boy," Jack told him. "Mind your Mom and Dad, and I'll be back to see you next weekend." He hugged the foal and kissed him on the nose. Then he and Nikki hugged and kissed everyone, and thanked the Wishmothers for everything.

"What about me?" Sparky asked. "Where do I live?"

Catman said, "It's been a long time since I had anyone to look after and keep me company. You want to live here with me, Sparky?"

"Oh, yes! I would love that!" said the young dragon. He nuzzled Jack and said, "See you next week!" When Catman held out his arm, Sparky flapped his wings, took off, and landed on Catman's wrist.

"You and I are going to be the best of friends," said Catman.

Sparky abruptly sneezed, and a bunch of sparks singed Catman's whiskers. "Oh, I do apologize!" said the dragon.

"I hope you'll grow out of that," Catman told him.

Champ laughed. "Sparky grow into big dragon!" he shouted.

Every day for the next four days after their return from Creepy Hollow, Jack went to Grandma Leandra's house to hang out with Nikki and Peggy, who had quickly become friends and were as close as sisters.

On Thursday, while they were sitting around the kitchen table having milk and cookies, Jack's parents arrived after an appointment with their doctor. They had come to take everyone out to dinner. Leandra made herbal tea, and they sat around the kitchen table, talking about sports, movies, music, and school.

"We have some wonderful news to share with all of you," said Jack's father, Frank. "Honey, you tell them," he said to his wife.

Mary Brady, Jack's mom, was a slender, beautiful woman with long black hair, green eyes, and a sweet smile. "Well, we just found out for sure," she said. "Frank and I are going to have another baby!"

Everyone cheered and congratulated Jack's parents, and the smile on Jack's face stretched from ear to ear. "That's awesome, Mom!" he said. "Is it a boy or a girl?"

"It's too soon to know, son," said Mary.

"Well, I wish for the baby to be a girl," he said.

Ding!

"What was that?" asked Jack's father.

"Was that a bell?" asked Jack's mother.

Jack grinned and exchanged glances with Nikki, Grandma Leandra, and Peggy. "It means my third wish was granted," he told his parents. "I'm going to have a sister, and I want to name her Mia."

Frank and Mary Brady looked at each other and shook their heads, totally lost and confused. "Jack, is this another one of your stories?" asked Frank.

"No, Dad. Cross my heart. It's true," Jack told him. "I made a wish and it was granted."

"Jack's telling the truth," said Nikki.

"Grandma, something's going on here," said Mary. "I can feel it. That bell rang loud and clear, and you have no bells in this house. It came out of nowhere."

"Oh, dear," said Leandra. "I guess it's time you were told the truth. I thought it best, for your own safety, to keep it a secret from you all these years. Please, forgive me."

"Forgive you for what?" Frank Brady asked.

"For never confiding in you," Leandra told him. "But first, let me tell you that last Friday night we found out that Angelina and Mike are alive."

"What?" Frank asked.

"They're...alive?" Mary asked, starting to weep with joy. "How did you find them? Where have they been all these years?"

"That's a long story," said Nikki.

"But it's exciting and filled with a lot of adventures, too," said Jack.

His parents stared at each other, uncertain what to think.

Grandma Leandra sighed. "Yes, it's time now to tell you everything," she said. She turned to Peggy Ward and looked at her for a long time, staring into her eyes. "You might as well hear this, too, Peggy. Something tells me you're going to be part of this family one day."

"That's okay, Grandma," said Nikki. "Jack already told her."

"Jack!" Leandra said, not knowing what to think or what else to say.

"Please, Grandma Sweet," said Peggy. "Don't be mad at Jack. He trusts me and I swore an oath to never tell anyone."

"I *had* to tell her, Grandma," said Jack. "Peggy, show her why I had to tell you."

Peggy smiled. "Okay, here goes," she said. She stared at her glass of milk for a few seconds, frowning as she concentrated on her thoughts.

Suddenly, the glass of milk lifted off the table, hung suspended in the air for a minute, and then slowly settled back down on the table.

Everyone except Jack and Nikki were stunned and surprised.

"My Mom told me it's called *levitation,*" Peggy explained. "I can pick things up and move them around, just by thinking about it. It's some kind of psychic power."

"Just like magic," Leandra said.

"It *is* magic!" said Nikki.

"Yep!" said Jack, smiling proudly at Peggy.

"Oh, my!" said Mary Brady. "I can't believe what I just saw!"

"Me, neither," said her husband. "Grandma, maybe you'd better tell us what's going on."

Before Leandra was even given a chance to speak, Jack told his parents, "Well, you see...once upon a time in the land of Creepy Hollow—"

Nikki jumped in and said, "Where bats and rats, and cats and gnats, no matter where you go will follow..."

The Authors

Erika M Szabo

www.authorerikamszabo.com

Erika became an avid reader at a very early age, thanks to her dad who introduced her to many great books. Erika writes alternate history, romantic fantasy, and magical realism novels, as well as fun, educational, and bilingual books for children ages 4-12 about acceptance, friendship, family, and moral values such as accepting people with disabilities, dealing with bullies, and not judging others before getting to know them. Erika also likes to encourage children to use their imagination and daydream about fantasy worlds.

Joe Bonadonna

www.dorgoland.blogspot.com

Much like Erika, Joe's dad introduced him to books, as well as movies and music, at a very young age. He was encouraged to write as soon as he could hold a pencil. While Joe writes mostly Heroic Fantasy, Sword and Sorcery, Horror and Science Fiction for an older audience, he decided to reach out to a younger audience and write something entertaining, as well as educational. In collaboration with Erika, this is his first children's book series.

Children's books by Erika